Cadillac
and the
Dawn of Detroit

D1371952

Annick Hivert-Carthew has spent the last fifteen years researching Cadillac and early Detroit. A native of France, her knowledge of the French language and culture allows and accurate study of primary sources about Cadillac. Her research has taken her to Canada, France, and throughout the United States as she works to uncover more information about the founder of Detroit.

An active historian, Ms. Carthew is currently working on an extensive biography of Cadillac with the President of the French Archeological Societyof Tarn-et-Garonne. She is also the author of *The Bells of Chartres*, a young adult historical novel, and *Marie-Thérèse Guyon Cadillac*, an audio cassette describing the life of Detroit's first First Lady. She is a professional speaker and reenactor and, dressed as Madame Cadillac, shares her knowledge of early French colonial Detroit with schools, museums, and historical associations.

Ms. Carthew lives in southeastern Michigan with her husband and two children. When she's not busy studying history and writing, she enjoys reading, visiting museums and attending the theater.

Cadillac
and the
Dawn of Detroit

Annick Hivert-Carthew

Wilderness Adventure Books

© 1994 by Annick Hivert-Carthew

Library of Congress Catalog Card Number: 94-19472
ISBN: 0-923568-38-7

Cover art by David A. Bredau
Photographs by Talley

Published by:

Wilderness Adventure Books
P.O. Box 217
Davisburg, Michigan 48350

Library of Congress Cataloging-in-Publication Data

Hivert-Carthew, Annick
Cadillac and the Dawn of Detroit / Annick Hivert-Carthew.
Includes bibliographical references and index.
ISBN: 0-923568-38-7 : $14.95
1. Cadillac, Antoine Laumet de Lamothe. 1658-1730--Fiction. 2.
Frontier and pioneer life--Michigan--Detroit--Fiction.
3. French-Americans--Michigan--Detroit--Fiction.
4. Pioneers--Michigan--Detroit--Fiction. 5. Michigan--History--
To 1837--Fiction. 6. Detroit (Mich.)--History--Fiction. I. Title:
Cadillac and the Dawn of Detroit
PS3558.I87C33 1994
813'.54--dc20   94-19472
                                                                CIP

Manufactured in the United States of America

To Max, my husband and friend, whose continuous support and love have kept me going. Thanks for putting up with a document-littered study room. I promise to tidy it up—some day.

To Paul and Jessica, my children, who have listened to more Cadillac anecdotes than they really wanted to. Thanks for yanking me back to reality when I need it.

Author's Note

Although this work is the result of ten years of research, its primary concern has been to catapult readers back to 1701 and bring Fort Pontchartrain and its indomitable first commandant to life. Pure History would not have described the guts and will it took to survive. Lusty pioneers, fierce Native Americans, they needed a story as vigorous as their personalities and emotions as tumultuous as their hopes and setbacks.

In *Cadillac and the Dawn of Detroit*, tales are spun around historical facts. Sometimes "improving" them to better portray its players, scenes are re-enacted through interpretation of original documents. History supplied the framework and I provided the drama.

Readers please note that characters' unfavorable opinions of certain people and places do not represent those of this author.

Acknowledgements

Many persons have given freely of their time, experience and knowledge. To all these I wish to express my warmest thanks, interacting with you has been a rewarding experience.

Thanks to :

Erin Sims Howarth, my editor, for her interest in Lamothe Cadillac, her belief in my work, and her ability to listen to new ideas.

Jean Boutonnet, President of the Archaeological Société du Tarn et Garonne, who has influenced my thoughts and writing style forever and unstintingly shared his vast knowledge. To his wife, Simone, who so warmly brought her support and help. They introduced me to the beauty and hospitality of Cadillac's home region.

Michèle Esperandieu, my sister, who unfailingly provided documents and information on demand and shared with me a memorable first visit to Cadillac's homeland.

Max Carthew, my husband, for his technical (and financial) support and positive comments.

The staff of the Burton Historical Collection, especially John Gibson, Manuscripts curator, who promptly answered requests, provided many documents and used their wits to locate others and provided suggestions when I hit a dead end.

The staff of the Detroit Public library for their help, and patiently retrieving long-forgotten and unused books from their vaults.

Frederick Stubb from the Detroit Historical Museum, for his help and enthusiasm.

Madame Husar, the owner of Cadillac's last residence, in Castelsarrasin, for so graciously opening the doors of her home and letting me absorb its wonderful atmosphere, walking, sitting or day-dreaming in the rooms where Cadillac lived.

Sharon Baker, for being my spiritual partner, and to her husband, Todd, who set me right on barn and chapel building.

Father O'Reilly, for sharing his specialized knowledge and guiding me through Ste. Anne.

Dr. William Phenix, Military curator of Fort Wayne, for answering so many questions on uniforms and military customs.

Mary Tedrake. Thanks for creating a wonderful Madame Cadillac costume to match the story of the book.

Carolyn Gillespie who encouraged me to take Madame Cadillac "on the road."

Laura Herrington, thanks for being so helpful and gathering material for me.

Many others have shared thoughts and provided illustrations and references: Art Staple—Sault-Ste-Marie Chippewa Reservation, Dick Cronin, Thatcher Campau Goetz, Ron Miller, Dick Lloyd, Andy Gallup, Ralph Nauveux, and Carl Gennette.

To any forgotten "assistant," may you forgive me for omitting to mention your contribution; you are the victim of an oversight, not an overslight. Your help was much appreciated.

Dramatis Personae

D'Auteuil, Ruette, Procurer-general of the High Council

De Bourgmont, Commandant interim for a short period in between de Tonti's departure and Cadillac's return (1706)

Callière, Louis Hector (de), Governor General of New France (1699-1703)

Champigny, Jean Bochart (de), Intendant of Canada (1686-1702)

Chenonvoizon (Quarante Sols), Huron Chief

Clairambault d'Aigremont, François, Inspector of the western posts (1708)

Dauphin de la Forest, François, served under Cadillac, and was given command of the fort after Cadillac's departure (1711). However, he was sick in Quebec, and Dubuisson assumed the post till his arrival (1712). De la Forest served from 1712 to 1714

Delhalle, Constantin, Recollect friar, Detroit's first "parish" priest, accompanied Cadillac in 1701 and helped found Ste. Anne

Deniau, Cherubin, Sulpician father, arrived in Detroit in 1706 to assist Father de la Marche

Dubuisson, Renaud, commandant interim at Detroit (1710) between Cadillac's departure and de la Forest's arrival

Frontenac (de), Louis de Buade, Comte de Palluau, Governor General of New France (1672-1682, 1689-1698)

Grandmesnil, Veron, Warehouse clerk and Cadillac's lawyer

Gueslis, Vaillant François (de), Jesuit father, came to Detroit with Cadillac in 1701 and left soon after

Guyon, Marie-Thérèse, wife of Cadillac

Laumet, Antoine, birth name of Cadillac before he assumed the name Lamothe Cadillac

Le Blanc, Jean, Ottawa Chief

Le Pezant, Ottawa Chief

Marche, Dominique (de la), Recollect father, replaced father Delhalle in 1706

Pemoussa, chief of the *Renards* (Foxes)

Picoté de Belestre, Marie-Anne, wife of de Tonti, friend of Marie-Thérèse Cadillac.

Pontchartrain, Jérôme Phélypeaux, comte de, Minister of Marine until 1715

Tonti (de), Alphonse, Cadillac's second in command (1701-1705) and the fort's commandant (1720-1727)

Vaudreuil, Philippe de Rigaud, Marquis de, Governor of New France (1705-1725)

Officers: Dugué, Chancornacle, Marsac, D'Argenteuil, de la Rané, de Tonti, de la Forest, de Bourgmont, Dubuisson, du Figuier

Soldiers: Jolicoeur, La Roze, L'Esperance, Francoeur, Laplante, La Giroflée

Table of Contents

List of Illustrations

Lac Supérieur

Chippewas

Ft. de Buade

Outaouais

Ba

Lac des Hur

Chippewas

Lac des Illinois

Renards

Pottawatomies

Saginaws

Outaouais

Pottawatomies

Ft. St. Joseph

Ft. Pontchartrain

Miamis

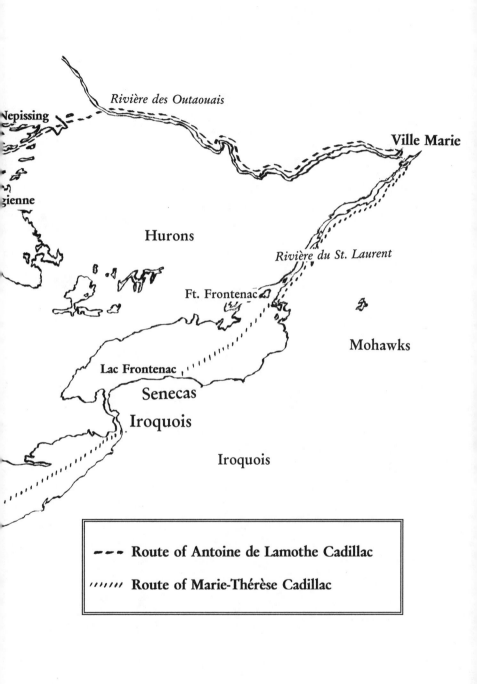

Rivière des Outaouais

Nepissing

Ville Marie

Hurons

Rivière du St. Laurent

Ft. Frontenac

Mohawks

Lac Frontenac

Senecas

Iroquois

Iroquois

--- **Route of Antoine de Lamothe Cadillac**

////// **Route of Marie-Thérèse Cadillac**

Foreword

Cadillac and the Dawn of Detroit is the story about a man with the vision to look at a wilderness and see a great city. It's a book about a man of courage, ambition, determination and love. Because little is known about him, Lamothe Cadillac has been portrayed as an arrogant, ruthless, grasping adventurer. This is the Cadillac of past literature, a caricature. Ms. Hivert-Carthew has shown us Cadillac as a real person. A person who exhibits great loyalty to his king, mentor, and especially his family. She shows us a man willing to fight to the end to fulfill his vision. Very much like the city he founded continues to fight to fulfill its destiny.

Cadillac and the Dawn of Detroit has changed my view of Cadillac; I used to believe in the caricature. The Cadillac in this book is a whole person, someone you can believe in. In the future when I discuss Cadillac it will be the man found in this book. A man of vision.

Frederick Stubbs
Assistant Curator of Education
Detroit Historical Museums

Prologue

The fur-trade reigned supreme over Michigan for a little over two hundred years (1634-1850), one hundred and twenty-six of which were under the French Crown (1634-1760). Michigan was destined to dominate for three reasons: its location, its rich hunting ground, and its cooperative trading natives.

At a time when a man could travel only by waterways in his birch bark canoe, this state lay in the center of the Great Lakes area. Four Great Lakes lap at its shores and hundreds of rivers and small lakes crisscross its land. If this was already not enough of an advantage, its territory was cut in two by the Straits of Mackinac, the only passage from the East to the waters leading to the Mississippi and its tributaries. It was the only route used by traders and trappers on their way to and from Quebec, where they sold their pelts and bought supplies.

France had already established a string of forts and trading posts in Michigan to control the fur trade: Fort de Buade (Michilimackinac), Fort St. Joseph (Port Huron), and St. Joseph (Niles). Of these three, one stood most commanding, most powerful: Michilimackinac. It ruled over the traffic between the Mississippi, Missouri, and Lake Superior. Michigan's fur supply reached the highest level of quality; thick and lustrous, it benefitted from an almost virgin continent with icy waters and numerous waterways.

In a matter of a few years, Indians had been propelled from stone age to iron age. They had developed a craving for European manufactured goods and were more than willing to barter their pelts for these items. This self-motivated, quite efficient fur gathering system sought to keep up with the increasing demand of a somewhat affluent and fashion-minded European Society.

The "get-rich-quickly" image of the fur trade appealed to many Frenchmen; a wealth in pelts meant a wealth in coins. Besides, it helped subsidize King Louis XIV's never-ending wars, the building of his precious Versailles, and in all replenished the rather depleted coffers of France.

Crucial to the French economy, the fur trade was equally important to the British. They had settled on the East Coast of America and were hungrily eyeing the French possessions of the Ohio Valley, the Great Lakes area and the Mississippi. Shortly after exploring the region, the British began infiltrating these territories.

While commandant at Michilimackinac (1694-1697), Antoine Laumet de Lamothe Cadillac, a shrewd and controversial French soldier and adventurer with a vision, developed a brilliant plan. He wished to build a post and permanent colony on the river linking Lake Erie to Lake Huron, closing the French control loop of the Great Lakes. The British had thought of it too, but Cadillac beat them at the gate.

On July 24, 1701, Cadillac planted the lily-strewn banner of France on the bank of the Detroit River. He thus placed one of the richest fur-bearing regions within the grasp of France and in the palm of his ruthless but capable hands.

He and his men cleared about one acre of land, parallel to the river, at present day Jefferson, between Griswold and Shelby. They built a fort which he named Fort Pontchartrain du Détroit, after the Minister of Marine who swayed King Louis XIV's mind in favor of the project.

And so Detroit, the city built on a dream, whose commanding

location many would covet throughout the centuries, began her first days under the command of a man who would set her ahead of all others. Although she would sometimes fall upon hard times, like a cat with nine lives, she would always overcome. Detroit would attract the bold, the smart, the hopeful and the opportunist.

The Night Before

Several campfires glowed on Grosse Ile, at the mouth of the Détroit River, near Lac Erié. It was late at night and underneath his woolen blanket a Frenchman tossed and turned restlessly. He called himself Antoine de Lamothe Cadillac, a far cry from the more common Antoine Laumet he'd been born on March 5, 1658, the younger son to a debt-riddled Gascon magistrate. Some secretly called him "le Faucon," Hawk, because of his prominent nose and his predatory pride. Indians referred to him as "mon père[1]." He had come for fame and fortune, both of which he wanted and needed badly; and no one—no one—took him lightly.

It was a blasted sweltering night; swarms of conniving, hungry mosquitoes hovered patiently, waiting for some exposed flesh. His favorite son, nine-year-old Antoine, lay beside him,

---

[1] Indians often addressed white officers as "mon père," our father, as a reminder that France had promised protection to her Indian allies against their enemies. Officers in turn called Native Americans "mes enfants," my children, acknowledging the agreement.

fast asleep. It had taken much persuasion for Marie-Thérèse, his young, beloved, Quebec-born wife, to let go of one of her precious children. But she had finally relented, and in May of 1701, after Cadillac had pressed a last loving kiss on her trembling hand, she had bid Antoine a brave *au revoir*. One hand resting on her protruding belly, she had watched her husband's party leave Quebec and her child's small figure disappear up *la rivière* St. Laurent, waving an embroidered handkerchief to the end.

She should have left with them, Cadillac had wanted her to, but she was weakened by the death of their one-year-old son, Pierre-Denis, the previous summer, and this seventh pregnancy. He had tried to delay his departure for Montreal until after the expected June birth, but higher authorities and common sense (much had to be accomplished before winter) had dictated the pace. Still, she had promised to join him as soon as possible.

All around them little groups of soldiers, traders and Indians curled near the glowing cinders, snoring, grunting and farting, seeking relief from pesky mosquitoes and prowling wild animals. Voyageurs had crawled into the shelter of their upturned canoes. Erecting tents took too much time and energy for one night. The pungent odor of hot, moist bodies and bear grease, used to ward off mosquitoes, hung above the party.

Cadillac turned on his side, pulling the blanket over his ears. A couple of mosquitoes danced over his glistening head, and he was up in a flash, swearing softly, swatting his blanket and giving up all attempts at sleep. He dropped in the campfire's pool of light, rubbing his weary forehead.

Sleep. He'd had so little for so long. Way back to late 1698, when he had fought tooth and nail at the court of Louis XIV for the right to establish a permanent *colonie* on the narrows of the river linking Lac des Hurons to Lac Erié. He had lived on borrowed money and, persuasive and courtly, befriended and won the support of the Comte de Pontchartrain. Pontchartrain was an enthusiastic young man of impressive lineage and

Ministre de la Marine, an advantageous patronage. The Ministre governed the Compagnies Franches de la Marine. These troops, the Independent Companies of the Marine, were in charge of guarding all aspects of France's interest in the colonies. Pontchartrain introduced Cadillac's scheme to King ("Roy") Louis. To win his cause Cadillac had thrown in some wild promises: the new *colonie* would be totally self-sufficient and cost the Crown nothing! Needless to say, Roy Louis had endorsed the project.

Cadillac had returned to Quebec in high spirits, the Royal Seal of approval and a grant of fifteen arpents at the site of the future fort in his pockets. He had brandished his triumph in the faces of the discomfited *Jésuites*, fully aware of throwing fat in the fiery battle between him and this powerful society. Since 1696, the Jesuits had filed charges against Cadillac for trading brandy for beaver pelts with Natives, contrary to royal decree. Ah, *les Jésuites*, who placed the saving of souls before all else and could not—would not—approve the trading of brandy with Indians for the luscious furs that poured gold coins into the depleted French Treasury.

During his absence, his staunch defender and supporter, Frontenac, the Governor General of New France, had died and been replaced by Louis Hector de Callière, a man cool to Cadillac's endeavors. Fortunately for Cadillac, Pontchartrain's opinion carried some weight. He was the direct boss of both le Gouverneur Général de la Nouvelle France, who headed the military of New France, and the Intendant, who handled judicial and financial affairs. Callière had had to bow, however ungracefully, to his superior and royal wishes, but his suspicious eyes were always on Cadillac, awaiting a falter and never providing quite enough support.

Back in May of 1701, Cadillac had left Quebec for Montreal to outfit his expedition. He accumulated maps and sketches, ferreting every bit of information he could lay his hands on. Then he and Alphonse de Tonti, his second in command, had feverishly selected their party. They chose two lieutenants, Chacornacle, a baron with a swift blade and devotion to his assignment, and Dugué, a handsome man of impeccable character. With them were fifty soldiers; fifty voyageurs, traders and artisans; one hundred Indians and two priests. Père Vaillant de Gueslis was a *Jésuite* who'd been foisted on the expedition but would nevertheless be useful to convert and teach French to the tribes. Père Delhalle was a *Récollet*, and would establish the colony's first little parish. Cadillac also brought his son, Antoine, and twenty-five canoes. By then he could almost sniff success.

He had selected the men personally, strong and hardy to withstand the hardships of the task ahead. Jacob de Marsac de Cobrion, the first sergeant, a huge man with a temper, would keep the men on their toes. Veron Grandmesnil, whom Cadillac suspected of being a bit of a rascal, especially with *les femmes*, excelled at numbers and legal problems. The brothers Jean and François Fafar deLorme were well versed in several Indian tongues. All bold and free men, whose allegiance he held in a tight grip. Only de Tonti caused him doubts. De Tonti, an Italian, had applied for the new post's command that Cadillac, more forceful and persuasive, had obtained. He had no proof of unseemly behavior, just a vague, uneasy feeling.

They had left Montreal in early June of 1701. To avoid unfriendly encounters with the Iroquois, with whom a new peace treaty was about to be signed, they had come by the route of the *Outaouais*. Their journey took them up the St. Lawrence, Ottawa River, Lake Nippissing, French River and Georgian Bay. This safer route consisted of thirty portages, not an easy trek.

They had paddled up the St. Laurent and used the chain of lakes and rivers as a natural path to the Détroit. The crew had endured the violent tossing of dangerous rapids. They struggled over portages with the crushing weight of their craft and belongings on their aching shoulders. At night the feral cries of wild beasts and the buzzing swarms of mosquitoes kept them awake. And always, in spite of the promised peace treaty, they had to be prepared for the silent Iroquois enemy feet.

The bloody hostility between the French and the Iroquois went back to 1609, when Samuel de Champlain, the founder of Quebec, had helped France's Native trading partners (Algonquins and Hurons) fight and defeat the fearsome and ever-warring Iroquois. The Iroquois then swore a lasting hatred of the French. The Iroquois confederacy, the most powerful of Indian forces, coveted the fur trade supremacy. The French blocked their way. Several peace treaties had been signed—and broken. The one in the making presented some serious hopes. It was paramount not to jeopardize its chances.

All night Cadillac pored over maps and paced amongst the slumbering groups. When, at last, a tiny fragment of sun peeked above the horizon, he gave orders to load the canoes. Young Antoine vaulted in with the voyageurs. The steersman called the beat of the oars. As they paddled up the river with its beautifully scalloped banks, retracing their voyage toward Lac des Hurons, straining against the strong current, they did not sing or laugh as was customary. The steersman's call and rhythmic splashing of oars were the only sounds breaking the silence of the country. Now and then de Tonti glanced at his commandant.

Cadillac appeared nonchalant, years of discipline keeping his taut nerves in check. Only his dark, sharp eyes betrayed his intensity. He keenly watched the land around him. Waiting and preparing for this moment had been a mixture of excitement, pleasure and pain. Eighteen years of honing body and sharpening wits had passed since leaving his native France as a young regiment cadet in 1683.

The thick forests and clear waters appeared as the travelers had described them, packed with animals and rich in fish and fowl, an inexhaustible bounty—the perfect location for a trading post. All he needed was a strategic position. From all sides the river beckoned him, glistening and coursing, majestic and life-giving, no less impressive then the Garonne, the river flowing through his native land. Ah, *oui*, he and rivers understood each other well. This one, with its scalloped edges, he decided, particularly so. He studied the land on both sides of it; in most places it was too uneven to build on, or the river was too wide.

Up, up they went. And then he saw it.

"*Là!*" He jumped up, pointing ahead to where the river tightened nicely, pulling at his senses. His canoe rocked, threatening to toss its passengers in the cold water.

"*Attention alors*! Careful!" mumbled soldier Laplante under his breath.

The men craned their necks and squinted ahead.

The head bargeman shouted, "*Tirez*! Pull!"

Excited, the oarsmen put on a spurt of speed. Soon they reached the place Cadillac had indicated. As the canoes hugged the shore, Cadillac eyed the land narrowly. Then he saw it—a ribbon of sandy beach tucked at the foot of the west bank. Above it, the ground appeared perfectly level.

"Closer! Quickly!" He commanded. The men swung their canoes. He jumped out before they pulled them aground and walked briskly up the beach, inhaling the rich scents of earth mixing with fresh water, de Tonti in tow. No one dared go ahead of him. He scaled the bluff and stood on the high ground, scanning the river, taking in the wondrous site.

The Founding of Detroit

"*Alors*, what do you think?" ventured de Tonti after a while. A proud smile lit Cadillac's face as he rubbed his hands. "*Parfait*, perfect location. It's too narrow for traders to go by unnoticed and our cannons can easily fire upon attacking enemies. We'll control the river. The trade is ours." He scooped a patch of soil in his bare hand, "The earth is rich, de Tonti. Touch it, *regardez*, see for yourself." De Tonti, whom he overshadowed and never quite trusted, followed his example.

He had been right, ever so right. It was during his stay as commandant at Michilimackinac that the idea had taken place, when more and more English infiltrated French territories and attracted trading Indians to their side with cheap rum. France, perpetually hovering on the brink of bankruptcy under the prodigal stewardship of Roy Louis XIV, threatened to close her northwestern posts, a gigantic mistake in Cadillac's eyes. He had studied maps, written detailed reports of all his expeditions along the Détroit de Mackinac and down Lac des Hurons, and coolly analyzed the problem. Then his finger and his brain pointed to a spot on the narrows linking Lac des Hurons to Lac

Erié; there would be the very place to stop British encroachments, catch "erring" Indians, and control the western trade. He
had evidence that the British had thought about it themselves,
but now, he, Cadillac, had beaten them.

Cadillac had big plans for this post, the future fortress of
commerce deep in primeval forests, the door to the western
trade; the gate he would guard. The French controlled the
Détroit de Mackinac, now, thanks to his vision, they would
dominate the whole traffic des Grands Lacs.

His plans went beyond the fur commerce. He realized that to
succeed, France must cease to treat the *nord-ouest*, any regions
west and south of Montreal, as a trapping area only. Trapping
and trading had generated a class of restless men, men who
often became lawless and debauched. *Non*, only a true *colonie*
that included farmers, artisans and families could anchor
France's grasp in this new area—a *colonie* that would encourage
tribes to settle around it, for Indians were the main fur suppliers.
He patted his empty pockets; a thriving post would soon fill
them.

"*Et qu'est-ce-que-c'est*? What is this?" he asked, following
the gurgling sound of water and tracing its course. "Even better.
A stream runs parallel with the river and elbows into it. We'll
be protected by water on three sides." He dashed about,
inspecting and gesturing in his usual energetic way. "It will be
a safe, thriving settlement." It was also too far for the *sacrés
Jésuites* to interfere in his affairs. He cast a dark glance at Père
de Gueslis, garbed in his black robe, scanning the river like a
raven on a perch. Patience, he told himself.

Cadillac was a soldier, an adventurer and explorer—a man of
action—but he was also a man of vision. As he gazed about
him, confident he would tame this wild forest, his eyes filled
with images of things to come—families moving about their
business; children laughing, carefree, protected by a high
palisade; farmers tending their land; Indians bringing in valuable
pelts.

Families settled land. Traders, soldiers and explorers conquered new areas, but men alone could not colonize them. Women and children were needed to establish permanent claims on the land. Families. He had not seen his for ten weeks, nor had he heard news of the birth of their seventh child. Although accustomed to long periods of separation, he missed sharing this critical moment with his loyal and loving wife.

Oui, he sighed. He had done well for his king. This little piece of *Nouveau Monde* was worthy of his homeland. He thought of the hardy Frenchmen who had tamed other parts of this Nouvelle France before him; Brulé, Cartier, Champlain, La Salle, and more. Ah, to have his name amongst theirs! A touch of fame attached to the financial rewards would be nice.

Cadillac removed his white-plumed tricorne, brandishing it regally, very much an aristocrat. "Lieutenant Dugué, bring the colors of France immediately." The *tambour* broke into a solemn "Le Drapeau," the call used to raise the colors. He thrust the staff into the virgin soil, "I hereby claim this land in the name of his Majesty, Roy Louis XIV of France."

The blue and gold Fleur-de-Lys[2] unfurled, caressed by an unexpected puff of wind. At the gentle stroke, this little piece of France fluttered and snaked into the air, lifting and twisting the hearts of the assembly with each movement. Proudly, Cadillac bowed to the colors of France. "I, Sieur de Lamothe Cadillac,

---

[2] The Fleur de Lys remained the heraldic emblem of France for seven centuries. At first many lys adorned the banner of France, but in the XIII century, the royal seal was downsized to three in honor of the mystery of the Holy Trinity (Three gold lys on an azure background). July 1789, in the midst of the French Revolution, a new flag was created, the "Tricolore;" three vertical blue, white and red stripes. The blue and red were the colors of Paris, the white of royalty. It symbolized the union between the king and the people; a union that did not last very long. France became a republic and shrieked at any signs of royalty. June 1790, the National Assembly banned the Fleur de Lys and King Louis XVI was beheaded the following year. The "Tricolore" has flown over France ever since.

vested Commandant of this expedition by the will of his Majesty, Louis XIV, decree that this fort be named Fort Pontchartrain du Détroit, after our sponsor and benefactor."

He turned to the men gathered around him on the riverbank. Piercing eyes fixed on the two priests, especially the *Jésuite*. He fell to his knees, and others followed. "*Messieurs*," he addressed the white men. "*Mes enfants*," to the Indians, mostly Hurons and *Ouatouais*, "Today *Dieu*, our Lord, has bestowed his favor on us. Let us thank him and pray he continues to bless this land." The two priests led the thanksgiving and benediction.

He genuinely thanked God for so many blessings, but deep inside he knew that his humble piece of devotion was influenced by a touch of diplomacy. True, he was a devout Catholic, and no one would deny his faith. But he supported the *Récollets* missionaries rather than the *Jésuites*, who put religion before anything else and hampered his trade. Cadillac had left Canada after many arguments with the *Jésuites* and was loath to have this ongoing feud mar his new enterprise.

The Bear

— July 24, morning, on the bank of the Detroit River

Cadillac walked about squinting at the sun, plan in hand. "Mmm, to be tucked between the river and the stream we need west, southwest orientation. Ah, *juste là*." He tapped his boot at the foot of a gigantic oak.

Not one to miss an opportunity to shine, he snapped his fingers and waited, hand open, for someone to pass him an axe. "I'll officially begin the clearing." A soldier, La Giroflée, handed him his tool. To free his movements Cadillac removed his white and blue *justaucorps*, *épée* and pistol, and laid them on the grass.

The tool was terribly heavy, but only slightly more than his *rapiers* and his trained shoulders did not sag under the weight. He lifted it waist high, with great distinction, and applied a fair blow to the oak. Satisfied, he relinquished the axe to his owner who said, "*Allez*, come on, Le Grand Pierre, you be next!"

"Le Grand Pierre! Le Grand Pierre!" chanted the crowd. They wanted fun and "Tall Peter" could always be counted on to provide it.

Le Grand Pierre, a Breton voyageur whose five foot nine inches had earned him his sobriquet, swaggered forward, towering over his comrades, all short and husky; long legs did not leave enough room for supplies in a canoe. As everyone gathered around him, he played to his audience, striping his buckskin vest. He flexed his muscles and displayed a hairy chest with a woman's shapely figure tattooed near his heart—Indians and white men alike favored tattoos to prove their manhood.

Muscles tensing, Le Grand Pierre raised his axe. It hissed through the air. Swivelling at hip and shoulder, he wielded the blade left and right over and over again in a mighty beat. The blade bit into the innocent flesh of the oak like a giant voracious tooth. Up the arm went, down came the wounding blade until the tree moaned, tottered and dove downward with a roar.

Le Grand Pierre's chest shone with sweat and, pinching his nose, he reeled backwards into the cool water of the Savoyard, leggings and all. Others followed. Tempted, de Tonti and the priests hovered over the water, and reconsidered after peeking at Cadillac's stern figure. Antoine pranced in the water, splashing and spurting like a young seal.

Cadillac ambled a little apart, peering into the thick, tangled foliage he planned to tame. *Beaucoup de travail*; so much work! But possible if all the men pulled their weight. He strode back to the group resolutely, "De Tonti, call the men to order and organize crews to fell trees. Chacornacle and Dugué, engage the Indians into clearing the brush!" His voice carried just enough authority to drag everyone out of the water. Behind the cool, commanding veneer lurked an impetuous, stormy Gascon temper that could be triggered into a full-blown gale at the slightest provocation.

The men, a hardy, rowdy and sometimes lawless lot, wiped their hands before honing their axes. Groups disappeared into the forest, bundles of tools on their shoulders. They had no horses or oxen to carry heavy loads, and no plow to clear the land. By supper-time sweaty bodies would ache and hands would bleed.

Without a word of explanation Cadillac pivoted on his heels and made for the wilderness; time to investigate along the river and record any fruit or nut-bearing trees to harvest for winter. He started to the left, forcing his way through brambles and tangled underbrush.

The forest smelt of warm leaves and bark, a scent that invited one to doze, propped against a tree trunk, and catch some sleep. As he pushed deeper, the air changed, from leafy and sappy, it became sweet and heady. Cadillac inhaled, thrilled.

As a boy, he'd crossed too many orchards around his native village, St. Nicolas-de-la-Grave, and plucked enough juicy fruit not to recognize the fragrance. He sniffed again. Plums, most probably. He could hear the humming of bees, and already had to shoo a few. There it was, a collection of apple and plum trees, growing wildly where wind and nature had sowed them, strangling vines crawling around their limbs. The plums appeared half ripe but the apples were still quite green and small. Bees buzzed frantically, suddenly disturbed.

Cadillac pulled at a vine. As soon as he could spare one, he would send a crew to hack those vines so . . . he paused, startled by the heavy snapping and crunching of brush coming from his right. And then he froze.

He identified the terrifying, musky scent of bear just as a massive black bear appeared between two trees and reared on his hind legs. The beast bared its teeth and raised its deadly claws. Beads of perspiration started running down Cadillac's face and neck and his heart beat savagely in his chest. Slowly, ever so slowly, he reached for his pistol and found it missing. *Pardieu!* He'd left it by the oak.

At that moment the bear growled savagely and charged. The happy image of Marie-Thérèse and their children fleeted before him. Whissssh. Just as he thought he'd die, Cadillac heard the hiss of arrows streaking through the air. He dropped to the ground and rolled away as fast as he could from the menacing, snarling beast. Whissssh, whissssh, more arrows hissed.

A slew of arrows in the chest, head and neck, the beast grunted, his snout raised in pain. He twisted and writhed and dropped on all fours. Two more arrows skewered him. With a bloodcurdling yell an Indian pounced on the wounded bear's back, plunging a knife deep inside its neck, and pushing it deeper still. Warm blood spurted on the Indian's face and he licked it with obvious relish. Cadillac grimaced. A second Indian watched, bow taut—two *Outaouais* from his party.

In agony, the beast reared up again with a thunderous roar, unsaddling his attacker. The bear raked his powerful, sharp claws on the leg of his fallen victim, ripping flesh and bones in one mighty blow. The other *Outaouais* released his arrow. It embedded itself into the beast's gaping wound with a thud. Sapped of his strength, the bear crumpled to the ground, part of the Indian's leg dangling from his claws, blood dripping, tendons swinging. And with a grunt and a twitch he expired. The wounded *Outaouais* collapsed. The other two people remained rooted in place, their brains slowly catching up with the events.

Cadillac was the first to recover. Jumping up, he stripped his *veste*, ripped at his linen shirt and raced to the fallen man— Dominique Crocs de Loup (Wolf Fangs), one of Père Vaillant de Gueslis's most recalcitrant would-be converts. The leg had been severed above the knee. Blood gushed out. Cadillac wrapped his shirt around the thigh and knotted the sleeves tightly. It needed cleansing with water and brandy, or most likely searing with a red-hot stick; *non*, the wound was too large, too bloody.

The other *Outaouais*, Aristide Dents Crochues (Crooked Teeth), his lips permanently distorted over tobacco-stained, overlapping teeth, leaned over, calmly inspecting his comrade, assessing the damage. "Work," pointing in the general direction of the clearing, "We smell a bear."

"*Mon frère*, I owe you my life. *Merci.*" Cadillac's words of gratitude were ignored; Aristide was already bending over the bear, separating skin and flesh.

Cadillac was not about to plunge his white hands inside a bear's bloody carcass; he dove back into the wilderness to recruit a rescuing team. Soon, others would be here, hoisting Dominique on a travois, helping Aristide cut the beast to pieces, scraping the skin, skewering big chunks of meat on sticks, and carrying the quivering fat in a woven basket. Well, they wouldn't have to worry about dinner that night!

Like the majority of Indians in the party, Aristide spoke French reasonably well. Many tribes had abandoned their Lower Michigan territories to escape the warring Iroquois who roamed lands east of Lake Huron and Lake Ontario. They had migrated to northern lands and came in close contact with French black-robed missionaries and traders. The white man's language and external worship of his God had become familiar. Most of them adopted French Christian names and happily endorsed a sobriquet derived from a physical trait or some peculiar mannerism. Many had relocated around Fort de Buade (Michilimackinac), the most southern post they dared penetrate.

Cadillac meant to change all that. His plan involved a major resettling of the tribes at the Détroit, a rival post to Michilimackinac, a post to grow into a proper *colonie* and cast the Michilimackinac in the shade. As anticipated, in 1697 France had closed Fort de Buade, recalling his garrison. Only the Jesuit mission had remained officially open. It had, by default, become the fortunate recipient of the *commerce des fourrures*, the fur trade, because the tribes and traders, indifferent to France's politics, continued business as usual, to the great contentment of the Quebec and Montreal merchants.

Cadillac expected loud protests from the *Jésuites* stationed there, who, seeing their fur gatherers and would-be Christians escape their influence, would decry their uprooting and the consequent blackening of their souls in what they called "citadels of lewdness and depravity"—any frontier posts.

Cadillac intended to outsmart them all.

Aside from the influential friends he had been able to secure at the court of Louis XIV and his own power of persuasion (he was extremely well educated, ironically enough, most likely by the Jesuits); a convenient ruthlessness; and a superior sharpness of mind and analytical powers, Cadillac banked on the fur trade and the cooperation of the native man to catapult his venture on the road to success. To many, the fur trade offered the chance to become rich and famous quickly. Human greed was all too familiar to Cadillac; he reckoned on its pull to work in his favor.

Pelts were in much demand in Europe; they provided warmth in drafty and poorly-heated houses, and displayed wealth nicely. Long fur caps kept the cold at bay, and ermine had long been a royal fur. This demand had increased drastically one day, when Louis XIV appeared in court wearing a broad brimmed beaver hat his tailor had especially designed for him. France was then the European leader of fashion—whatever Roy Louis did, everyone imitated—so started a mode that would spread to other European countries. The trend would last close to two centuries, filling many empty pockets, including the depleted coffers of France, and costing the lives of countless wild animals.

Animals were trapped and hunted in winter, when their furs had grown thick and lustrous. Trappers scattered in the wilderness, either alone or in a two- or threesome, never more, for an area supplied only a limited harvest of pelts. They paddled their canoes on uncharted waterways, wintered with the tribes, and established new routes. In spring they emerged from the wilderness to barter their peltries, coloring trading posts with their bright sashes and woolen *tuques*, roistering until early hours of the morning, gambling and squandering a whole winter's profit in a matter of days, but also pulling rough sketches and maps out of their frayed pockets.

That caught everyone's attention.

Visions of glory danced in the eyes of explorers and adventurers, always on the lookout for the elusive shortcut to the spices of the West Indies and China. Soldiers marched to claim new territories and reap promotion. Trappers encountered new tribes—more souls for the missionaries to convert, teach, and open missions for. Aristocrats connived and contrived to sponsor expeditions to enlarge Louis XIV's kingdom and hopefully glean a reward. For the rest of France, mostly famine-stricken farmers, the fur trade represented escape from ever increasing taxes and extreme poverty.

It operated under a monopolistic regime: all profits belonged to the king. Wealthy men bought a license from the French Treasury and they, in turn, issued a limited number of permits or *congés* to trappers and voyageurs. This system proved extremely difficult to enforce; too many hands grappled for some of the profits outside governmental controls. *Coureurs de bois* (runners of the woods) were the unlicensed trappers, the modern-day poachers. When caught they were flogged and branded.

One self-motivated group contrived to satisfy most of the European glut for pelts: the Native American. In a matter of years after the discovery of this "new" continent by Christopher Columbus, Indians had been propelled from stone age to iron age. They developed a craving and a dependency for European-manufactured goods that rendered their lives easier: woolen blankets, clothing, tools, cooking utensils, iron pots, guns and powder, and unfortunately *eau-de-vie* (brandy), and were more than willing to barter their pelts for these items. Hooked on a slew of French commodities, many of them cast aside their traditional nomadic livelihood and ceased to roam in small bands to anchor whole tribes around French encampments. They did not know it, but they were gradually becoming dependent on the white man and his trade for survival, making the return to their old ways almost impossible.

An Evening by the Fire

At nightfall, Cadillac sat around the spit, picking at a juicy morsel of roasted bear. A last one. Like everybody else, he'd eaten too much. The men stretched their weary limbs, puffing on their pipes, yawning and rubbing their bloated bellies. From their left came the beat of incantations. Dominique's friends were applying plants and root salves to his wound, chanting to the Great Manitou.

Across the leaping flames, Le Grand Pierre spiked one last oozing piece of charred meat with his knife and dropped it into his mouth. His lips snapped around it greedily and droplets of grease spurted on his chin. He dabbed at it with a dirty rag, then, reclining on his elbows, replete, belched heartily. By the voyageur's account it had been a good day. Voyageurs, who penetrated deep into the woods, cut off from their civilization, would often adopt Indians ways, discarding French clothes in favor of buckskin tunic and leggings. As Cadillac often said, "When you live with wolves you learn to howl." The band was a colorful lot whose most precious belongings were contained in a brightly beaded bag hung from the sash they wore at their waist, things that meant so much to the owner and so little to another man.

A voyageur brought his canoe close to the firelight for repairs. He laid several strips of birch-bark to patch over a hole, holding them with one hand and sewing them in place with stringy red spruce roots with the other. Later, he would seal the seams with white pine gum. While working, he hummed to himself. Another had rolled up a log and began to hollow out a *pirogue*, the fast and easily-maneuverable one-man craft used for fishing and quick transport.

"Eh, anyone for a song?" called Marsac, mending gigantic holes in his socks.

"*A la claire fontaine?*"

"*Pourquoi pas?* Why not?"

"*A la claire fontaine, m'en allant promener* . . . By the clear fountain, I went walking . . ."

Soon, the little clearing hummed with the men's voices, always ready to intone their favorite French songs filled with love and bravery. It was time to pat rounded bellies and fill their minds with stories about their homeland—their favorite moment, and one of Cadillac's too. When the men had exhausted their repertoire of all-time favorite yarns, they created their own; wondrous tales of adventures in the wilderness tinged with hope for a nest-egg and a good woman to share it with. Sometimes, the songs grew rowdy and lewd.

Cadillac decided to meander among the various groups. He relished the opportunity to get to know more about his men, their hopes and their personality traits. He approached several mixed clusters of white and Indian men bartering possessions, learning each other's language and trading hunting secrets. When he first joined them, the groups quieted somewhat, uneasy and subdued by his aristocratic figure. Soon they relaxed; months at the court of King Louis XIV had polished his diplomatic skills, he could be so charming and courteous, lulling one to believe him almost harmless. He smoked a pipe with Aristide Dents Crochues, inquired about Dominique Crocs de Loup, and sat with a trader sharpening his tools. Mixing so, he also gathered useful tidbits.

Cadillac had a reputation of ruthlessness and arrogance. But do soft men lead bands of willful adventurers through the wilderness? He thought not. These men risked much for gain, and they believed he would help them fill their pockets. And his own. He had an ever-growing family to feed and a fortune to establish.

The younger son to a large family, he always had to fight hard for what he wanted, even more so after his older brother, of a quarrelsome disposition, had forced their parents into ruinous litigations that depleted the family resources. By then his education had been more or less completed. Ambitious and restless, he had pinned his hopes on the *Nouveau Monde* and the vast possibilities it offered. Somewhere on the Atlantic, the plain Antoine Laumet had become the more impressive Antoine de Lamothe Cadillac. The name would impress people, give him credibility, and open powerful doors.

He had landed at Port Royal, the capital of Acadia, in 1683, and indulged in some privateering while studying the East Coast and infiltrating British colonies. In 1687, he engaged in shipping with François Guyon and married the gentleman's niece in Quebec. He obtained a grant in Acadia (Bar Harbour), in 1688, where he settled his bride. In 1689 he dashed back to France to provide the ministry with firsthand information on the Atlantic seaboard. Meanwhile, his extensive estate was ravaged by the British and his destitute but stalwart wife had to dodge the enemy and trudge back to Quebec with one toddler and a newborn. Marie-Thérèse, twelve years his junior, was then only twenty.

The period from 1689 to 1694 could be named the "years on the rise." Determined, ruthless and arrogant, the Gascon spared no energy gathering crucial information, making himself useful at the court, ferreting introductions to influential people, and zipping back and forth between the New World and the Old. At last he had been appointed, by royal decree, captain in the marines as well as ensign in the navy, and given the post of commandant at Fort Michilimackinac. Full power had come into his hands.

He had stayed at this post until 1697, mapping the area and gathering arguments for the establishment of a post on the Detroit River to counter the importance of "Manathe," whose seizing he strongly advocated.

Always so astute, controversial and forceful in his views, always treading on many toes, and very mercenary, he acquired many enemies. His worst mistake would be antagonizing the Jesuits over the trading of brandy to the Indians.

Cadillac's letters show him as a fastidious, highly educated man of a superior intelligence and biting humor, a considerate husband and a concerned father, with an incredible talent for landing himself in trouble. It is not surprising that such a man inspired extreme feelings in his contemporaries and historians. Scoundrel or visionary? A probable mix of the two, he was now poised for his *coup de maître*: the founding of Detroit.

An Indian Burial

Several crews worked on the palisade and four corner bastions. Laplante unloaded the tents and directed their pitching, their homes until cabins could be built. Jean Delorme uncovered a honeycomb in some wild vines and carefully removed it outside of the future fort's perimeter. Honey would make a nice change from maple syrup for seasoning.

Cadillac was mulling over a gift for Dominique Dents de Loup. He could have easily picked a trinket from the treasure chest his party had filled with religious medals, Jesuit rings, tin mirrors and beads to trade with Indians, but something honorable in his hardened soul told him to make a personal offering. His dagger, with its ornate silver stock embossed with his family crest? A crest he had unabashedly designed himself. *Non.* Indians and white men did not value objects in the same fashion. Whilst Europeans appreciated silver and gold for their beauty and their worth, Indians might prefer a mirror for its newness and mystery.

An idea pounced in his head. One of his gold-edged tricornes with its white plume, part of the Compagnie Franches de la

Marine's uniform and a symbol of authority; besides, Indians loved to parade in a white man's garb. He seized the oldest.

Dominique was lying on a pallet, his leg stump swaddled in buckskins packed with pungent herb and bark pastes. The acrid stench of near-death, mixed with decayed blood and putrid flesh, socked Cadillac in the face. Swarms of filthy black flies buzzed over the blood-soaked and pus-filled wrappings. The beautiful coppery skin had turned grey.

Hardened by months aboard merciless sailing ships, Cadillac did not bat an eyelid. He knelt by the dying man and ceremoniously placed the tricorne over his head. "*Pour vous. Merci.* For you. Thank you."

A weak hand reaching for the plume, Dominique opened his eyes, eyes glazed with pain and approaching death, yet calm and unafraid. "*Mon père . . . Moi*, Long Walk," he murmured.

"I know, my son. I shall recommend your soul to the Great Manitou, the spirit of all things, and I shall call upon Mother Earth to greet you. When it is time for shadows to dance around us, I will recognize your soul amongst them and praise such a courageous hunter."

Dominique smiled faintly. "*Moi . . .*" he paused to gather his energy, "*Moi*, Long Walk . . . bear claws," he pointed weakly to the necklace of wolf fangs adorning his neck.

"*Mon fils*, I shall . . ." Cadillac stopped. Dominique's eyes, fixed by death, were staring at the brim of the hat protecting his brow.

Aristide, who had been hovering around the pallet, picked up his drum and started beating on it, calling everyone to dance and sing in honor of Dominique's death. In the forest, Indians dropped their chores and rushed to the clearing. Some tied dried gourds around their bodies, shaking them with supple movements, dancing and chanting.

"*Les pattes d'ours*, we need the bear's claws," Cadillac shouted in Aristide's ears. Seeing Aristide's blank face, he raised his hands and, fingers clenched as claws, growled, "*Un*

ours, rrrr, rrrr," and felt extremely foolish. Aristide passed the
drum to a buddy and disappeared. Cadillac waited patiently, at
least he appeared to. Inside he was boiling with frustration,
assessing the damage to the men's spirits and estimating the loss
of working hours—all of his men would have to attend Dominique's burial.

"De Tonti," he shouted, "Get the *tambour* to call the *Assemblée*. Bring some spades."

Aristide returned, a stinky bear paw in each hand, and hailed
another *Outaouais* to help him. They settled to the gruesome
task of separating the claws from the partly decayed flesh.
Meanwhile two Indians loosely wrapped Dominique's body in
skins, chanting with the dancers. This done, they carried him to
a makeshift travois, the beautiful white plume of his tricorne
swaying lightly.

Animal Effigies
Manufactured by European silversmiths for the fur trade, these
effigies were highly prized by Native Americans. The shapes
represent the Natives' spiritual helpers.

"*Par ici*, this way." Cadillac led them away from the clearing, to a distant part of the forest he had calculated to be outside the fort. He certainly did not want the settlement to interfere with Indian burial grounds—the surest route to hostility. Indians respect their dead, even though they do not weep and mourn for days as white men do. One day of chanting and dancing; except today he would have to hasten the celebrations, he could not afford the time.

His instrument wrapped in a black wool cloth as a sign of mourning, the *tambour* pounded the Burial, "Enterrement." Dugué ordered some men to dig and the Indians started lining the grave with birch bark. The body was gently deposited inside. The white men removed their hats and remained silent while Père Delhalle recited Christian prayers, his voice drowned by the chanting and dancing, "*In nomine Patris et Filii et Spiritus Sancti . . .* Amen." They crossed themselves.

One by one the Indians deposited a gift on the body; snow shoes, bracelets and beads, and some Indian corn and a pot to boil it in, so Dominique would not go hungry on his Long Walk. Aristide arranged the bear claws on the dead man's chest and straightened the white-plumed tricorne. Pale eyes, not without envy, speculated on its being there. Cadillac's stone-face kept them guessing.

Cadillac blew his cheeks and started pacing; the celebrations would go on all day unless he interfered, and fast. He jumped squarely in front of the crowd and bellowed, "*Mes enfants.*" Only the white men, trained to answer the commandant's orders, paid attention. "My children," he roared again, his voice this time dripping with impatience. The crowd quieted. "*Mes enfants,*" he repeated a third time with great command, "Today a great hunter passed away. Dominique Crocs de Loup appreciates all our gifts for his Long Walk. Indeed they will sustain him. But the Great Manitou, Master of all things, is waiting for him and Dominique yearns to be with him. Let us not delay him. O Mother Earth and spirits of the east, west, north, and south, hear me. Take our prayers to the ears of the Great One and guide Dominique on his journey." He threw a handful of bark over the body and invited others to do the same with a wave of his hand.

As the bark fell on the body, hiding it from view, Cadillac ogled the white plume sticking out from the coarse covering. Every time bark fell on it, it sprung up again, unwilling to surrender and bend, much like its previous owner.

What a day! In a few hours he had lost one brave, one excellent hat, and several hours of good working light.

One of the largest Indian burial places was the Navarre farm, later known as the Brevoort Farm, on the Potawatomi village and burial compound. The Natives deeded the entire farm to Robert Navarre in 1771, ". . . that he may cultivate, light a fire thereon, and take care of our dead; and for surety of our word we have made our marks, supported by two branches of wampum."

Later, when Detroit expanded and farming land gave way to roads and buildings (1867), thirty skeletons were exhumed and several artifacts discovered: pipe-bowls, tomahawks and flints. Catholics were buried inside the fort, in a little cemetery next to the church. The records of Ste. Anne's Church show that persons of distinction (priests, commandants, etc.), were even buried within its walls.

Unrest

All afternoon, fueled by anger, Cadillac worked his Gascon blood into a frenzy—marching relentlessly through the clearing, supervising and ordering, pointing and directing, driving everyone close to their limit, and beyond. He barked commands; axes hissed, hacked and split, backs bent, hands bled, jaws stiffened and eyes hardened. Weary cinnamon and white skins touched, sharing labor, mixing sweat. The two priests pulled and carried, soothed and prayed, shrugging off Cadillac's show of temper as being part of the package. By early evening, exhaustion had dulled brains and knotted muscles. Overtired and resentful, the men became careless.

"De Tonti, how—" a distant shout in the forest, followed by a thundering thud, snapped Cadillac's attention. He felt a slight tremor roll under his feet. Panicky, urgent cries broke the ensuing silence. The men around Cadillac dropped their tools and bolted in their direction. Without thinking he ran with them, stumbling, ignoring snarling roots and stabbing branches.

"It's Émile! He's under there," someone shouted.

The logging crew had gathered around a gigantic felled tree amongst a heaped debris of limbs, splintered boughs and flying leaves. Cadillac came to a halt, a quarrelsome arch to his brow. "Ah, Laplante, what's happening?"

Laplante, the soldier in charge of the logging crew, squirmed and raked a dusty hand through his hair, "It's been a long day. Émile, er, he did not get clear," he blurted to the ground. Cadillac had worked the men unreasonably hard, Laplante knew it, Cadillac knew it. The accusation hung in the air, but awed by his superior, Laplante could not spit it out.

Le Grand Pierre was not hampered by such qualms. He shoved his way to the front, his voice rising to a shout. "It was bound to happen. He's been pushed too far, we all have, and look where it got us!"

Cadillac glared at him and growled, "*Assez*, enough!"

Le Grand Pierre's shoulders tensed. He spat contemptuously on the ground, "Only because it's Émile . . . otherwise—"

Cadillac rummaged through the clutter, "Is he underneath all that?" Laplante nodded. "Is he alive?"

Laplante lifted his shoulders helplessly, "*Je n'sais pas*, don't know yet. Must be knocked out."

Le Grand Pierre began clearing the mess, "It's going to take a while to cut our way carefully through. *Allez, aidez-moi*! Help me!"

By the time Émile was freed, the moon had draped a silvery lace over the forest. His buddies stretched a blanket between two poles to bring him close to a campfire and assess the damage by its light: open fractures with bones sticking out, a profusely bleeding gash on the forehead, and probable severe internal damage. Blood oozed steadily from Émile's ears, nose and lips. Nothing they'd not seen before. Nothing they could do, but wait and pray.

The others trooped to the main fire and sat in a circle around the big iron kettle filled with a thick dry pea and salt pork soup; breakfast fare. There had been no time to roast the juicy pieces of bear Aristide was willing to share. The Indians had had enough of the "Père;" they gathered separately.

Although they shared the circle, backs were turned on empty spots at Cadillac's sides. There would be no singing and storytelling tonight. The resentment hung around the fire; Cadillac appeared not to care.

Suddenly, Le Grand Pierre, who'd been sullenly cleaning his teeth with the point of his knife, shoved his wooden plate aside and vaulted up in one supple motion. Enough is enough. Le Grand Pierre had had his fill of Cadillac's hard driving. He hurled his shiny blade through the night where it flashed a silvery arc before embedding itself at Cadillac's foot, shortly followed by its swaggering, powerful owner. The flames painted menacing shadows across Le Grand Pierre's face and the fire crackled and spat, warning of peril, harsh words, clenched fists and flickering weapons. A hush fell over the groups.

Cadillac's stare never wavered, but his calculating eyes noticed, registered and committed to memory. He would remember each and everyone's reaction. His second in command, de Tonti, sneered quite openly. But Cadillac shrewdly controlled his temper; Le Grand Pierre could sway a crowd. He drew on his pipe, which had gone out, and tapped it against his shoe, staring at the other man in the pool of light. Raising slowly he picked up the blade and wiped it with his own kerchief. "Yours, I believe? You appear somewhat careless with such a fine blade; mind it does not stray one time too many."

Père de Gueslis, emerging from the dark, yanked Le Grand Pierre back with a force he did not know he had. "*Mon fils*, it is indeed a fine blade, use it wisely." Le Grand Pierre tugged himself free and snatched his blade. Torn between his anger and the words of a godly man, he hesitated.

Père Delhalle pounced in. "Did you all know that a blade—not as fine as this, of course—might have started the fur trade? Commandant Lamothe, could I entreat you to bring your enlightened knowledge to mine and help where I falter?" Cadillac eyed him coolly, nodded and regally resumed his place. With a gentle, persuasive hand, Père de Gueslis coerced Le Grand Pierre to sit. He sat, his hard stare glued on Cadillac, who shrugged it off.

The crowd, deprived of a good fight, grumbled but settled back, always ready for a *conte*. These yarns represented news, knowledge and entertainment. Who got killed and who was where, what new stream and new place had been discovered, and what wondrous deeds had been done. A *conte* always started from true information, but as it passed from mouth to mouth, it was embellished, improved upon and often reinvented. It grew from report to yarn to tall tale, and the men relished it. A good trapper was appreciated, but a gifted raconteur was loved and sought out.

Père Delhalle launched into ardent storytelling while he controlled the company's volatile temper. "After Christopher Columbus discovered this continent, in 1492, a frenzy of adventure overtook Europe, and rulers dreamed of conquests and wealth. Each wanted to be the first to claim the shores of this *Nouveau Monde*. Most headed south. But *we* headed north . . ." Boisterous cheers cut him short. Hands raised, he commanded silence.

"Enough with rulers and long words, get on to the fine blade!" quipped Francois de Lorme around the clay pipe hanging from his mouth.

"Er . . . the blade, *oui, tout de suite*. Immediately. But let me start my story. If I don't place it in time, it won't mean any-thing." He cleared his throat. "Even in those times, Breton fishermen (other loud cheers and a smug smile from Le Grand Pierre, who came from St. Malo, a fishing port in Brittany) ventured far north into the Atlantic, near Newfoundland, in search of cod. That's where my story starts."

"About time, too!"

"Let him finish," commanded Cadillac.

Père Delhalle bowed gratefully. "One day a fishing boat left its cozy little harbor off the coast of Brittany. As the women and children waved and the priest blessed them, the fishermen dreamed of all the cod they'd catch and the comfort the money would bring to their families.

"Driven by need and dreams, they ventured further and further north into the Atlantic. They were near Newfoundland when a furious storm tossed their hapless vessel on the snarling ocean." Père Delhalle was on a roll, he held his audience captive in a chain of words and glowed with pleasure. "Frozen, hungry and disoriented, the men sought shelter from the bashing waves. They found the opening of the Golfe du St. Laurent in our present Nouvelle France. They anchored their boat and rowed ashore. There, they tried to build a fire to warm their chilled limbs and dry their clothes. Later, when the storm had abated, they would hunt for meat and seek fresh water. All listened to the whispers and cries of an alien land, nervous fingers curled around daggers. One man raised his eyes and jumped up, raising the alarm. They'd been noiselessly surrounded by copper-skinned men carrying clubs and arrows, watching them with open curiosity. Neither side had ever confronted men of different skin color. Each group of men eyed the other wearily. Boldly, one Indian stepped forward, and pulling a thick animal skin off his shoulders, dangled it on a stick toward the frozen fishermen. 'They're friendly! *Regardez*, Look! This one is offering us his garment!' cried one fisherman, extending a trembling hand toward the gift, retrieving his dagger from his sheath with the other. '*Pour vous*, for you,' he said to the Indian, presenting the blade on his open palm.

"And thus started the first trading. Many followed in the fishermen's footsteps. And all this because of a blade."

Père Delhalle stopped to watch the reaction. The crowd nodded, but was plainly hungry for more. "You followed in the fishermen's footsteps," he improvised, "Enduring a trying passage . . ."

"In stinking, freezing boats, with many of us dying of *mal de terre!*" interrupted Marsac.

"Rotting food and dank water laced with brandy that gnawed at my belly . . ."

"Retching and spitting my teeth overboard!" A few rolled

over with laughter.

Cadillac shuddered at the memories of his own miserable crossings in dark, airless and dismal quarters, the pungent stink of wet wood burning his nostrils. He had better recollections of his privateering days, when he had reserved himself the best living quarters.

"Peeing in an overflowing bucket of slop!"

"Winds and storms steering us off course . . ." Le Grand Pierre added.

"What course?" cracked Dugué.

"Our ships were bulky and difficult to maneuver." Cadillac remembered only too well the challenge of navigating François Guyon's ships. "We tried to follow maps of sea routes showing known wind directions to fill the sails, but currents and storms threw us off course. Our compass and backstaff were not enough help." Cadillac's authoritative tone dominated all voices. No one knew what a backstaff was and they were not about to ask; Cadillac was enough of a show-off. Besides, they were still seething.

"I have heard that at the Greenwich Royal Observatory they're researching something called longitude, but don't know how to chart it," remarked Père de Gueslis.

"That's interesting, how . . ." Cadillac started. The crowd whistled and grumbled. They wanted stories about people, not science. Cadillac stopped, one eyebrow arched dangerously.

"Commandant Lamothe, why don't you tell us about our ancestors, the first explorers to tame this land?" soothed Père Delhalle rather quickly.

Cadillac crossed his legs at the ankles and stroked his mustache. The nonchalant position brought him freedom from his otherwise starched composure. But the relaxation was only apparent, because while his mind whirred to cull its knowledge of history, his keen eyes continued to observe the gathering. The company shifted and stretched, seeking a comfortable position before settling into another *conte* session. Some refilled their pipes.

"Once the mouth of the St. Laurent was discovered, the call of the river enticed bold men farther and farther up its stream. Using natural waterways, and in spite of many hardships, they gradually rowed their way into Mishegum, between Lac des Hurons and Lac des Illinois. . . ."

Brass nested French trade kettles, two small kettles, and a French hand forged steel yard balance with a wooden arm. Kettles were packed inside one another to conserve space. They were one of the earliest and most popular trade items of the Natives, and were traded by weight.

Sainte Anne

Today a warehouse and church had to be erected. As a precaution le Sieur de Lamothe Cadillac decided to build the *magazin* first and the church second. Gun powder and casks of *eau-de-vie* required securing as soon as possible. Then more time could be dedicated to the church. A church to offer solace to the men, appease the *Jésuites* and provide Père Delhalle with his little parish.

"*Vous* . . . You . . . *et vous*," he said, pointing to groups of renown hardworking men, "Take the longest logs to the southeast corner and start hewing. For the church we'll lay them on their sides," he patted one. "White oak. Hard and heavy as iron."

His duty accomplished, Cadillac searched for Père Delhalle. He spotted his grey garb amongst Dugué's group. "Ah, *mon Père!*" A high-spirited back slap accompanied his words. The unsuspecting priest pitched forward. Unabashed, Cadillac caught him by the sleeve and continued his train of thought, "What's the patron saint of the day?"

Startled, the priest faltered, "Today . . . er, today, ah! July 26, is the first day of the feast of Sainte Anne."

"What does Anne mean?"

"It's a good name, meaning 'grace.'"

"So be it. With your permission, of course, your little church will be named Ste. Anne."

"The name brings me joy and I am certain our Lord would approve."

Cadillac bowed and strode back, in high spirits, to the southeast corner to direct the building of the walls. Nothing roused more excitement than walls going up.

Le Grand Pierre was there, hewing a white oak, energetically sweeping his finely sharpened adze over its surface, each bite revealing the buttery, smooth surface of the wood, woodchips falling on his moccasins. "What length do you want it?"

Cadillac warmly eyed the cleanly hewed wood and ran knowing fingers on its flat flesh; ah, to transform the rough into the smooth, to bend nature and men to his will. "My plan says thirty-five feet long by twenty-three feet wide. We'll raise the walls today. The roof and chinking are for tomorrow."

All day men strained, hewing and cutting, rolling and lifting logs into place with braces. By late afternoon, the side walls reached almost seven feet. Holes had been cut for the entrance door and two small windows.

Cadillac sent for the two priests, requesting their immediate attendance. "*Tambour, l'Assemblée*"! Call the Assembly! *Soldats, en garde!*" They formed two disorderly rows, *justaucorps* and *vestes* discarded, chemises opened at the neck, sleeves rolled up.

He bid them in after the priests with a grand gesture of his hand, barely containing his pride and excitement. The others, a mixed lot of Frenchmen and Indians, trooped in behind, hair plastered to their foreheads, sweat streaking down the deep grooves of their weary faces.

They piled in, mopping their brows with the back of their forearms. Their senses filled with the sharp scent of freshly cut wood and the pungent smell of sweat, grease and grime, they glorified in their deed. Inside the four walls, light pierced through the timbers, distributing dappled brilliance across the interior and frolicking on the trampled grass and the men's white and cinnamon skins, hair and clothes. Above the walls a fringe of foliage danced merrily against the clear blue summer sky. The building stood as proud and entrancing as a cathedral, a tribute to man's endurance and the power of his dreams.

Mind racing, Cadillac envisioned the little chapel as it would soon be, placing here and there the articles of devotion they'd brought with them. Here would be the colors of France and the altar on which he would place the silver chalice purchased with his own funds. And there would go the confessional—the confessional, *sacrebleu*, had not yet been unloaded! No confession, no communion tonight. That would not do.

Nouvelle France had been created partly in the name of *Dieu*, although Détroit was established for a commercial and political purpose. But French colonists were nevertheless very religious. Their social life centered around the family and the church; a wise decision in a time when Church and Government were not separated and disobeying religious code was breaking civil law. The penalty came twofold. If a person was caught or reported eating meat or doing manual labor on a Holy day (there were over fifty in addition to Sundays—most of them falling in summer, a season of intense farming activities, forcing families to toil fifteen to twenty hours a day to make up for lost time) the guilty party could lose a year's earnings. Those accused might endure public humiliation, crawl on their knees to the altar to confess their sins to the assembly, and pay a hefty fine to the accuser.

Taking communion without confessing one's sins was an even bigger one: a Mortal one, a sin that sent you straight to Hell. This sin was so severe that people never traveled without their precious *certificats de confession* that entitled them to receive the sacrament of communion and a Christian burial.

Confessions were heard by the priest who delivered penance in a practical form: helping the poor, nursing the sick or the keeping of silence for slanderers. In this wilderness, *Dieu* only knew what price sin could bring.

Cadillac clapped his hands, breaking the precious moment irreverently. "Le Grand Pierre! We need to unload the confessional, take some men and bring it over."

Le Grand Pierre eyed Cadillac wearily. His mind quickly reviewed some of his deepest offenses, not liking the forthcoming task one bit. The other men showed their dislike of the task by squirming uneasily. He ambled away heavily, three men grudgingly following him.

Cadillac organized his sins into categories and, in his usual arrogant way, dismissed some, reduced others and gracefully left a few intact. One by one, men discreetly shuffled out, not quite tiptoeing, mumbling about pressing work, and darting through the door to freedom.

A few minutes later Le Grand Pierre and his companions returned, huffing and sweating heavily, burdened in more ways than one by the weight of the solid oak confessional. The two priests stood by the door, a Bible in hand. The crowd remained cautiously outside. After depositing the confessional on the ground with a loathing expression, Le Grand Pierre and his companions bolted toward the exit.

A hand gripped Le Grand Pierre's shoulder. "Ah, *bien*. Our first men to reconcile their souls with our Lord," said Père Delhalle. Trapped as ermines by hounds, the four froze, horrified. As one man, they bunched up.

"Come, my son." The hand applied more pressure. Resigned, Le Grand Pierre turned to the confessional, his Adam's apple bobbing up and down a few times. The others bolted wildly outside.

Père de Gueslis organized a line and when Le Grand Pierre emerged from the chapel, the men trooped in one by one to unburden themselves of their sins. Excessive wenching—none of that these past ten weeks—drinking, swearing and generally adapting the rules of their church to fit their needs. They would return to their old ways soon after the magical moment had passed.

When all the men had prepared their souls for communion, including Cadillac, who had walked in with the light, confident steps of a man having little to confess, huge fires were banked for a feast. The *tambour* joyously burst into "La Prière," the Prayer, calling them to their first mass at the new fort. Meanwhile, the non-Christian braves saw to the roasting.

The Colors of France were brought in and placed with great ceremony near a makeshift altar. The Fleur-de-Lys stood still, a bright gold and blue patch against the creamy logs.

Flanked by the two priests, Cadillac stood by the altar. "*Messieurs*, by the power vested in me by our gracious Roy, Louis XIV, and by the good fortune bestowed on us by our mighty Lord, I hereby declare this church be named Sainte Anne. This day, in this place, we hold in our heart our God and our country. Indivisible." Heads bowed. "Prepare to thank our Lord for all his bounty with an open heart. Père Delhalle, pray officiate." Ah, if only greed, love and ambition did not cause humans to deviate and fall.

The Fight

Père Delhalle proclaimed the mass ended. The men erupted from the church like a charging herd of buffalo. Cadillac stepped out regally, not at all offended by the unruly behavior; biding his time, fully aware of what was to come and welcoming it.

As most men of different races and situations do when forced to live together for a long time, the band needed a release for their hot tempers and hot blood craving for a woman, a drink, warm food, and a good fistfight. At last they were given the chance to even gripes and settle disputes. Women missing, tonight they would double the drinking and brawling.

Cadillac gestured Marsac and two soldiers to follow him. Père de Gueslis noticed and made as if to follow but thought better of it. The men returned carrying caskets of *eau-de-vie* on their shoulders. They were hailed as heroes. Cadillac grinned smugly under his prominent nose. Be damned! *Que le diable emporte* Père de Gueslis's self-righteous soul! Père Delhalle winced at the sight of the brandy.

Le Grand Pierre grabbed a casket and noisily guzzled the amber liquid, not stopping for breath. Men waited their turn, smacking their lips, eyes darting down the line. "*Vite*, Pierre, pass it on!"

The fires' dancing lights illuminated their flushed faces. Dark, damp patches grew on their vests. Mosquitoes hovered and landed. Indians applied their paints and brought out the drums. Fat dripped, flames spat back. The stench of sour breaths and sweat sat on the clearing. Greasy fingers grabbed juicy bits and shoved them into half-filled mouths, wetting the lot with generous swigs of firewater.

Cadillac moved from group to group with the casket, passing the fiery drink to eager hands. More food, more *eau-de-vie*; more and more, to make up for weeks of backbreaking work and privation.

A gentleman would have gagged. Not Cadillac. He looked about him, satisfied. It was the smell of men enjoying themselves. Except for a few graceful swigs to prove the men he was one of them, he did not indulge. He was accustomed to a more expensive, smoother brandy—Armagnac, Gascony's own brand—one he could swirl around in his mouth; all silk and sweet fire. Besides, tonight required all of his wits.

Satiated, bellies stretched and brains heated, the men challenged each other to games, any game a man might beat another in; racing, shooting, spitting, peeing and more. Émile and a cask of *eau-de-vie* had been propped up with grass-stuffed blankets. Dragging with fatigue, befuddled by brandy, some of the men crawled in the bushes to retch and slumber, then shook their buddies up and dared them to do it all again.

"Anyone ready for a *jeu de main*?" Le Grand Pierre retrieved a tiny emblem in the shape of a woman carved in bone from his bead bag. He kissed it before hiding it in one of his hands behind his back.

A whole season's earnings were gambled and often lost on this hand game, with only a fifty percent chance of winning. Some Indians gathered around Le Grand Pierre, bringing moccasins and buckskin vests and whatever else they could bet. Others searched their clouded minds to recall anything worth betting. Coins being scarce on the frontier, they used baubles, Jesuit rings, religious medals and playing cards as markers.

Le Grand Pierre passed the brandy around, "*Buvez, mes amis, buvez*; drink, my friends, drink." Spirits enticed boldness and foolishness; bets became wild and could fatten up a clever player's pockets.

Cadillac sat next to Aristide Dents Crochues, drawing on a pipe. White smoke billowed around him. "Le Faucon is busy," someone murmured.

Sitting cross-legged, Aristide was already rocking precariously. Cadillac nudged him. "*Encore*, more brandy?" Drunk, Aristide babbled on and on. Cadillac knew enough *Outaouais* tongue to decode his slurred words, mostly valuable information about the *Renards* (Foxes) he hoped would settle around the fort.

Loud, angry voices erupted from a gambling group, a few men were already exchanging drunken punches. Cadillac craned his neck in their direction and pushed more brandy on his companion. Aristide crumbled to the ground and snored loudly.

"You bastard, you've broken my nose . . ."

"And I'll break a lot more before I'm finished."

At that point everyone felt they had to take sides. Which side did not matter. They all needed a good brawling. They slugged and punched and reduced each other to bloody messes.

Cadillac watched, not one bit put out. Oh, the pain tomorrow! But tonight months of frustration were disposed of. Here and there some collapsed in breathless heaps. They would have gone on fighting until their strength had gone and their fists became too weak to raise. But Père de Gueslis darted amongst them, pistol in hand, cunningly avoiding wild blows. The fighters stopped at the second shot in the air, most of them in ruin, all of them startled. "*Mes fils*! My sons! Cease immediately. Commandant, I entreat you to stop these men killing each other."

"They're hardly killing each other, they're enjoying it."

The cutting edge to Cadillac's voice further angered Père de Gueslis. "Drunk. All drunk, on the *eau-de-vie* you provided. A disgrace to our Mother country."

Jesuits had exerted pressure on France to abolish the brandy trade for a long time. Early colonists had introduced liquor to the native Indians, who by now had become hooked and demanded it as a trading item. Unfortunately, Indians had no resistance to alcohol, and apart from the unpredictable behavior triggered by it, they were cheated by traders who gambled and bought pelts at a pitiful price. After a whole season's work, an Indian was often left with no other reward but empty pockets and a mighty hangover.

This provoked the outrage of the Catholic missionaries, whose purpose reached far beyond converting and teaching: they wished to stop the abuse and oppression of the Natives. The Jesuits had pushed for the abolition of the brandy trade. The anti-liquor faction had won; a royal decree forbade the trading of liquor to the Indians.

Stationed at Michilimackinac at the time the decree was issued, Cadillac had not agreed, protesting vehemently and scheming feverishly. The Indians wanted alcohol; they had not sworn loyalty to the French, and began trading with the British, who were not so hampered by ethics and were willing to oblige. The Northwestern fur trade could easily change hands. The fur trade had become big business and several tribes and countries competed for its profits. Cadillac was reported ignoring the royal command on several occasions.

Cadillac turned frigid, eyes as dark as sloe, "They needed it. This is *my* fort and these are *my* men. I am the commandant, I act as I see fit, without your meddling." The tone had risen and boomed in the now quiet clearing.

"The Church will hear of this, and the court. You are forbidden to give spirits to the Indians by royal decree. *Eau-de-vie* brings lewdness, violence and exploitation! It robs Indians of their dignity."

Cadillac snorted. "Are your eyes and mind so closed to believe that in our efforts to bring our civilization to this *Nouveau Monde* we could purge it of all its vices and shield the native man from our faults? Even a mother cannot stop her child from acquiring knowledge of the world. These people are sharp-witted, I cannot forbid one race to partake in what another so freely indulges." He shook his head in frustration. Such a sense of déja vu! He'd used the same argument to placate Père Carheil, the *Jésuite* missionary stationed with him at Fort Michilimackinac, the one he'd had great trouble keeping his fist away from after many similar quarrels.

"I cannot ignore such a blatant transgression of Roy Louis' will. I shall write to *sa Majesté*."

Cadillac planted himself in front of Père de Gueslis, regal, icy and commanding. Mere inches apart, the two men glared at each other, body and mind wound in such a tight coil it threatened to spring and hit. Cadillac visibly pulled a tight hold on himself.

"You may act as you please. I am liked at the court. Powerful friends have sponsored me. Indeed, Roy Louis himself has placed the royal seal on my mission. You look after the souls, I take care of the men . . ."

"They're one and the same . . ."

"*Non.* Some men don't want a soul. *Pardieu*, an uncomfortable thing a soul can be." He dismissed the priest with a disdainful gesture of his hand and marched away.

Père de Gueslis would not be shaken off. "Commandant Lamothe, your powerful friends will not be able to shelter you from your folly. The Church will see to that."

Cadillac turned, a purplish, dark shade creeping on his face. "You can write all the letters you desire, report on all the meager things your narrow mind accuses me of. But remember when you fall that I warned you."

Several years later le Sieur de Lamothe Cadillac was to eat his words. Father de Gueslis became the Jesuit Superior in Quebec, a powerful position. Cadillac continued to claim a little too loudly that clerics had no business interfering in State affairs. He was guilty of being ahead of his time. France would agree with him in 1789 (fifty-nine years after his death) during the French revolution, when Church and State were separated. Cadillac's intense anti-Jesuit sentiments would precipitate his downfall and follow him to the grave. He and the powerful Society he called the "Roue Infernale" would file charge after countercharge against each other and appeal to the King of France for arbitration. Louis XIV, fatigued by their constant bickering, sent strict orders to the Gouverneur Général de Nouvelle France to settle their quarrels. An agreement was reached in 1702 that neither side respected. And the merry dance continued. . . .

Detroit remains one of the rare posts not founded by the Jesuits. Father Delhalle had been nominated parish priest. Father Vaillant de Gueslis departed soon after the arrival in Detroit. Several historians claim Cadillac contrived to provoke a public argument, accusing Father Vaillant of treason and inciting the settlers' anger, leaving no choice to the Jesuit but to depart. And yet, a letter written by the missionary only a few months later displays no rancor. Cadillac claims to have dismissed the Jesuit on grounds of ill health. What really happened? No one knows. Whatever the reasons, their forced "cooperation" in Detroit must have strained their tempers to the limit, and we can safely assume several fiery arguments flared between the two.

The Morning After

When the sun burst unto the clearing the next morning, many pairs of bloodshot eyes blasted it a dirty look. Cadillac squinted at it. Soon, he would give orders for *la Diane*, the wake up call. His packed schedule did not include sick time. He counted on the cool water of the river to revive this pitiful lot.

Dieu, his head pounded! He massaged it. Aside from the few swigs he'd taken for show, he and the two priests had not drank, and yet he was left with a bitter taste. A sour, long-lasting taste placed by the argument with that *sacré* Père de Gueslis.

Groups ambled to the river. Soon a moist, hot wind ruffled their hair and played with the leaves. In the north, smoky, puffed up clouds rolled angrily toward the clearing.

The first roar of thunder cracked over their heads as they started delving their wooden spoons into pots of boiled dried peas flavored with a meager portion of salt pork. The sky darkened and a breath of storm snatched Cadillac's tricorne and danced with it, twirling its white plume. Antoine chased after it. Heavy drops of rain began to drum a mad tempo on the party. Men grabbed the cooking pots and took refuge under canoes and tents, followed by their hungry buddies.

Facing each other under different tents Père de Gueslis and Cadillac locked glances; Cadillac confident, imperious and challenging, and Père de Gueslis tense, outraged and determined. While a violent, mighty storm ripped furiously through the clearing, renting their clothes, whipping their faces, tearing at their hair, it was nothing compared to the silent battle raging between these two formidable men.

As abruptly as it had started, the storm ended. The sun, brilliant and triumphant, resumed its merciless beating on the sodden crowd. Their soggy clothes steaming in the sudden heat, men separated into weary crews. Only Cadillac showed great force and energy, marching between groups, bending over work, listening and encouraging. This little patch of land was more than mere boggy soil and tangled trees. This clearing stood in the center of their dreams—the heart and control of the fur trade. And he would let nothing—and no one—snatch the dreams that kept him and his men going. He would endure, resist, survive and conquer, and he would make sure his men did as well.

The evening was a disturbing mixture of elation and resentment. The *magazin*, albeit missing a roof, had been closed off and the powder casks rolled in, Laplante guarding them. The church's roof had been completed and three quarters of the palisade erected. This should have been the occasion for much rejoicing, but as the men stretched their weary bodies and rubbed bear grease on their raw hands, the fatigue, the tension between Cadillac and Père de Gueslis, the relentless demands of their commandant, came to claim their minds and rob them of joy. Cadillac sat on his own, outwardly unaffected, penning his report to Governor Callière.

Monseigneur,
    You will see appended the plan of Fort Pont-chartrain du Detroit. . . . Its position is advantageous; it is at the narrowest part of the river, where no one can pass by without being seen. Our humble little church has been completed and our joy is great. . . .

The tradition states that Ste. Anne's church, named after the patron saint of the day, as was the French custom, was erected first. This wonderfully romantic concept is most likely untrue for two reasons. First, as a seasoned soldier, Cadillac would have ordered the immediate construction of the palisade as protection. Second, gun powder and pelts required securing, and the colony's first year survival depended on the supplies they had brought with them. Sheltering them from inclement weather and thieving hands became a top priority, hence the warehouse and powderhouse. Ste. Anne must have been the third building to grace the new settlement.

It is doubtful that this original building reached a high degree of sophistication. Time was not on their side. Waterway traffic closed toward the end of October, when winter took earth and water in its icy grip, paralyzing all communications. The settlers had to complete the housing and the planting of the following year's crop before this ominous time.

Social life centered around the family and the church. A parish was sustained by the "tithe," an unpopular tax levied on the villagers and sent directly to the Upper Country archdiocese.

The parish priest was the spiritual leader of the community. His main function was to administer the sacraments, but in a remote post like Detroit, he taught religion to the white and native children, kept an eye on the adults, attended to the sick and the bereaved, converted the tribes, helped in the fields, and enforced traditions and morality. His importance ranked second only to that of the commandant.

The Arrival of the Hurons

Sitting at a newly-hewn table in the privacy of his dwelling, Cadillac reviewed the reports from the Delorme brothers. He had sent the pair to deliver an invitation to tribes of the Hurons, *Outaouais* and Oppenagos to settle around the fort. The report said the Huron elders had agreed to enjoy his protection and a large tribe had begun its exodus toward their new home.

He had moved into this roughly-built abode about a month ago, the first one erected after the *magazin* and the church. The interior was dim, with only an orange, opaque light filtering through the thinly scraped skins stretched over the window openings, and he kept his door partially open for extra light. The tangy fragrance of the naked logs did not quite cover the musty scent of the earthen floor, and neither could the slight breeze whistling between them. But home it was, with its welcomed privacy.

For now, the colony was racing against winter, swiftly building shelters for everyone. Outside, the pounding of running feet, shouting, hollering and general commotion told him a packet of voyageurs from Quebec had arrived, bringing fresh news, supplies, and letters, and for him, no doubt, orders from Governor Callière.

"Commandant."

Cadillac almost jumped a foot.

A wooden box on his shoulder and a letter in one hand, a voyageur eyed him with a twinkle in his eyes.

"Leave them here," he barked and shuffled his papers in a busy manner.

"M'sieur Cadillac, Sieur Grandmesnil sends his respect and begs for your attendance at the *magazin* to check the supplies you requested."

"Tell him I shall be there immediately."

He tore the seal of Governor Callière's letter. As usual the missive was polite but cool. Not too many rebukes about his complaints of the *sacrés Jésuites* this time. At least he did not have one living here anymore, breathing fire in his back. He had cleverly contrived the departure of Père François de Gueslis a few weeks before.

He needed to step outside, to shake the darkness of his home, to be part of the bustling, to absorb the sounds of men going about their business. His boots crunched on the crisp, dry soil of the main street, Ste. Anne. The crackling of gold-speckled leaves told him he and his men must hurry, hurry, because although today was a dazzling early autumn morning, winter already sent warning signals that it was preparing to settle its heavy frozen cloak over the clearing.

In Rencontre, a perpendicular alleyway to Ste. Anne, workers sawed and hammered under Le Grand Pierre's directions, quickly putting together cabin after cabin on the twenty-five-foot square lots he'd marked out. Several voyageurs loitered by them, smoking, gesticulating and guffawing, their bright sashes splashing rainbow colors on the upright logs. Between the pounding of his hammer Le Grand Pierre cracked jokes and sent everyone into roaring fits of laughter.

Within its tall palisade the fort was vibrating with excitement. There was much yelling and cheering and back-slapping. As Cadillac strolled to the *magazin*, men saluted him. The *magazin* was teeming with people and he had to jostle his way inside. The noise, the heat, the reek of leather, untreated furs and sweat, socked him in the face. The newly-arrived voyageurs were unloading the goods sent from Quebec; guns and barrels of powder, woolen blankets, cooking utensils and an array of tools. Veron Grandmesnil stood in their midst taking notes, his assistants rolling barrels and stacking the merchandise under his direction. Several Indians watched the whole proceedings, eyes following goods they might later trade their pelts for. Piles of furs lay in every available space. Shelves overflowed with wooden boxes of goods, leather straps, and baskets and sacks of grains.

Cadillac walked to the grain stock, elbowing his way through the crowd. He untied a sack and ran his finger through the seeds of wheat they had brought from Montreal in June. It was dry and healthy, ready for the second planting he anticipated in the spring. There had been no time for individual farming, so the men had cleared fifteen arpents of communal land outside the stockade and hastily sowed the first crop.

Veron Grandmesnil spotted him and beckoned him over. Suddenly the voice of a soldier boomed from the doorway. "Commandant! Commandant, *ils sont là*, they're here!"

"*Qui?* Who's here?" Cadillac craned his neck over the many heads blocking his way.

"Indians! Hundreds of them!"

Cadillac darted out of the *magazin* as if it were on fire, raced to a corner bastion and climbed its ladder. Then he saw them, hundreds of them walking out of the wilderness, approaching the fort with remarkable ceremony. Hurons! He recognized them by their hairstyle, a crest of greased hair standing on their head. He clambered down as fast as he could. "De Tonti, where is he? Find him," he yelled at someone standing by. "Tell him to bring a battalion. Dugué, Chacornacle, follow me! Marsac, guard the bastions!" Except for the running soldiers, all activity had suddenly ceased, the chatter had quieted, men stood rooted in place, beholding the incredible sight through the open gates and bastions. The field workers handled their tools nervously, wiping their hands on the cotton *sarraux* covering their frayed woolen pantalons. Those harnessed to the plough dropped the leather straps, torn between making a dash for the protection of the fort or staying in place. At last Cadillac marched out of the fort, a puffed-out de Tonti by his side, and a quickly-assembled battalion behind them.

Cadillac raised his hand. "Halt!" He watched the approach of the Hurons with awe.

In the first row marched the young men with bows, arrows and painted shields slung over their shoulders, prancing on their loose, long limbs, oozing energy and excitement from every pore of their cinnamon skin. Behind them marched the men, magnificently dressed in their doe and elk skins, leggings decorated with porcupine quills, their proud faces painted, jet-black eyes unwavering, and hands filled with hatchets, knives and wooden clubs. Bear claws and carvings of buffalo horn and tufts of hairs from their enemies swayed at their waist with every step. Next came the elders, unpainted and covered with long buffalo robes touching Mother Earth, walking at a slower pace but with great dignity. Each elder carried a peace pipe in his hand. Then, a distance behind, came the women, loaded like packhorses, papooses on their back, dragging travois burdened by the tribe's possessions; fur blankets, baskets, cooking ware and rolled-up bark to cover their wigwams.

The human tide came closer, and closer, and halted several yards from Cadillac. The procession split to let the elders through. The women rushed to hand them beaver skins which they set in front of Cadillac.

After the customary exchange of greetings, Cadillac directed them to the area he had preselected for their village; to the right of the fort, across the river, where he would collect rent.

The women built the wigwams in less than three hours, including a makeshift meeting lodge where the elders and some braves awaited the arrival of the commandant and his men. Cadillac, de Tonti and the two lieutenants, the priest, Veron Grandmesnil and the interpreter Fafar Delorme, arrived with great pomp, each carrying pistols, daggers and gifts. They stooped inside and sat on bear skins around the kindled fire, laying their weapons at their sides.

A Huron elder stood and gravely set an adorned, lit peace pipe in front of Cadillac. Removing his buffalo robe, half-naked, he started singing, praising his "Père," putting his tribe under Cadillac's protection, promising peace and help against his *Père's* enemies. He placed the robe on Cadillac's shoulders and presented more gifts of beaver and buffalo skins.

Cadillac rose and through Fafar Delorme's singing translation explained that their *Père* from across the big salted lake had come to offer peace and protection. "*Mes enfants*, I accept your gifts. In return, I bring you many peace offerings. This kettle to cook food in so 'my children' never go hungry. These hatchets to help them defend their women and children against their enemies; and four looking glasses, ten needles, and six combs to thank *mes enfants* for a safe passage through their country."

He picked up the peace pipe and, untying its painted eagle feathers, replaced them with six small knives. In great silence Cadillac deposited the pipe on the ground and surrounded it with his—and his men's—weapons. The elders nodded and solemnly passed the peace pipe around. Served quietly by the women, the feast began.

When their bellies were full, they stepped outside to continue the celebration. Settlers and soldiers joined them. Huron women danced and sang around fires, elders beat their drums and young men tried their luck at climbing a greased pole. To please them, Cadillac fought a mock duel with his rapier. He was a fine swordsman, much better than anyone in his regiment, and knowing it he'd chosen de Tonti as his opponent.

As was their custom, one elder threw a handful of tobacco on the flames and watched it sparkle, crackle and pop. *"Pas mal,* not bad," muttered Laplante. "But watch white man's tobacco!" and he tossed the content of a little leather pouch on the embers. Instinctively Cadillac and his companions scrambled up.

In a thundering spit, the fire exploded, blasting sparkling, bursting embers on every side, peppering the air with detonations and clouds of smoke. Terrified, the Hurons scattered. Soldiers, voyageurs and traders whooped with glee. After a while the Hurons, always ready to enjoy a good joke, returned to the fire and joined in the merriment.

All evening and most of the night until early morning, Cadillac prowled from group to group. The point of his boots glistened with dew as he listened, registering and remembering, looming over each bunch of men like a starving bird of prey. "Le Faucon," Hawk, they called him behind his back, and indeed that name was whispered many times that night.

Cadillac granted lands to the Hurons, planting the boundary markers himself, well within his fort's domain so he would keep control of the land and watch their every move. Oppenago (Wolves) settled to the left and Ottawas half a league (about 1.2 miles) further up, and also north of the Hurons. Miamis and Pottawatamies migrated also. All tribes, in accepting their grants of land, shouted *"Vive le Roy!"* three times with Cadillac. As a peace offering and at the chiefs' demands, especially Cheanonvoizon, the troublesome Huron chief, his men erected French-style cabins for the Indian leaders.

Cadillac claims that six thousand Indians wintered at Detroit in 1701 and 1702. This was an incredible feat considering he would have been responsible for their welfare (food, health and peace). By 1708 three hundred fifty-three acres of land had been cleared for cultivation by Indians and soldiers; one hundred fifty-seven owned by Cadillac, forty-six by settlers, and one hundred fifty by the Hurons. Sometimes supplies ran short and canoes were sent to Michilimackinac and Fort Frontenac (Lake Ontario) for provisions—an expensive exercise for a commandant who had claimed self-sufficiency and was bound to his words by a tight-fisted Louis XIV.

These tribes had previously been rivals and nomadic. Now, sedentary around the fort and forced to live in close proximity with one another, sporadic bloody skirmishes flared up. Occasionally a few innocents died in the crossfire.

Although the French and the Indians had established a working relationship—each side used the other for its own purpose—it required patience, skill and goodwill to understand each other. When Cadillac resided at the fort, he held both sides tightly in an iron grip, but during the two occasions (1702, and November 1704 to June 1706) when he was recalled to Quebec for an extended period of time, bloody clashes exploded.

Cadillac—the Seigneur

They should have long gone to bed, but Cadillac, his officers and Veron Grandmesnil were still playing cards in his cabin. The fort more or less completed, they lazily basked in self-indulgence, a warm sense of satisfaction wrapped around their chests.

They had dragged the table close to the fireplace to play in its light, preferring its amber glow to the stinky, smoky rushes dipped in bear or fish oil they normally used, the puffing of their pipes burying its brilliance in grey clouds.

Cadillac swallowed a swig of smooth Armagnac, especially imported to Quebec. He had brought only a few caskets with him and served it sparingly. A pani, a gift from the Hurons, tried to refill his mug. He waved the native servant away.

Soon after the Hurons, several other Indian Nations had come to settle around the fort; the Miamis, Oppenago, four nations of *Outaouais* and Pottawatomis, even a few fearsome Iroquois, and he'd granted them land to settle. Within a league four forts and villages had been built.

"Ah, I miss *les jolies demoiselles*—fair-skinned ladies with all their fineries. It will be a long winter without their company." Grandmesnil gave a heartfelt sigh that brought a broad smile on his companions' faces.

"And it will be duller soon, when the more challenging Indian males go hunting and trapping and hole up somewhere for winter, leaving the women and children in the care of the elders," remarked de Tonti idly.

Cadillac snorted and bit hard on his pipe. It was so easy for de Tonti to say so. It was he, Cadillac, who kept the many Indian Nations around the fort in a relatively peaceful state. The situation—as explosive as forcing the French and the British, who had been at each others' throats for several centuries, to cohabit pleasantly—required careful handling. It was he who ruled over it with an iron grip, always on the alert, always anticipating. But skirmishes at the fort suited de Tonti, they threw a cast over his superior's capabilities. To the delight of Gouverneur Callière and the *Jésuites*, conflicts boosted de Tonti's hopes of Cadillac's removal and his own promotion to the vacant post. *Et, bien*, we shall see who ousts the other first. The commandant's shrewd eyes nailed de Tonti to his chair.

"Dull? Surely, de Tonti, you mean 'peaceful,' a happy state we *all* have been working for." The rebuke sliced icily through the gathering's congeniality and the evening took on a sharp edge. De Tonti bowed slightly, eyes dipped low to hide their hatred, "*touché*." The others squirmed uncomfortably on their seats.

"This game is growing tedious." Cadillac disdainfully threw his cards on the table, pushed his chair back and started pacing. Eyebrows furrowed, fists clenching and unclenching, lost in his thoughts, stopping now and then to glare into the fire as if expecting a reply to whatever clouded his mind, he continued his furious treading, unmindful of his guests. Ignored, feeling spurned, de Tonti, Marsac, Dugué, Chacornacle and Grandmesnil glanced at each other and prepared to leave, de Tonti gritting his teeth, perpetually resentful and envious of his commandant's authority.

The noise snatched Cadillac from his daze. He raised an imperious hand. "*Non. Non. Restez.* Stay. I shall show you my plan." He took a map from his desk and unfolded it on the table. "De Tonti, I haven't discussed this with you but I am sure it will meet with your approval." De Tonti bowed woodenly. The others exchanged quick knowing glances; no love lost between those two.

"Here is the fort at its present size. *Dieu* granting safe passage to my wife and Madame de Tonti, I shall apply for the royal permission to call for your wives," he said to the three officers who were married. "Grandmesnil, being a bachelor, you'll have to take your chances with the *demoiselles* we can convince to join us. Dugué, pray, hold the top corners."

He pointed to some lines outside the fort on both sides of the river and perpendicular to it. "Look. See these lines? This is land I will grant to any deserving man who intends to farm it. Each lot has a narrow river frontage, so all can have access to water, but goes back a league or two. They look like ribbons."

Unlike the British, who relished their privacy and far-off neighbors, French pioneers, very sociable, preferred to live in close proximity, calling to each other from their doorsteps at night, "*Tout va bien?* All's well?"

De Tonti pursed his lips and hissed, "You need Royal permission to grant land."

Cadillac leveled him a smug look. "*Oui*, of course. And I applied to that effect in my last letter to Gouverneur Callière, who will duly pass my request to His Majesty. Until then, the men will receive oral grants from me. Any more questions?"

A worry line stretched across Chacornacle's forehead. "Wouldn't it be dangerous for these families to live so far from the fort?"

"Not if they tend to their land during the day and return to the safety of the fort at night."

"Will these families own the land?"

"Ah, Grandmesnil, *toujours pratique*. Always practical. I am a seigneur, this is my fief. This land was granted to me by *sa Majesté* and I, in turn, will lease it to the farmers."

"What about cattle and horses?" asked Marsac.

"I'll buy some from Quebec and Montreal as soon as we've established a secure route for all our goods. The watermill I was duty bound to construct as a seigneur is almost complete and proudly stands by the river."

"And some festivities, dances and soirées!" exploded Veron Grandmesnil.

"What about a . . ."

Cadillac lent only half an ear to the ensuing exchange, which had turned from the serious to the frivolous. He could see them, well-tended fertile fields of wheat and corn, rich pastures and fat cattle, rosy-cheeked youngsters and beaming parents. And when the time came, in May, to pay homage to their Seigneur, the contented villagers would gladly plant a proud pole in front of his house and a sturdy youth would climb it swiftly, crying, "*Vive le Roy! Vive le Seigneur du Détroit!* Long live the King! Long live the Lord of Détroit!" Sturdy youth. Antoine! He glanced at his son's empty pallet. *Pardieu*, he had forgot! The boy was becoming slippery as an eel, always in the communal kitchen, picking up swearwords and singing bawdy songs with the men. He'd been so preoccupied with the fort, he'd not paid much attention to his son's ragamuffin manners. Marie-Thérèse should be here soon. What a raking she'd give him!

The mighty Cadillac, fearless explorer, undaunted adventurer and iron-fisted ruler of a fort, wondered how many days remained before his wife's arrival and prayed it would be enough to squeeze some refinement out of his son.

He hurriedly rolled up the map. "*Messieurs*, the night is late. *Bonsoir*." Before they could say anything, he briskly ushered his startled companions out of the room. Seconds later, Cadillac raced to the communal kitchen.

Antoine, dishevelled and flushed, was standing on a table in the center of a spirited chorus bellowing a drinking ditty that Cadillac himself had known well in his younger days.

" . . . *A boire et à chanter,*
Jamais se marier,
Car le mariage,
Est une vie d'esclavage,
Nourrir fe. . . ."[3]

Marie-Thérèse's disapproving face flashed in front of Cadillac and, white at the mouth, he clamped a hand over his son's lips and dragged him, bucking and kicking, all the way home.

The bulk of Cadillac's oral grants were recorded in 1707, others were added in 1708, 1709, and 1710. To obtain a conveyance one was required to first pay a fixed yearly rent to the seigneur (Cadillac). If a property became delinquent or its owner did not maintain actual possession of it, it reverted to Cadillac's ownership. An owner could not borrow against his land without consent nor sell without giving Cadillac the first right to purchase. Second, because Cadillac had exclusive rights of trading at the post, anyone involved in a trade or craft had to pay a tax for the privilege of practicing it. Streets of Detroit are named after the first landowners: Beaubien, Casse, Campau, Chesne, Rivard, Livernois, etc.

In 1710 sixty-eight habitants "owned" lots within the fort, thirty of whom also rented stretches of land by the river, and

---

[3]   An old 15th century song addressed to bachelors, advising them of the pitfalls associated with women.
"Never to marry,
Because marriage,
Is a life of slavery,
Feeding woman and child . . ."

thirteen cultivated gardens outside the palisade. Settlers who leased both obtained a discount. Of the sixty-eight settlers, twenty-nine were soldiers, including Jacob de Marsac, who traded his uniform for a plow. All soldiers belonged to the Compagnie de la Marine, and served a dual role as policemen and soldiers. Anxious to see them integrate in civilian life, the Ministry of Marine encouraged them to settle after or even during their service.

Immaculate garden plots dotted the outside perimeter of the fort. Although the region offered abundant meat and fish, vegetables were an important part of the French diet. Families, even the Cadillacs, carefully tended their own little patch. The main street was Ste. Anne, which ran parallel to the river. That the Cadillacs lived there we have no doubt—lots around that area reached a higher price than anywhere else.

Cadillac conveyed a plot inside the fort to a woman, Marie Lepage, and a tract of land on the river to his daughter, Magdeleine; a most unusual move for the period. Was Cadillac a liberal for his time, or were these women especially smart? Both. Cadillac had no tolerance for fools and since he conveyed them important land, Marie and Magdeleine must have earned his respect one way or another. That Cadillac was a visionary and a free thinker has already been proven by his actions. Married to an independent, capable and smart woman with a good business head, Cadillac used her talents unabashedly; he had soon realized it gave him the freedom to pursue his gnawing ambitions. Very early in their marriage, he gave Marie-Thérèse full power of attorney to handle all his affairs during his many long absences, wrote about her with great esteem, and never doubted her capabilities, however impossible the task or precarious the situation. She was asked to hire voyageurs and canoes, send supplies, write to so and so, close this deal and begin this one. And, alone in a then "man's world," Marie-Thérèse dealt with each request efficiently.

Madame Cadillac's Arrival

Lately, Cadillac had taken to amble by the river bluff, waiting for the arrival of his wife, whose coming he had privately requested before his departure. The days went by and the sky turned leaden grey. Crackling russet leaves twirled in a nippy little wind that grew more ferocious each day. He wrapped his woolen cape closer to his body and concern crept on his face. The river, the lifeline whose moods he perceived so well, would soon become a foe. His attachment to Marie-Thérèse set aside, her coming held a critical and commercial value.

Frenchmen had three enemies in Canada. The first two, a long and harsh winter and the fierce Iroquois, they were learning to adapt to. The third was more insidious and harder to face for arrogant seventeenth and eighteenth-century men—the lack of white women.

Traders, soldiers and explorers conquered new areas, but men alone could not colonize them. The task was too big, too lonely. Married men longed to get back to their families in Old France, bachelors dreamed of the maidens they had left behind. A few *coureurs de bois* lived with, or married, Indian women, but so far away from home, so cut off from their own civilization, most yearned for a companion of their own culture, a little bit of home in a foreign land. Most misbehaved, drinking, gambling and fornicating with native women, only a few wanted to settle. Women and children were needed to establish permanent colonies.

French women were the keepers of the faith, culture and traditions—the upholders of morality. They kept "the old man" on the straight and narrow. Women could toil through a load of chores assigned to their sex by society, then cross over to the male side. They could sweat behind a plow and reload their mates' muskets—a crossover rarely performed by men. Forced by babies and day-to-day duties to be less nomadic than their mates, women planted roots. Men could seize land, but women held on. to it.

Their stabilizing influence on the male population had not escaped the Crown. At one point, France allowed only married men to immigrate and imposed fines on parents whose sons were not married by the age of twenty and daughters by the age of sixteen. Women produced the next generation, the country's natural growth. Without them, there would be no posterity, and posterity mattered tremendously to white men and the future of the new colonies.

Indians, the Indians whose pelts the French relied upon, had grasped these facts long ago. They viewed the arrival of French women as "the most vital proof of their wish to settle an area in earnest." Convincing the native man to migrate to the Détroit, and enticing French and Canadian men to plant roots there to develop a flourishing colony, would require the presence of women.

But many horrifying reports of death and hardship in the Northwestern territory had reached the women's ears and they feared leaving the relative safety of established towns for what could be death on the river. Marie-Thérèse was to set an example, pave the way for others, because this fort had to succeed, it could not be allowed to fail.

And so, as promised, Cadillac had received confirmation that early in September 1701, his wife and Marie-Anne Picoté de Belestre, the wife of de Tonti, had boarded two canoes. Accompanied by a handful of men to protect them, they began their critical expedition. The message had brought him joy but also sorrow. On June 5, two days after his departure from Montreal, Marie-Thérèse had delivered a little girl, Marie-Anne, who died a few days later. She was their second consecutive child to pass away, and his heart had grieved at their loss and for the woman he loved and was not there to comfort.

As days went by without a sign of Marie-Thérèse, Cadillac, all too aware of the enormity of the task he had required of her, became tired and anxious. He barked and growled, as pleasant as a mother bear watching her cub being attacked.

The new peace treaty having recently been signed between France and the Iroquois, the authorities had advised she travel by the shorter route: up the St. Laurent, through Lac Frontenac and Lac Érié; seven hundred fifty miles through uncharted Iroquois territory—to show France's faith in the recent pact. She could have been raped, tortured, scalped and murdered.

The voyage would last close to six weeks—six weeks of constant fear of an Iroquois attack, of physical endurance, coarse food and no privacy. Cadillac imagined her sitting for ten to fifteen hours a day on the hard seat of the birch-bark canoe, goods and personal belongings heaped around her and no room to stretch. He knew how restless and bored their six-year-old son, Jacques, would grow, whining for constant maternal attention, pulling on her frock, fidgeting on her lap. He could see them clearly at night, beaching the canoes and bivouacking at the water's edge, all wrapped in furs and woolen blankets, close to the campfire, eating their ration of boiled dry peas and salt pork, always listening and watching for a possible attack. His heart would beat savagely, guilty of demanding so much in the name of success.

One morning, only minutes after his return from his quiet vigil by the river, just as an unseasonably hot sun melted the morning frost, the blast of a musket jolted him into action. Laplante shouted, "Canoes approaching!" Cadillac raced to the river, as did many others. Way down the Détroit the silhouettes of two heavily laden canoes were slowly pushing up against the current, the singing voices of the paddlers piercing the distance.

Cadillac sprinted back to the fort, hollering and gesticulating. "De Tonti—our dames are here! Dugué, rout the Indians. Chacornacle, prepare a row of honor. Marsac, ready the canons!"

Everywhere men raked feverish fingers through their mussed hair, straightened their jackets and tucked their shirts in their leggings. Cadillac donned his uniform, tricorne, gaiters and rapier; all kept immaculate by his pani in preparation of this moment. The native servant handed him his gilded *gorget* and long, curly wig, which he had not bothered to wear in this wilderness. He donned them and eyed himself critically in his looking-glass, then turned to inspect his son.

Cadillac and Antoine stepped down to the beach followed by hordes of vermilion-painted Indians, scrubbed traders and excited voyageurs. Père Delhalle stood so close to the water it nibbled at his grey cassock. Cadillac glanced back at the bluff where the canons' black mouths were waiting to spew their blank fire. Soldiers stood straight and proud around the Fleur-de-Lys.

The canoes neared; the canons were blasted one by one, spitting smoke and roaring, sending tremors under everyone's feet. Indians whooped and danced and beat their drums; *Français* and Canadians threw their hats in the air, a few fired their muskets; many coughed from the smoke. Cadillac strained, eyes seeking one face.

As the canoes swung toward the beach he saw her, or rather he first recognized the coiffe, a pretty confection he'd brought her back from his last trip to Paris. Underneath it, one hand clamped over her mouth in a disbelieving gesture, the other soothing a skittish Jacques clinging to her frock, Marie-Thérèse's brown locks curled softly around her pretty face. His heart missed a beat.

"I can see *ma mère*," cried Antoine, waving and bouncing. Standing beside de Reaume, the valiant *sieur* in charge of her safety, Marie-Thérèse's eyes roamed over the assembly, and spotting her son they paused to assess his well-being. Satisfied, they lifted and locked with Cadillac's, happiness sparkling on her face. Cadillac's features softened, and his piercing eyes used to bore and intimidate caressed and wooed.

The voyageurs vaulted in the water to beach the canoes. Cadillac did not wait. He leaped into the river, uncaring of his highly-polished boots and the frigid water snaking its way inside and he plucked his wife from the craft, leaving Jacques empty-handed.

Following his example, Antoine splashed in the water, wading toward Jacques, who, bereft of his mother and surrounded by chaos, cast watery eyes about him.

"Eh, Jacques. *Saute!* Jump!"

The boy pouted and shook his head. Antoine had been with their father too long; he was a young man of actions—he hauled his brother overboard and dumped him in the water, indifferent to his shrieks.

In her husband's arms, Marie-Thérèse tensed.

"*Detendez-vous ma mie*, relax, they're all right," her husband whispered against her hair, for the sake of breathing in her musky vanilla scent. Cadillac carried her to dry land gripping her close and tight, one of his hands wrapped firmly around her hip, the other slyly creeping up her round breast.

Seven pregnancies had padded Marie-Thérèse's body in all the right places. She had ceased to wear *paniers* around her hips and *derrière* after the birth of their fifth child. Nature had taken over to display her fecundity and her husband's wealth, unlike thin women who had to pad themselves heavily lest one mistook their small proportions for a lack of affluence.

Marie-Thérèse raised an eyebrow and moistened her lips, parting them slightly. He stared. He badly wanted to kiss her. Tonight, he promised himself, in their cabin, the boys fast asleep, she would be his. Breathing faster, he tightened his grip.

A humorous smile softened her face and she looped her arms loosely around his shoulders, her fingers discreetly reaching under his wig to stroke his neck. "*Ma chère,* you seem bent on tormenting me," he whispered and stared hard at the men ogling them.

"*Mais bien sûr, mon ami.* But of course, my friend. With no one to tease you, I'm sure you have grown complacent," she whispered back in his ear and wriggled her behind in his hand.

He released her abruptly and she stepped for the first time on the soil of her new home. *Pardieu,* it was so good to be loved and teased and not be taken too seriously, he thought as he bowed over her hand to greet her officially. "Madame, welcome to Fort Pontchartrain du Détroit."

Marie-Thérèse Guyon-Cadillac

Cadillac turned to Marie-Anne Picoté de Belestre. "Ah, *ma chère* Madame de Tonti, our new *colonie* is indeed very blessed to be graced by two such charming ladies." He courteously kissed her wrist under his wife's watchful gaze.

In late August he had tucked a lengthy epistle to Marie-Thérèse in a list of supplies he required. In it he had explained his suspicions of de Tonti, and his resolve to be on his guard. The accusation must have pained her. She and Marie-Anne had met in childhood at the Ursulines school and had remained fast friends since.

Not unaware of his own uncompromising and full-blooded temperament, he realized Marie-Thérèse feared he would extend his wrath to his rival's spouse. His gracious greeting having set her mind at rest, a tremulous smile of gratitude trembled on her lips. He grinned like a schoolboy and dropped Marie-Anne's hand. "I must not keep you, I am certain *sieur* de Tonti is anxious to show you your new home. We shall see you later."

Grabbing his wife's elbow he swung her around before she could protest.

"Madame Cadillac!" Lifting his grey cassock with both hands, a broad smile on his kind face, Père Delhalle rushed toward them. "Madame, what a pleasure."

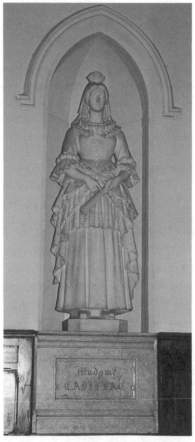

photo by Joan Sankovich

Statue of Marie-Thérèse Guyon-Cadillac
Madame Cadillac Hall, Marygrove College
Detroit, Michigan

Sharing his joy, Marie-Thérèse dipped slightly at the knees, "*Mon Père*, it is so good to see you again."

Cadillac and Père Delhalle had met on and off for several years in Quebec, and the priest had been an occasional guest at the Cadillacs' table. The Récollet, a gentle, dedicated, peaceful aristocrat, had entered the priesthood in middle life and won over whomever he met, including the hardened commandant. He had been personally requested by Cadillac to participate in the expedition.

"We're having a special mass in your honor this evening. For now I must go to the Huron village to talk to their chief, Chenonvoizon. I feel he may convert some day."

After Père Delhalle's departure, Cadillac, always a grand seigneur, introduced Marie-Thérèse to everyone present, his dark eyes registering every move, every word; this was *his* lady, the first First Lady du Détroit.

Years of schooling at the strict couvent des Ursulines in Quebec had instilled excellent manners and boundless graciousness in Marie-Thérèse; she unfailingly rewarded everyone with a kind word, a smile, a gentle gesture. Indians—the ones who had settled recently around the fort and were less used to seeing white women—caressed her hair, tugged on her frock and stroked her white hands. She calmly withstood their touch.

Cadillac beamed. Another good judgment. When the time had come for him to choose a bride, he had made a decision of the head as well as the heart. Oh, Marie-Thérèse was pretty enough, very pretty indeed, she had wriggled into his heart quite easily, but she had won him over several unofficial "contestants" due to some other attributes.

Quebec-born, Marie-Thérèse had had several advantages over her competitors. Cadillac had been a young man on the make; impatient, rash and ambitious, he had no time for fussy or simpering *demoiselles*. Unlike freshly landed French women, who panicked and gagged, the smells, the jostling, the shouting of trading posts were part of Marie-Thérèse's life. She did not have to adapt to this *Nouveau Monde*, she was born to it. She had grown up with the daily encounters with Indians and rough trappers and the reek of untreated furs. Marie-Thérèse could handle pelts, barter with traders, withstand long, icy winters and torrid summers. She could eat bear grease without batting an eyelid and spend hours in a canoe without complaining. That was the type of companion he needed, and that was what he had chosen.

Twelve years her senior, impeccably dressed, ambitious, and extremely intelligent, Cadillac had lived at the French court and mixed with powerful men, and had deliberately set on his course to sweep her off her feet. How could she not have fallen in love, fourteen years ago, when this dashing, rather arrogant French soldier asked for her hand? She was seventeen and, although born into a wealthy merchant family, had never really mixed in high society. Quebec-born, she felt a little provincial next to him. She had been extremely impressed—and still was.

Holding her elbow, he guided Marie-Thérèse to the fort's open gate, the one on the riverside, used to unload canoes. "Look at this perfect location. The fort is protected by water on three sides, one by this gigantic river, and two by a stream that elbows into it. And it's all as I guessed. The river abounds in fish, the forest teems with deer, moose and caribou and the fort is surrounded by wild fruit trees and creeping grape vines. We shall be superbly self-sufficient." A slight breeze toyed with the white plume on his hat. "Ah, what a proud moment it was on July 24 to select this site!"

Marie-Thérèse looked up to his excited face and smiled, a wan, sad, brave little smile. He caught its wistfulness and squeezing her elbow gently, brought her closer to him. His glory had a price—insecurity, hardship and a dispersed family. He hoped, they both did, that the challenge ahead of Marie-Thérèse would soothe her grief over the death of their two babies.

At thirty-one Marie-Thérèse had already given birth to seven children. Two, Pierre-Denis and Marie-Anne, had died in infancy. Her oldest three remained in Quebec, two daughters, Judith, twelve, and Magdeleine, eight, at the Ursulines convent, and one son, Joseph, eleven, awaiting a position of *enseigne* at his father's fort. Their youngest, Jacques, six, she had brought with her, and Antoine, nine, had come to le Détroit with his father. Between child-bearing, she had run his affairs, executed his requests, made decisions in a man's world, and picked up pieces wherever and whenever they were lost. They had had much sorrow to overcome, and no doubt, *Dieu* would inflict more, but like her husband, she'd learned to bend and adapt. She was resolute to tame and conquer, only her weapons would be smiles, gentleness and Christianity.

Jostled by the exuberant crowd, they passed through the gate, an eclectic group of followers tagging behind them. Within its palisade, the fort was exploding with hollering and cheering and running. The *tambour* and the fife beat a merry tune while everywhere burst happy cheers, *"Vive Madame Cadillac! Vive Madame de Tonti! Vive le seigneur du Détroit!"*

"All this was done in three months," said Cadillac with a grand sweeping wave of his hand. "Palisade, bastions, *magazin*, church, mill, cabins, and of course, our first planting for next summer's harvest." She appeared truly amazed.

"Let's go to Ste. Anne. That's our main street. We have two other streets parallel to the river and each hugging one side of the palisade, St. Louis and St. Joachim, but they are much narrower." He pointed to an alleyway perpendicular to Ste. Anne, lined with roughly-hewed cabins packed close to each other.

"We have three north-south alleyways, Rencontre, St. Antoine and St. François. That's where the men live. The de Tontis and we live on Ste. Anne, tucked between the church and the *magazin*. They are next to the church and we are next to the warehouse. It's more spacious. And this is the communal room," he explained, indicating a larger log structure. "We had no time to build chimneys inside the cabins. Instead, the men come here to share warmth and cooking. Next to it is the outdoor communal baking oven."

Marie-Thérèse stopped in her steps, horrified. No heat, and winter fast approaching? She swallowed hard. Her husband noticed her dismay. He squeezed her hand and hastened to add, "Do not concern yourself, our own abode is graced with a chimney." She sighed with relief.

"*Par ici.* This way." The communal room was empty, but it had a homey disarray. A large kettle hung in the chimney, tables and benches hugged the fireplace, pipes and tin mugs dangled from wooden pegs. Here and there a scarf, a pouch, a dirty plate, an empty goblet laid, abandoned by its owner. A violin rested on a small shelf. This was a room where men warmed their aching bodies and mended their spirits.

"Now, let me show you the king's *magazin.* One must not forget all furs belong to Roy Louis," sieur Cadillac quipped rather drily. "I have a clever fellow, Veron Grandmesnil, running it. He also keeps the public records." He bent close to her ears. "I suspect he is a little too fond of *les femmes.*"

All day they stood side by side, visiting, receiving gifts from the Indians, feasting and rejoicing, listening to speeches, and singing. Marie-Thérèse had traipsed across miles of wilderness. She was dusty, overwhelmed and exhausted, but she forced a smile.

Later in the evening, when at last they could take leave of everyone, she was past caring that their dwelling was a dismal, hastily-built hut of logs with a rickety loft, chinked with grass and mud, and covered by a roof of bark. A chimney of sticks and mud stood at one end of the main room. Doeskin was stretched across the window opening, a nasty little wind whistled between the logs and the beaten-earth floor felt cold and damp under her feet. All she wanted was to crawl underneath her fur blanket and curl to sleep, but not before setting her mind on improving this place and ordering glass panes from Montreal the following spring.

Cadillac had other ideas.

The pani had kept the fire roaring. The flickering flames danced on his wife's hair. It shone and glistened. The cabin overflowed with trunks, bundles and bags. Utensils and furniture were stacked in every available space, signs of the comfort Madame Cadillac brought with her. A wonderful carpet had already been spread next to their bed. Their bed at last! Cadillac clapped his hands to dismiss the pani, who from now on would sleep in the communal kitchen. He bolted the door, shoved his children up the ladder, tucked them into bed, dumped the smoky rushes in the chimney and virtually leapt on his wife.

She giggled and set her tiredness aside to welcome him into her arms. They had waited months for this happy reunion; besides he was rather set on providing the fort with its first white baby. He figured the de Tontis would be similarly occupied, throwing spices into the race.

She would have preferred to defer another pregnancy, to let her body regain strength, but the need of being loved, of erasing months of sorrow, overwhelmed her and she pulled him hard against her. They felt like children, kissing in semi-darkness, letting their hands roam on each other, careful not to make any noise.

"How long before the boys are asleep?" he whispered against her mouth. His hands unlaced her frock.

The awful shriek made them jump. "Ma . . . *ma mère*, I am afraaaaaiiiid!"

Jacques! The boy screamed louder. "*Mèèèèèèère!*"

Cadillac swore under his breath, "*Sacrebleu!*" Marie-Thérèse quickly laced up what Cadillac had so eagerly undone. Jacques was already at the top of the ladder, howling, his little chest shaken by hiccups. "*Mère*, hic . . . I, I sleep, hic . . . with you, hic . . . tonight." Next to him Antoine rolled his eyes.

Marie-Thérèse scooped up her crying child and hugged him on her bed. Jaws set, Cadillac cast his younger son a jaundice eye, then without a glance and a good night, stomped up the ladder and dropped on Jacques' pallet.

In the morning, unaccustomed to have his plans thwarted, Cadillac was in his most reserved and least communicative mood. Oh, he smiled at Jacques and his wife—a smile that would have frozen water on a hot summer day.

But his mood improved drastically by the time he'd wheedled an invitation for his sons to sleep at Père Delhalle's. He spent the rest of the day with a vibrancy to his every move, cussing at the sun for not retiring sooner.

The next day Cadillac strutted about with a spring in his step and a contented smile under his hawkish nose. Ten weeks later Marie-Thérèse was *enceinte*—expecting—trailing a month behind Marie-Anne de Tonti. . . .

Departure For Quebec

On their way to the canoes awaiting to take him to Quebec, Marie-Thérèse looped one arm over her husband's. "*Mon ami*, please select one good woman, strong, hard working and firm in her resolve. Offer her a contract for at least three years; I do not want to instruct a servant for a shorter time. Ask Mother Superior at the couvent des Ursulines, she will help you. I could not abide a grouch, and with this baby," she patted her protruding tummy. "I need help."

Cadillac squeezed her hand. "I shall do my best." He bent close to her ear, "Take care of this new baby. It means a lot to all of us." They exchanged a smug and yet concerned look. Both remembered only too well one dark night in late March, when an agitated de Tonti had aroused their household with his frantic banging on the door.

White and copper skin trappers having long left for the hunting season, their departure had thrown a blanket of silence and tedium over the village. It grew worse after Le Grand Pierre's leaving, the last rowdy left in the fort. At first he had resisted the call of the wild; it was late in the season and he'd promised Cadillac to reject his old vagabond ways and set up a store. He would stand by his door and let the wind toy with his hair, caress his face and creep up his nose, filling him with the scents he recognized so well. He'd sniff one last time and, jaws set, turn around and bang his door shut.

Then nature had sent a last warning, a warning animals heeded well; some flew away, some hid deep in the woods, several burrowed, and quite a few curled up, noses tucked in their warm thick winter coats. Aristide Dents Crochues had left, beckoning him as he paddled away, "*Vite*, Le Grand Pierre, hurry!" At that Le Grand Pierre lost it all. He hastily packed his bag, hopped in his canoe and paddled and paddled to catch up with Aristide's party, the door of his cabin flapping in the wind.

Winter had marched into the clearing, blowing, snowing and freezing, locking land and water in its powerful grip, robbing the fort and its surrounding Indian villages of a food supply. No more berries and wild game. They had to survive on shrinking rations of smoked meat, fish, wild rice, corn and nuts, praying for an early thaw and its subsequent arrival of supply canoes from Quebec. Fortunately Cadillac's party had brought sufficient wheat to last the season, but not enough to let every man have his customary two-pound loaf of bread. They were given six thick slices a day which they spread with bear grease and devoured hungrily.

Loneliness had gripped their hearts, especially Marie-Thérèse's and Marie-Anne's who had no female company but each other, and even that grew tiresome; their husbands' constant rivalry frayed their nerves.

Outside the Cadillacs' cabin, a fierce, frigid wind had been pounding the logs, snaking its way between them, whistling its victory and licking their limbs with its icy tongue. They'd hauled their bed and the children's pallets close to the fireplace, but the glowing embers could not loosen the claws of privation and iciness on their thinned bodies.

"*Vite! Vite!*" The door moaned under the pounding. "My wife! The baby!"

Marie-Thérèse had recognized de Tonti's voice and the urgency in it. She had leapt out of bed, and wrapping a fur blanket around her chilled body, had yanked the door open. A flurry of snowflakes buzzed around de Tonti's worried face. "I'm coming immediately. Time to dress," she shouted and banged the door shut and dove into her clothes, mentally counting the months of Marie-Anne's pregnancy. Five months! Too early. *Mon Dieu!*

Ever since her arrival, her status of "Dame du Manoir" had assigned her the duty of *docteur*. For months now she and Marie-Anne, whom she had recruited, had applied all the knowledge, nostrums and cures their mothers and nuns had taught them to heal and cure whatever wounds and sickness befell white and Indian people. They combined their wisdom with a touch of Indian lore, listening intently to the tribes' medicine men. During late fall, they had feverishly gathered and dried all the plants they required for the coming winter and strung them from their cabins' rafters: wild angelica for indigestion, spruce bark for failing kidneys, garlic against cholera, and, of course, the essential clear golden pith of fir balsam, the native Algonquin remedy for frostbite and sores. Many a trapper lost his fingers, toes and nose to a harsh winter; they simply dropped off.

They had followed the medicine men's advice and brewed decoctions of young shoots of spruce to fend off the violent attacks of dysentery brought on by the meager and unvaried winter diet. Last fall a malaria outbreak had struck several men, and as the two women cooled the feverish foreheads of its victims with wet rags, they were told it would last until the first frost.

In winter, the dreadful *mal de terre,* scurvy, loosened their teeth and bloated their limbs. They coughed, sneezed and spat blood with indigenous chest ailments, and their joints creaked with arthritis and rheumatism, all aggravated by the cabins' upright logs which brought the dampness of the soil in the homes. They put on a brave fight, nothing was too repulsive to save a life; not even animal excreta, crab eyes and wood lice.

Before departing from Quebec, Marie-Thérèse had filled her medicine chest with dried herbs and precious jars of seneca oil. An Iroquois nation near Albany collected this oil. Skins were laid around the spring to soak in the liquid, then wrung over containers. Pioneers and Indians alike used it as an unguent for wounds, aches, and pains.

She reached for it. Cadillac had anticipated her move and handed it to her. She grabbed it and, remembering that Père Delhalle was away at the village of the Oppenagos, she snatched the jar of *eau bénie* next to the wall crucifix, and dashed out in the cold clutching the blessed water.

Marie-Anne's baby was born an hour later, a minute, wrinkled creature mewing for air, too cold, too small, too unfinished. And yet, they were not ready to relinquish him to death. Marie-Thérèse bathed him in the warm water de Tonti had heated over the fire before she had sent him to Marsac's for the night; birthing was a woman's business. She feverishly swaddled the newborn in a beaver skin and pressed him to her chest, hoping to raise his temperature.

Meanwhile, although exhausted, Marie-Anne had unlaced her chemise and squeezed her breast to activate milk production. If only he could suckle a few drops of this life-giving nutrient! She squeezed and squeezed, but not even a trickle would come out. Finally she shook her head, eyes luminous with tears and frustration, and stretched her arms toward her son.

Then only herself a little over four months pregnant, Marie-Thérèse, against all odds, tried to express some liquid out of her own breast. Nothing! Defeated and helpless, she slumped on the bed and wrapped her arms around her friend.

The tiny creature tucked between them, the two women rocked and sobbed, their chemises wide open, breasts red and sore. Marie-Thérèse wiped her eyes with a corner of her chemise. "I'll get the *eau bénie*," she whispered. Marie-Anne acquiesced silently. She unswaddled her son's head to ready him for baptism.

The Catholic Church granted a religious burial only to those who were baptized, so when a priest was not available and a baby was born, a neighbor baptized it to ensure his place in heaven. With the elevated mortality rate, the ceremony was performed shortly after birth.

Marie-Thérèse opened the phial and poured the cool water over the baby's forehead. "*Je te bénis, au nom du Père et du Fils et du Saint Esprit*. I baptize you in the name of the Father, the Son, and the Holy Spirit."

Praying, they resumed their vigil, watching the baby's life ebb away. He expired in the early morning and they wrapped him silently in white linen, ready for burial. With him had died the first hopes for a pioneer baby. Now expectations rested on Marie-Thérèse.

Two weeks later, when several days of sunshine had melted the ice and the river started to flow freely, groups of trappers and Indians began drifting back into the fort, jerking it back to life.

"*Prenez soin*. Take care," Cadillac reiterated solemnly.

"Yes, of course. Give my letters to Judith, Magdeleine and Joseph and assure them of my love, and *s'il-vous-plaît*, bring them back. And you, *mon ami*, will you be all right?" she peered anxiously into his dark face.

Cadillac and the *Jésuites* had relentlessly filed charges and countercharges against each other. They accused him of trading *eau-de-vie* to the Indians and debauching the souls they tried so hard to convert, of wanting to annihilate Fort Michilimackinac, their missionary stronghold. He countered that clerics should not meddle in politics, smoothly suggesting that they move to the Détroit and work with the tribes here, knowing full well they preferred to deal with him from afar. True, he had cleverly fiddled with the books to account for the extra *pots d'eau-de-vie* that had seen their way to the fort and down some eager Indian gullets. Finally in a heated moment, in his usual brash way, he had charged the Society with offering Nouvelle France to England on a silver platter. Besides, he had spat to Père De Gueslis, could he really forbid one race to partake in what his indulged in so freely?

Ron Miller of the Compagnie Franches de la Marine du Detroit
in the typical garb of the *coureurs de bois*

He met Marie-Thérèse's inquisitive glance and drew her closer to him, "Do not fret, I can handle Gouverneur Callière. His summons says he has organized a meeting in Quebec between Père Vaillant de Gueslis, who is now the Jésuite Superieur, and entirely opposed to the resettling of the tribes here. You know how meddlesome the *Jésuites* are in my affairs."

She stared up at him. He forced a smile. "It might be uncomfortable but not unsurmountable. *Non*, the real fight will be the dispute with the Compagnie de la Colonie." Cold, dark anger hardened his features.

"Roy Louis—the ungrateful bast . . ." he caught himself in time. "Forgive me, *ma chère*." She smiled at him.

Cadillac smiled grimly. "After all I have done for France, Roy Louis has decided to brush aside all my work and his promises. He has granted exclusive rights—my rights—to all of *my* fort's *commerce des fourrures* to his own Compagnie de la Colonie; no doubt to replenish his coffer for another war, another wing of his palace." His voice was bitter. "But I shall fight, rest assured. We shall not be robbed of our dues."

"I really wish people knew you as I do, and ceased to treat you so wrongly."

The warmth in his wife's voice made Cadillac lose some of his tension. He fell silent for a moment, feeling a little uneasy over her blind faith. Most of the accusations were right even if he staunchly refused to admit it to others and to himself. Victory and power came to the most focused, the least unencumbered by principles, and he qualified on both accounts. "While I am gone, do not entrust your thoughts to anyone but Père Delhalle. *Do not* go to de Tonti, you know I suspect him of treason. I have noticed letters going back and forth between he and the *Jésuites*."

Marie-Thérèse tugged herself free. "Marie-Anne is my friend. I intend to keep our friendship. We're the only two women here, and we need each other."

Cadillac retrieved her hand and brought her back to him. Stalwart Marie-Thérèse! Prickly as a bear when he became overly peremptory. He added smoothly, "The feud is only between de Tonti and me, and so far he is unaware of my suspicion. Any change of attitude would only alarm him and make him more cautious. *Non*, keep your friendship, but for my sake do not confide in the ears of my foe's wife."

Marie-Thérèse stiffened against him. "As if I would!"

"I forget I have an independent wife."

Piqued, she huffed. "*Mon ami*, see if you could traipse across the wilderness and settle forts and disappear for months with a dependent wife hanging around your neck!"

Another set down, he reflected wryly. He was getting used to it. "*Ma mie*, let us part friends."

Still miffed, she grudgingly offered her hand. "*Oui bien sûr*, although you do not deserve it."

He winked, nipped at her skin and vaulted in his *bateau*. "Let's go!" he cried to his bargeman, Sans Rémission.

In his report to the French Ministry dated September 25, 1702, Cadillac wrote from Quebec that "Madame de Tonti's child died for want of milk which she had not anticipated. I fear the same might happen to my wife who was about to be confined when I left."

Detroit had no cattle, so cow's milk could not be substituted to save the baby. In any case artificial feeding was unknown, wet-nursing being the usual answer. It leaves us with a few unanswered questions. Since no white woman was available, why not recruit an Indian woman? Did the French and Indians harbor some outlandish fears of pouring the milk of one race inside another? Did some taboo prevent them from doing so? Maybe. But most likely the baby was born prematurely or with some difficulty (forceps were not invented until 1733), and there was no time to walk to a nearby Indian settlement, especially at night, when the fort's gates were closed for safety.

In spite of Cadillac's repeated requests, no nursing sisters were allowed to come to Detroit to found a hospital for "the sick and infirm savages" (the first hospital, St. Mary's, was founded only in 1845). Cadillac delved into his own pockets to provide a medicine chest to treat habitants, soldiers and Indians, thus abiding by the French policy to provide treatments for the native men "in order to gain their friendship." Although its motive lacked nobility, the policy nevertheless benefitted the tribes who were fighting imported diseases to which they had no immunity (smallpox, typhoid, etc.). The British did not share this policy, and ceased all treatments when they came to power, with disastrous consequences for the native man. In 1767, in Detroit, an Ottawa pleaded to the British:

> *"Father, when the French had this country, they always provided a doctor to attend to our sick people. We have lost a number of our people. We therefore beg you'll let us have a doctor to attend us when sick."*

The petition was ignored.

Return From Quebec

The full glory of a receding autumn painted the whole region with gold and scarlet. As the river undulated softly beneath his *bateau*, Cadillac let his eyes roam about him, fixing in his memory the beautiful sight of the fort—his fort—jutting proudly over the bluff, its neat little picketed gardens surrounding it. He bent to his daughter Magdeleine and oldest son, Joseph, whom he was bringing back from Quebec. "This is ours, and will be yours one day, Joseph. The rapacious Compagnie de la Colonie may control it for a while, but not for long." *Non*, indeed, all his energy will be spent on getting back what was rightfully his; his vision, his creation.

Cadillac bunched his fist to his sides and glanced darkly at the three figures standing in the *bateau* behind him. The older one was garbed somberly and the two younger ones held on to their powdered *perruques*, their ruffles flapping in the wind. Idiots, he sniggered under his breath, and patted his own queue, sensibly encased in an eelskin bag.

He heard la Giroflée sound the alert from his *chemin de ronde*, "*Bateaux* approaching! Flying our pennant!"

A throng of people poured from the gates. He peered and squinted and craned his neck, letting his eyes rove over the scalloped beach and the assembled crowd. Marie-Thérèse was not there! An uneasiness gripped him. She should be there—he expected her there—brandishing their new child swaddled in a beaver blanket. In four months he had received no messages confirming the birth in late July and he was anxious to learn the gender of this new offspring.

"*Plus vite!* Faster!" he barked.

Grunting, his voyageurs accelerated their rhythm, muscles bulging under buckskin vests, increasing the distance between their craft and the others lagging behind, laden with supplies. They beached the *bateau* and he sprung out. Hardly on dry soil, with his usual arrogance, he was already issuing orders. "Sans Rémission, see to the unloading. Ah, Le Grand Pierre, take my children to their mother."

Le Grand Pierre pounced on the job like a cat on a mouse. "Commandant, with your permission, I'd like to show them the *magazin* first, we have some new snow shoes." Cadillac eyed him suspiciously and nodded. Le Grand Pierre was clearly relieved to be out of his eyesight.

The arrival of fall provisions was always the cause of much excitement. Goods were eyed and handled speculatively while interested buyers figured a way to purchase them. Today, it seemed to him that the crowd, usually rowdy, was unusually restrained, eyes shifted and glided past his hawkish scrutiny, souls squirmed under his stare. A frightening anxiety crept up his neck. Where was his family? He forced the nagging question out of his mind; urgent business had to be taken care of. His officers saluted him.

"Ah, *Messieurs*, allow me to introduce you to these 'worthy' *sieurs*," the voice dripped sarcasm, "Monsieur Radisson, Nolan and Arnault, commissaires de la Compagnie de la Colonie." Dugué and Chacornacle exchanged a quick puzzled glance. Marsac scowled. De Tonti bowed stiffly.

"Marsac, please show *ces messieurs* to their quarters. Let us all meet in my council chamber in an hour. Dugué, Chacornacle and de Tonti, report to me while we walk to my quarters." They trooped uneasily beside his commanding figure. "How was the wheat harvest in July and did you sow another crop in September as I had instructed?"

Before de Tonti had time to answer, Père Delhalle stepped in Cadillac's way. "Commandant Lamothe, we are happy to see you again. But pray, a moment of your time, before you go any further."

Cadillac frowned. The others fidgeted and became suddenly fascinated by the points of their boots. "*Mon Père*, surely the matter can wait . . ."

"*S'il-vous-pla ît.*" Père Delhalle insisted, looking him straight in the eyes.

The old anxiety rushed back to his chest.

"*Messieurs,*" he bowed to the others. "Rendez-vous in an hour. De Tonti, bid Grandmesnil to join us." Like hares suddenly freed of a snare they bolted out of sight.

"It's my wife, isn't it? Why isn't she here?" He could not ask the ultimate question; the one he feared most. They walked past his auspiciously quiet house and he made to stop but the *Récollet* pulled him by the arm and lead him to the church.

Inside its musky shelter Père Delhalle faced him squarely. "*Oui.* It is about your wife." Cadillac paled. "She took to her bed, weak and frail after the birth, then contracted the ague. But she is all right now, although still very fatigued. It's the baby." He paused. "It died the same day it was born, in July, in spite of Madame de Tonti's efforts. It was baptized and buried. Madame Cadillac bore it with great dignity."

Cadillac regarded him in raw silence. Three dead babies in a row. And, again, Marie-Thérèse had borne this tragedy alone. The weight of guilt, of sadness, wrapped around his chest like a giant iron manacle.

"I know how much this child meant to you, to all of us in

fact. I'm sorry." Père Delhalle placed a gentle hand on the commandant's arm.

Cadillac was not one to share his pain. Years of military training would cage it in his heart, where it would hurt and strain against its closed door. His face unreadable, he freed himself. "*Merci, mon père*, for giving me the truth. Now, if you will excuse me, my family needs me."

Propped on her pillow, eyes wide and misty, Marie-Thérèse smiled bravely. "*Mon ami . . .*" Her voice cracked to a whisper.

He slumped on the bed and gripped her hand tightly, depositing a tender, moist kiss on her white knuckles. Later, their entwined hands promised, later, when the pain is not so raw, we'll speak of our grief.

Marie-Thérèse rested her forehead onto her updrawn knees. After a shattering pause, Cadillac lifted his wife's face. "We'll pull through," he muttered between his teeth. "I brought Joseph and Magdeleine back with me." The news brought a warm glow to her pale face. "They should be here soon, Le Grand Pierre is showing them *le magazin*, no doubt to give us privacy."

"What about Judith?" she inquired anxiously.

"Judith preferred to remain at the couvent des Ursulines. She sends her love and begs you to understand." Ah, *Dieu*, what a sense of irony you have, he pondered, chastising me for my anti-*Jésuite* feelings. You've given me a church-abiding spouse and two intensely pious daughters, Judith and Magdeleine. Both, he was sure, would eventually become nuns. It won't work, you know. I'll never give in. *Jamais!*

"And now," he added with the clear, efficient mind of a military man who knew when to return to his duty, "Tell me. How were things in my absence? I see our home is much improved; tiles on the floor, carpets and skins hung on the walls. This salon is much bigger, the glass panes you desired are in place, quite comfortable." He peeked round the door. "You had two rooms added?"

"A scullery and a bedroom for us."

He snooped around the scullery. "Hummm, you've been busy. What are all those jars I see?"

Marie-Thérèse brushed her face with the back of her hand and, catching his mood, forced a calm smile on her lips. He rewarded her with an admiring glance. "Madame de Tonti and I collected some of the wild fruit around the fort. We made plum cheese, pear jam and even some peach brandy. The pani and one or two soldiers came with us, but we did not venture too far. We had many skirmishes between the tribes, especially between the *Outaouais* and the Miamis, some of them quite bloody." She did not add that without his iron will and leadership, tension and nervousness had crept into the fort, nor that she had fretted over the jittery soldiers, wondering how long before they became trigger-happy.

His penetrating stare read it all. He balled his fists. So, de Tonti, always so ambitious and eager to fill his place, had not shown true leadership after all. He would have to do something about that. "What about the July wheat harvest? Was another crop sown in September?"

"As you suspected the July crop was rather poor, but at least it proved this land can be farmed. And *oui*, Indian corn and wheat were planted in late September as you had instructed."

"Has Grandmesnil collected my fees from the settlers who used my *moulin* to grind their grain?"

"*Oui. Oui.* To all of that. But what about you?" She peered eagerly into his stern features. "How did you fare?"

He started pacing the room like a Field Marshall reporting on his latest battle. "First, a *contretemps*. No sooner had Chacornacle joined me in Quebec for his short stay, that he quarreled with the sieur de Hauteville. The two, being rather too swift with their swords, fought a duel. Rumors of the secret meeting escaped and only my word saved him from disgrace. Chacornacle is a hot-tempered but worthy man. Fort Pontchartrain needs men of his caliber." He stroked his mustache pensively.

"Then?" prodded his spouse.

"Gouverneur Callière squeezed a sort of truce out of the *Jésuites*; they will urge rather than deter the resettling of the tribes around the fort and all complaints about me will be sent to him rather than to the court." Wryly he added, "In exchange I must be *un gentil garçon*, a good boy, and make no trouble."

"*Gentil garçon*" could not describe Cadillac's behavior at the best of times. Wisely, Marie-Thérèse made no comment. "What about your *commerce des fourrures?*"

"Ah, *cher* Roy Louis! How grateful I am to our mighty king. Let me do all the work and now graciously removes the rewards from my pocket to his coffers."

While pleading his case, Cadillac had trod on many toes, delivered too many truths, and was altogether always too clever. Louis simply refused to handle any more bickering, Callière would have to arbitrate all complaints. People started ganging up on him and accumulating evidence to his discredit; the knowledge that he was still the protegé of the powerful comte de Pontchartrain was the only restraint holding the final blow. "I was forced to sign a contract handing over my exclusive rights to the *commerce des fourrures* from this fort to the Compagnie de la Colonie and accepting their yearly payment of two thousand *livres* for our subsistence. De Tonti gets only 1,303. Should deflate his overpuffed Italian chest." He grinned. "That reminds me, I have called a council in my chamber." He prepared to leave.

"*Mon ami*," she called. "What about settlers? Are any coming?"

Halfway out of the door, he answered. "*Oui*, next spring. Several families; a few wives, Marsac's, the others I can't remember. Mère Supérieure selected two maids for you; one plain and one quite comely. The comely one, she says, is quite enterprising. I'm hoping one of the traders or voyageurs will snatch her up and start a family here."

Although the reference to family reminded her of their recent loss, Marie-Thérèse chuckled and raised a teasing eyebrow.

"Commandant, short of *commerce des fourrures*, have you slipped in the matchmaking business?"

"*Mais bien sûr*, of course," he winked. "I have an expensive *femme*. I must do what I can to keep her content."

She threw a pillow at him. He grinned, caught the pillow, tossed it back and flew out of the door.

The drafty, austere room in the barracks—a square box scantily furnished with one long wooden table, eight chairs and a few rolled-up maps—could hardly qualify as a council chamber, and yet it was Cadillac's territory, a room where one felt incapable of escaping the piercing scrutiny of the hawkish Gascon.

Sitting at the head of the table, his wig formally in place, Cadillac waited solemnly for the three *commissaires* and his officers to sit. He dispensed with niceties and lunged straight into the core of the meeting. "Grandmesnil, take note." Grandmesnil grabbed one of his many cut quills and opened a pot of ink he'd defrosted over the fire. "Sieur Radisson, *s'il-vous-plaît*, state your business so it may be recorded."

Radisson cleared his throat and stated pompously. "We, commissaires de la Compagnie de la Colonie, in accordance with the agreement signed by sieur de Lamothe and the said Compagnie, have come to oversee the *commerce des fourrures* at Fort Pontchartrain. By orders of the Gouverneur and the Intendant, and the will of his *Majesté*, we demand that all ledgers and records of transactions as well as all future commerce be immediately handed over to us. In reward of your compliance, Roy Louis will finance the fort's garrison, and la Compagnie de la Colonie will maintain the expenses of its commandant and officers. This must bring you great relief, *monsieur* Cadillac; this brilliant endeavor must have sorely depleted your funds."

"Brilliant endeavor" of course it was, why else would the Crown grab it for itself, if not for glory and retribution? Coldly, Cadillac rose to his feet. "*Messieurs*, the state of my finances

remain my affairs, and solely mine." Radisson bent at the waist
in a piqued manner. "Indeed the offer is too 'generous,'"
sarcasm could not be mistaken. "My rights have been trans-
gressed; my possessions removed from me; but who am I to
protest what his *Majesté's* hand has sealed?" The slanderous
tirade smelt of treason and could land him—again—in dire
trouble, but he could not tame his petulant Gascon blood.

The three *commissaires* frowned darkly. Jaws hardened,
Cadillac ignored them. A corner of his mind noticed Grandmesnil had not recorded his last comment. "Still I am not yet set
to relinquish my rights, my possessions and privileges, especially with my faithful officers standing by me, all fast men with
their swords." Dugué, Chacornacle and Marsac nodded in
agreement. De Tonti swallowed hard. "Trouble, de Tonti?" At
the thrust, de Tonti winced.

"Commandant . . ." objected Radisson. Arnault shot up and
opened his mouth to protest. Nolan coughed uncomfortably.

Cadillac silenced them with a peremptory hand. Arnault sat
back grudgingly. "Have no fear, *messieurs*, although what is
rightfully mine has been grievously snatched from my devoted
hands, the sieur de Lamothe has no intention of bringing you
harm and deception." A pointed stare pinned de Tonti to his
seat. "My sword and my loyalty belong to our *Roy*, and until I
can clearly defend my case and extract retribution I shall bow
to *sa Majesté's* command. However," he jabbed a warning finger
toward the *commissaires*, "Do not infringe upon my military
prerogative; I am the commandant and *seigneur* of le Détroit. I
shall not hesitate to enforce my authority." With that he stalked
out of the chamber, all of his officers but one in tow, just in
time to subdue his explosive temper. De Tonti remained seated.

In the stunned silence of the chamber, the only noise was the
scratching of Grandmesnil's quill trying to catch up with the
virulent diatribe.

The Arrival of Other Women

Marie-Thérèse and Marie-Anne remained the only two women at the fort for almost two years, relying on each other heavily. Having each lost their baby, they raced to conceive another one.

Since Cadillac's return, the animosity between the two husbands had grown fearfully; the commandant treaded coolly around de Tonti's suspected treachery, slowly slipping an inescapable noose around the Italian's calculating head. Overshadowed by the overbearing Gascon, de Tonti spent increasingly more time planning to overthrow his boss and accumulate some wealth. A most unwise move around the hawkish Cadillac, who, as a good bird of prey, circled over him, accumulating evidence and sharpening his talons.

The electricity-charged situation put tremendous stress on the two wives. They bore it as well as they could and defused many an awkward moment. When they cried, it was on each other's shoulders.

There was, however, very little time for sorrow. The day started at sunrise and was filled with arduous tasks, tending to the sick, sewing and mending clothes. They helped Père

Delhalle teach French and catechism to Indian children side by side with their own offspring. Cadillac believed in full assimilation, the same way he encouraged intermarriages and enticed Indian males to join the French garrison. Under the watchful eye of la Giroflée, the two women held weekly sewing classes for Indian maidens, with little Magdeleine, already a precocious, intensely religious child, reading from the Bible.

No doubt their diligence and manners were a great asset to the fort and their grace helped stabilize the French male population. But two ladies cannot control the behavior of one hundred men over which they have no rights, especially the voyageurs and trappers who were a law unto themselves. Cadillac threw a few miscreants in the garrison's prison to ponder over their crimes, and Père Delhalle brandished the fear of eternal hell in their faces. However, the fur trade had developed a volatile breed of men who balked at curbing their drinking, brawling, gambling and fornicating with Indian women in the woods.

Behavior set aside, it was still paramount to convince the Indians of the permanency of the post. And that could not be achieved by only two women. Madame Cadillac and Madame de Tonti had paved the way for others, but royal permission had been slow to come in spite of Cadillac's several requests. At last in 1703, six families, a few wives (one or two refused to follow their mates into this wilderness), and a maid for the Cadillacs, arrived in Détroit.

Getting them there had not been easy. The lack of white women had been a great problem for Nouvelle France from the beginning. The first French woman, Dame Hébert, had arrived in Quebec in 1610, ten years before the landing of the Mayflower. However, the number of French women emigrées did not approach the population of their British counterparts (neither did the men's). The French temperament did not—and still does not—aspire or thrive on emigration.

Countless women had heard or read missionaries' reports of

the harshness of the land, the constant threat of Indian attacks and the day to day struggle to survive. Not a very compelling package. A few, the intrepid and the daring, especially the poor, the orphans and young widows with no hope for the future, responded to the challenge.

Of the few applicants, many were soon disqualified. The men, whose very dark souls they were to pluck from hell, and whose comfort they were to provide, turned picky. Candidates had to be comely, between the age of fifteen and thirty, healthy, sweet-tempered, intelligent, hardworking, pure of soul and body, and intensely religious. Predictably, the number shrank considerably.

A trickle of brides-to-be crossed the Atlantic. Competition rose to a high pitch amongst commoners—traders, farmers and enlisted men. One can imagine a few tricks were played and a few blows exchanged before a winning suitor could carry his bride away. The picture was even more trite for officers and aristocrats for, in a class-conscious society, their brides needed to be of "good breeding."

The shortage of qualifying volunteers threw the Crown, ministers and clerics into a panic; France could not relinquish her hold on this *Nouveau Monde* and its lucrative market through lack of French women. Something had to be done to encourage emigration, and quickly. King, ministers and clergy put their heads together and came up with a splendid reasoning: the clergy professed it was a Christian woman's duty; the ministers, a civil obligation; and the King promised a dowry. With the assurance that they would find husbands suited to their own station in life, some highborn women agreed to emigrate. A committee reviewed their applications before applying the seal of suitability.

Patrician young ladies generally faced a rather dismal life; they were mere commodities in a business transaction between their parents and a future husband whose alliance would profit the family. Love marriages did not exist at their level. They could refuse and return to the convent for life. Emigration blessed by the Church and the Crown opened the door to what their parents called sacrifice, and the young ladies freedom.

These bunches of ill-assorted young women, rich and poor alike, with spunk as their common denominator, would be known as the "King's Daughters." The scandalmongers had a field day, the colonists got a few brides, and France kept her fur trade.

Detroit had very few single ladies emigrées, only a couple of Nouvelle France widows and two or three maids for the Cadillacs. The port of arrival for all women was still Quebec and, due to the intense competition, by the time they reached the western posts they had been snatched by eager bachelors.

By the mid-seventeenth century, there were several Canadian-born maidens available in older, established towns such Quebec, Montreal and Trois Rivieres, but they were well protected and spoken for rather quickly. Men were granted permission to return to Quebec to seek a spouse. The approximate dates of arrival of the frigates from France were issued, and eager swains did not stray too far from the harbor.

As soon as the ship was sighted, the more determined males would jump in their birch bark canoes and paddle vigorously, keeping an eye on the competition, and climb on board to snatch the comeliest demoiselle. Aristocrats were protected by a wall of nuns who shepherded them to the convent where they would wait to be formally introduced to prospective husbands, officers and well-to-do merchants, at an official ceremony hosted by the Gouverneur. Consequently, most Detroit women were new brides or wives joining their husbands with their families. The situation improved when "imported" children grew to adulthood, and with the first Detroit-born generation.

No wonder that one bright spring afternoon the habitants and neighboring tribes abandoned their chores and dropped their tools at the first cry of "Flotilla of canoes and *bateaux* approaching!" Decked in his dapper uniform, his lady in all her fineries on his arm, Cadillac ambled to the beach, regal, resplendent and smug. Now, in spite of Quebec's coolness and Callière's lack of support, his *coup de maître* was under way. In a few glorious moments, Fort Pontchartrain du Détroit would cease to be a garrison. With the arrival of wives and six whole families it would truly become a colony—his. Born of his vision, wrestled from the wilderness and hostility of the merchants of Montreal and Quebec who saw it as a rising star to rob them of the fur profits. And, of course, they were right. Under his leadership, le Détroit, so strategically placed, would dethrone all others. He, who attracted the most tribes, would control *les Grands Lacs*. What really rankled most of these righteous souls was that *he* had thought of it first.

Cadillac had relentlessly applied for families and wives, for a *docteur* and nursing sisters to found a much needed hospice, and for a teacher to teach the children, pioneers and Indians alike. However, the *Jésuites* and merchants had exerted their negative influence on the Quebec authorities. Callière had discouraged all would-be applicants, intimating the approaching closure of the fort. Still, some had believed Cadillac, and ignored the threatening message. The absence of de Tonti and his family, who were in Quebec reporting to the Compagnie de la Colonie, rendered his glory even sweeter.

Pandemonium reigned on the beach. Trappers had returned only days before and had already roistered nights and days. Red-eyed and sour-smelling, they dragged their weary but eager bodies to the river. There they stood, idly scratching their crotches in between foul hiccups and resonant, nauseous farts. The Hurons, Ottawas, Miamis, Oppenagos and Pottawatamies all danced, vermilion paint on their faces, drums and gourds in hands, the women and the children staying way back. Soldiers, trappers and traders hollered, spat and waved their hats, hailing the voyageurs to go faster and faster. Husbands waded in the water, eager to grab their wives from their vessels. Bachelors hovered close by, hoping against all odds that a few demoiselles had reached these shores, even Le Grand Pierre, who was not in the market for a wife, but always hoped for a little bit of fun. The officers, Chacornacle, Dugué and Marsac, lined up on the beach, swords dangling at their waists. Père Delhalle had brought a wooden cross and held it before him, ready to bless the newcomers. Above them on the bluff, a wind-whipped Fleur-de-Lys twirled around its staff. Ah, the colors of France, placed there by his own hand almost two years ago. A proud sight, a proud moment.

The canoes and *bateaux* swung to the beach, and for the first time he saw them all clearly; eager, slightly frightened faces of men, women and children who had defied danger to share in his vision and seize the dream. This was home, a home worth fighting for.

He welcomed each family formally, very much a grand seigneur. Behind every smile lurked a shrewd appraisal of the newcomers' qualities, swiftly filed to be used in due course. The large François Bienvenu family, dit Delisle, disembarked. "What a healthy *garçon*, a pretty *fillette*. *Bienvenue à tous*. Welcome to all of you." The Guillaume Bouches, the le Tendres followed. Two more trooped out, wide-eyed. A few single men saluted him as they stepped out. "Guillaume Labarge," "Joseph Lande," "Jean Michel," all farmers, judging by the tools slung over their shoulders. "Jean Raymond, hunter," "Claude Rivard, interpreter." Ah, *bien*, he is the one who spoke the tongue of the *Renards*. One more bowed to Marie-Thérèse, "Bertrand Arnault."

Marsac, beaming, brought his wife.

"Madame, charmed."

Marie-Thérèse left his side to join Père Delhalle and bid the settlers to the blessing and on to a repast in which everyone would take part.

The neighing of a horse brought Cadillac to the largest *bateau*. He had ordered several cows, pigs, chickens and three horses. They would bring him nice earnings to supplement the

Compagnie de la Colonie's paltry annuity, a payment a lesser man would think ample but one that could never sustain the lifestyle he deserved and to which he had grown accustomed. The horses he would lease for heavy chores; the cows would calf and produce milk, pigs the bacon and the chickens eggs.

"*Allez,* come on!" Sans Rémission tugging roughly on his reins, a thin, sweaty, mangy and neighing horse rolled his eyes with fright.

"Cover his eyes! Put a blanket over him!" Cadillac lowered his voice as he approached the terrified animal. Back in St. Nicolas he had always had a horse. "Whooa, *doucement,* gently, whooa." Horses were so much like humans. You soothed them, lulled them, before making them do what you wanted. "*Doucement.* Whooa. What shall we call you? You're the first, here. Mm, what about *Colon*? Colonist? Perfect name for you." Patiently, he appeased the horse and guided him on the unloading plank where he handed him to la Giroflée. "Take good care of him." He turned to Sans Rémission. "Where are the other two?"

Sans Rémission's face turned purple. "Died. The shock of the voyage . . ."

"All of them? The cows, pigs, chickens?" The voice dripped iciness, the eyes assessed and accused. At best he was not a happy loser. To see part of his profits evaporate did not humor him. "*Pardieu,*" he exploded, "You must have been devilishly careless!"

Sans Rémission mustered enough pluck to spit back, "Eh, *mon Seigneur,* this is a difficult voyage. Two pigs and a few chickens have survived. Be content."

Cadillac eyed him up and down haughtily. The bargeman did not flinch. "*Bien,* Sans Rémission. Be in my chamber in an hour, we shall review your contract." Cadillac pivoted on his heels, leaving the threat hanging in the air. Fuming over this contretemps, he marched back to the fort.

Meanwhile, Grand Pierre, accompanied by Aristide Dents

Crochues, loitered by the canoes and *bateaux*, looking the women over, checking if all were accounted for. He'd heard of two maids coming to work for the Cadillacs. The first one, Françoise, a plain maiden, he'd accompanied to the Cadillacs' abode. The other, rumors said, was quite comely.

Having delivered Françoise with considerable speed, Le Grand Pierre had zipped to his cabin to scrub every visible patch of his body. He patted his hair and beard with saliva, batted the dust out of his old *tuque* and tied his brightest sash around his waist.

Then, he coolly ambled back to the beach where throngs of men still dawdled expectantly around the *bateaux*. Upon seeing him, they, no fools—the same reason kept them there—at first stared, guffawed and whistled, not too loudly—only a man bent on self-destruction would provoke Le Grand Pierre. But then their eyes had darted between him and the last canoe. A plump, feminine silhouette caught their attention. All hell broke loose. Men who had stuck together for months through danger and privation suddenly threw aside existing relationships. It was every man for himself. The fiercest battle had yet to be won.

A grin on his face, Aristide watched the contest.

Le Grand Pierre shoved and elbowed and took every bit of unfair advantage his height and reputation gave him. First in line, he stood like a big bear sniffing honey, drooling over the coming pleasure and yet assessing the danger. Behind the elbowing crowd, Aristide was slapping his thighs with glee, making him feel foolish.

He never remembered what he noticed first, the squealing, pink, plump piglet tucked underneath Rose's equally round arm or the firm, protruding breast it rested on. Piglets grew into large pigs; pigs meant bacon in the soup for many nights; a breast meant softness, wet kisses and fun.

He stared at Rose as she climbed steadily out of the canoe, large-hipped and surefooted, two wide streamers laced with ruffles swinging from her cotton *coiffe*, a sure sign of blessed singlehood. As soon as a girl reached marriageable age, she added the streamers to proclaim her eligibility and catch the attention of young men seeking a wife. In spite of himself, Le Grand Pierre's heart missed a beat; the *coiffe* was a *bigouden*, a lacy starched-up cylinder from his own Brittany.

He spat on the ground and swallowed hard. Her eyes dropped to the wet patch of soil, and to his horror, under her withering stare, he found his foot grinding over it, trying to erase it. Deep inside he knew then that the bacon and the breast had a price.

A toss in the hay, he would like; a houseful of brats he'd gladly leave to others. Disgusted, he swung on his feet. His eyes collided with a wall of hungry, prowling stares raking the young woman's promising figure. Through their leering eyes he saw it all; open features facing the world squarely; wide hips promising healthy children; sturdy arms and legs to pull and scrub; and underneath the stretched cloth, two round breasts for his work-roughened hands to rest on; and of course, the bacon. It awoke his hunter's instinct; coveted by so many others, the prize's value immediately soared.

Heedless of the warning screaming in his head, he swivelled on his feet and darted back to the maiden. He bowed. "Le Grand Pierre at your service, Mademoiselle." His hand, which had not felt anything pink nor round for a long time, hovered a few inches above breast and pig, attracted to both, in fact more to one than the other, and was actually making its descent toward Rose's chest, when it was slapped by the demoiselle's hands.

The two exchanged hot, knowing stares. Le Grand Pierre's hand remained hanging in midair, drawn like a magnet to the softness of the pig and the breast and yet fighting it, knowing full well that the smallest touch meant the end of his drinking, swearing and wenching days.

Eyes glued to the spot where he could have sworn a nipple strained against her bodice, he heard himself say, "What a nice, er, animal, you have here." And sweating profusely, he watched his hand drop to the pig and seal his fate in one single motion.

With a sigh of relief he thanked his lucky star; his hand at least knew how to keep its owner out of trouble. "And what would be *votre nom?*" he croaked in a thin voice.

"Rose Garec," she replied, shrewdly following each stroke of his hand.

The other men groaned and grudgingly made their way back to the fort and left him to his courting.

A Marriage

"**R**atataaa, ratataaa . . . ratataaa . . ."

In front of Le Grand Pierre's cabin, *le tambour* in the Roy's full livery, a blue *justaucorps* lined with red *veste* and culotte, routed the habitants with a lively "Marriage" on his blue drum painted with gold fleur-de-lys. One by one, they sauntered from the darkness of their homes, hailing each other, blinking at the sun and oppressive heat of this July morning. They'd just donned their Sunday best, yet dark patches already spread under their arms and in their backs. A bright, glistening flush lit their tanned cheeks, but no earthly promises could have kept them away. Too much excitation hung in the air. Contagious laughter burst every which way. Their natural *joie de vivre* would catapult them through the day, singing and dancing. The women hitched baskets filled with homemade gifts and samples of their favorite recipes on their swaying hips, children skipping ahead, men trailing behind, exchanging greetings.

Under the sparkling eyes of the vibrating assembly—a dozen families with a few well-scrubbed children and close to sixty bachelors—Jean Raymond wiped the broad grin off his face and solemnly rapped on Le Grand Pierre's door. Guillaume Labarge opened it from within and thrust a starched up groom outside. "Oooh, *qu'il est beau!* How handsome he is!" cooed l'Esperance in a voice that would have earned him a black eye a few days ago. Paul Chevalier whistled and the children shrieked with delight.

Hair combed, beard neatly trimmed, a clean bright sash at his waist and beaded moccasins on his feet, Le Grand Pierre, looking as comfortable as a dancing bear facing a circus crowd for the first time, raised a challenging eyebrow and bunched his fist.

Paul Chevalier reeled backwards in mock terror while Claude Rivard and Jean Raymond gripped Le Grand Pierre, and signaling to the *tambour* to begin the procession, tucked him behind the musician. His *Outaouais* crony, Aristide, appeared at his side, gliding along with supple strides.

They marched gaily through St. Louis street, turned on Rencontre and again on Ste. Anne. There, in the shade of the porch of the commandant's residence, stood his beaming bride, buxom and sturdy, surrounded by the Cadillacs and the officers' families. She held a fragrant bouquet of pasture roses and swamp milkweed against her breasts, shielding unwittingly the two pink things that had provoked his downfall and tormented his dreams. During their courting his mind, hands and lips had often strayed that way, bringing them both tremendous enjoyment, but these heated moments over, doubts tormented him. Freedom and he had lived comfortably for close to twenty-eight years. It was like losing a close friend.

Cadillac caught Le Grand Pierre's dazed countenance but if he smiled inwardly, his face did not betray his thoughts. Imperial, he handed Rose to Fafar de Lorme, for although he was pleased by the wedding, his rank would not allow him to walk a servant to church. He bowed to Marie-Thérèse and, feeling magnanimous (de Tonti was still in Quebec, and he had caught two of the Compagnie's menial clerks cheating), generously ceded his rights to the front of the procession to the bride. As was the custom, Le Grand Pierre came last with his witnesses and friends.

The *tambour* picked up the beat once more, and the *cortège*, colorful and regal, now that Cadillac and officers had joined it, filed on to Ste. Anne church.

Père Delhalle waited by its threshold underneath a festoon of spruce intermixed with black-eyed-Susans, a large cart by his side. A veiled object, about three feet tall and draped in a length of fine damask matching Marie-Thérèse's intricate dress material, lay in the middle.

Cadillac, not one to miss a chance to shine, left the *cortège* and plunked himself ceremoniously next to the *Récollet* who, unlike most people, seemed unaffected by his imposing presence. Cadillac oozed energy and strength; the tilt of his head, the hawkish features, all bespoke of strength and authority. It cast a shade on people and made them shrink and grapple for self-confidence. He knew it and capitalized on it, barely subduing it for his superiors.

Sword dangling by his side, he removed his white-plumed tricorne with great flourish, fixing his piercing sloe eyes on the assembly. "Today God is bestowing two favors on his humble servants. We are gathered here to bless our bell. We pray it peals for many happy occasions as it will today, celebrating the first wedding in Fort Pontchartrain du Détroit[4]."

Dugué, the senior of the half-pay lieutenants, marched to Madame Cadillac, and, clasping the staff of the colors of France, brought the bell's official godmother forward. Marie-Thérèse, radiating charm and grace, clasped the material and unfurled it. The bell, an ornate piece of bronze work imported from Paris at Cadillac's great cost, caught the sunrays and burst into a sparkling hue. Père Delhalle beamed. The villagers grinned smugly and shielded their eyes. Now, at last, the true heartbeat

---

[4] The first marriage contract was recorded in 1707

of the village had arrived. Above their heads, like a protective angel, it would call for gatherings and warn of danger, happiness and sorrow[5].

After Père Delhalle's blessing, the bell was wheeled, the wedding party jostling behind, to the center of the small parade field laying in front of the church, to where a little tower had been erected next to the communal well. Unlike its Old World sisters, the bell could not reside inside the church. Being the most powerful means of spreading the alert, it had to be heard from afar and remain accessible to all.

It took four men to hoist it in place. Madame Cadillac was offered the first pull. She was not sufficiently strong; the bell clanked timidly, quite a disappointment. Faces drooped.

Cadillac hooked a finger at his two younger sons, Jacques and Antoine. The two lads gave a mighty tug. An enormous chime, clear as crystal, exploded, rattling loose teeth. The children clapped. Père Delhalle grinned broadly and beckoned everyone back to Ste. Anne.

Madame Marsac, the village's best baker, deposited her basket of cut up communion bread on the altar. The bride and groom took their places at the front.

"Demoiselle Rose, Hortense Garec . . . take as husband sieur Pierre, Etienne Le Pennec, voyageur . . ."

Rose dimpled and said "*Oui*." Le Grand Pierre's Adam's apple visibly bobbed up and down while his eyes roamed wildly about him, as if considering a mad bolt.

"Sieur Pierre, Etienne le Pennec . . . take as wife Demoiselle Rose, Hortense Garec . . ." Le Grand Pierre froze, mute as a rock.

Père Delhalle prodded him gently, "Pierre le Pennec . . . *pour épouse*, Rose Hortense Garec?"

The congregation held their breath, Cadillac cleared his

---

[5]   This bell mysteriously disappeared in 1712 and was never found.

throat, and Rose—well, Rose knew what to do. She deliberately but delicately rubbed one breast against his arm, leaned over and whispered, "I'll share my pig."

Le Grand Pierre swallowed hard. "*Oui*," he croaked weakly.

The mass over, the village children raced wildly outside to the bell, fighting over its rope.

The *tambour* picked up his tool and Marsac his fiddle. They all filed in an unruly procession through the village and onto the river where a feast of *tourtières*, roasted quails, fruit and cool, crunchy grated cucumber for dessert—a real treat—was laid on tables under shady trees.

Cadillac good-humoredly proposed a toast to the newlyweds. The groom's hand was pumped up and down, his back whacked, and the bride was thoroughly, and occasionally lustily, kissed. Barrels of *eau-de-vie* were tapped, wooden and tin plates were heaped. Indians arrived in little groups and meandered amongst the guests, sampling food and gulping brandy under Cadillac's watchful eyes. He went to speak quietly to the *tambour*, who seized his drum and loudly announced a game of "baggataway" (lacrosse). Indians loved the game. Many had arrived at the feast racquet in hand. The match could last the rest of the day. Meanwhile they would refresh themselves with ladles full of cool water instead of firewater. Aristide dragged Le Grand Pierre to the common, half of the fort's male population in tow.

It was a lazy, sultry afternoon. A cluster of dames, sleeves rolled up and bodices somewhat loosened, rested in a heap of hitched petticoats on the scorched grass around Rose, "oohing and aahing" at her gifts and providing unrequested marital advice. On the beach, two boys rolled in the dust, exchanging blows while others, pioneers and Indians, frolicked around, sweaty hair plastered to their heads. Men, those too satiated to play, sat in mixed groups of elders, farmers and artisans, tugging at their sticky shirts, puffing on their pipes, discussing crops and general problems. Others had crawled quietly underneath a bush, and collars loosened, hands crossed underneath their heads, snored the afternoon away. Now and then a clamor erupted from the common and they would grunt and shift position. Cadillac's group was more subdued. The ladies sat in the shade of a giant oak on chairs brought by the panis, their skirts spread around them, subtly lifting the hem now and then to let some air under. In a circle around Marie-Thérèse, they chatted and gossiped behind their fans. Breviary laying open on his stomach, Père Delhalle smiled benignly, taking gratification in his flock's pleasure. Cadillac and his officers sat a little aside. The men, taking their cue from the commandant, had abandoned their wigs and unbuttoned the two top buttons of their uniforms.

A disparity existed between the Cadillacs' palates. He'd been brought up in the heart of Gascogne (Gascony), a land reputed for its rich food (Cassoulet and *paté de foie gras*) and full-bodied wines. She was a *Nouveau Monde* lady, accustomed to plainer, wholesome dishes, but whenever possible his taste prevailed. Today she had outdone herself. Under her direction, Françoise had concocted a delicious marinated wild duck roast, and Cadillac had opened three bottles of his French wine and liberally passed around his best Armagnac to "dissipate bilious juices" and loosen tongues.

The Cadillacs' offspring had been granted permission—indeed encouraged—to leave and mix with Indian and village children. Their father recognized the inestimable value of an upbringing amongst "the People." He had himself been on the receiving end of such an education. Son of a magistrate, how else could he have learned about crops, nature's fauna and flora, but with the local swains who taught him to love the land and la Garonne, the wide river stretching through his homeland?

Ah, rivers, how he understood them! Even this one, coursing through primeval forests, unaffected by wars, rivalries and ambitions, quietly but unrelentlessly providing life, communication and power. Especially at the Détroit, where he who controlled the traffic on the river held the northwest *commerce des fourrures* in his hands. She, the river, had let him do that.

Abruptly he stood and ambled toward it. Marie-Thérèse briefly glanced up and resumed her conversation. She perceived his loneliness, deeper in the midst of festivities—the type of malaise and isolation created by power, superior intellect and ambition. The sun shone full on the water, turning it to amber and emerald as he took in the splendid sight. He dragged a hand in the shallows and scooped some of the soil—brown earth and rocks. How he missed the smooth, white pebbles from his *chère* Garonne. *Non*, he chided himself, don't think of it. St. Nicolas had not enough room for you. Your aspirations needed a wider playing field. But this—he swept a proud glance around him—this is yours to hold and pass on to your heirs for generation after generation.

Marriage amongst habitants was indissoluble—aristocrats were more likely to cheat, and straying outside its vows was severely frowned upon. The banns were read three consecutive Sundays to rout any impediments. The women did not take their husband's surname. They kept their maiden name to which they added, "wife of . . ." The main goal of marriage was procreation to populate and settle this vast land, procure working hands to help parents in their tasks, and produce a young generation of caretakers for the elders.

Family consisted of many children, often over ten. This was not a difficult task in a time when contraception was quite basic and forbidden by the Catholic faith, although some bloody abortions were sometimes performed at great risks in secrecy (no record of any in early Detroit). Abortionists were tried as witches and burnt at the stake, not to speak of the mother who often bled to death or succumbed to infections.

Children's mortality rate was high, and yet lower than in France; issued from a sturdier stock (only the strong survived the transatlantic voyage and the harshness of the land) they in turn submitted to nature's natural selection. Winter babies were weaker than others due to their mother's seasonal malnutrition. Children were cherished but brought up strictly; corporal punishment followed a long lecture. Their wardrobe consisted of two changes of clothes: working clothes and Sunday best. Their parents crafted all their toys in wood or rags. At night they climbed pell-mell up the loft to share straw mattresses with their siblings. Duties were stereotyped, girls with mother, sons with father. Children attended catechism classes given by Père Delhalle, assisted by Marie-Thérèse and daughter Magdeleine. Since there was no school, parents were the prime educators, a system which perpetuated illiteracy for the unfortunate ones.

The Cadillac children had attended schools in Quebec. At the Détroit, they were tutored by their parents and also very likely by Père Delhalle. All could read and write very well, their signatures in Ste. Anne parish registers are firm and flowing. In education as well as in many other areas, Cadillac was ahead of his time. A real integrist, he had plans for a school where white and Indian children would learn their ABC's side by side.

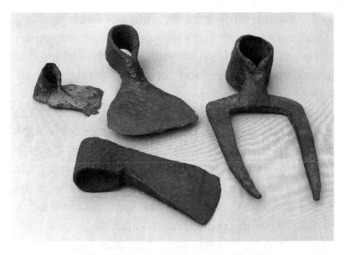

Gardening and Farming Tools
French hand forged hoes, hand cultivator, and belt axe
Gardening tools were also popular trade items.

To survive, the family operated as a team. They worked, ate, prayed, struggled, danced and mourned together. Their lifestyle was regulated by the two main seasons and their characteristic labor. Tilling, planting, hay-making and harvesting happened between May and early October, a cycle during which many holidays occurred, forcing families to toil into the night to make up for "lost" hours. No hand was too small, too old or too mighty to participate. Their industry and the weather dictated the level of comfort, or hardship, for the group that winter. Many additional jobs needed doing during these months; the land had to be drained and ditches dug. The cabin needed rechinking, the cart greasing, and the vegetable patch tending.

Winter came and the family closeted together, keeping warm around the hearth. *Le père* crafted the next season's tools, improved the living quarters, smoked his pipe, argued politics with his friends and complained about the commandant. *La mère*, baby balanced over her hip, wove, sewed clothes and blankets, cooked, gave birth and passed on to her children whatever she knew. If educated enough, she read the Bible to her family. Sickness and diseases, famine and death, danger—all of these parents spent a considerable amount of time fighting. A daunting prospect.

Little is known about the Cadillacs' progeny, but when we look at the family's accomplishments and interpret documents, we realize the whole family abounded with vitality. Both parents had received an excellent education and were of lively intelligence. We can be sure many arguments flared up between the quarrelsome and autocratic Cadillac and his independent wife, for a woman given full power to run her husband's affairs and make decisions in a man's world does not bow meekly.

Fire

In the middle of the night a frenzied strike of the bell made him roll over, batting with a lazy hand at the inopportune clamor. Bang! Bang! "M'sieur Cadillac! M'sieur Cadillac!"

Someone was hammering and kicking and shouting at his door. Jolted out of his sleep, Cadillac sat bolt upright, the ringing and the urgency in the voice waking his senses in one split second.

"What is it?" whispered Marie-Thérèse, clutching his arm.

"Shhh. *Écoutez.* Listen." He cocked his head.

From a distance, muffled by the thickness of the walls, came the cries of panicked voices, "*Au feu!* Fire!" and everywhere the pounding of running feet and banging of terror-driven hands. "Wake-up! *Au feu! Au feu!*" and the throwing open of doors. Above it all rang the wild toll of the bell.

"*Le feu*! Oh, *mon Dieu*! Marie-Thérèse, get out, get the children out!"

Galvanized into action he vaulted out of bed, fumbling for his clothes in the dark, throwing them pell-mell over his nightshirt, clambering to his door and wrenching it open, his heart hammering, Who? Where?

Pierre Roy the trader, pounding on the door, almost hit Cadillac in the face with his banging fist.

"Whose place, where?" They joined the throng of half-dressed people spilling into the street, carrying buckets, thundering past his house.

Next to him, Pierre Roy wheezed, "The . . . bastion . . . the church . . ."

He hurtled down the street, whipped by a whistling wind, past de Tonti's abode, heart racing wildly; the acrid stench, the heat of burning wood scalded his throat and lungs.

A gigantic, fiery tongue was greedily devouring the church, spreading its deadly appetite to the vicarage, throwing a hot amber glow into the night, painting frantic faces with glistening sweat and grime.

"*Comment*? How?"

Pierre Roy was somber. "It started in the barn, the one just outside the palisade where we keep hay and farming tools, and the wind spread it to the bastion and the church. La Giroflée was on guard duty sharing his time between this bastion and the one by the river." Cadillac swore under his breath. They were grossly undermanned; an envious, vengeful Quebec had pressured the Crown to recall most of his soldiers, leaving him a paltry garrison of fourteen men to defend his colony. Fortunately Chacornacle and Dugué, both men of valor, were still by his side. They made up for de Tonti's lack of support. "La Giroflée gave the alert, but it's engulfing everything in its path. Now, even the vicarage—" Discouraged, Pierre Roy dropped his voice.

While digesting the explanations at a record speed, Cadillac's mind had nimbly jumped ahead to cause and effect and appropriate action. Only de Tonti's home, next to the vicarage, stood between his house and the fire. His was strategically placed next to the *magazin*, so he could keep a sharp eye on all its activities. The *magazin, pardieu,* filled with pelts and provisions, also housed the King's ammunition. Ammunition! *Sacrebleu,* they must move fast!

Checking his dread, Cadillac had never looked so fierce and dangerous, his eyes so piercing and resolute. Foes. It would have to be. Barns do not ignite on cold, damp nights without help. Which of them possessed the blackest soul? Who hated him the most?

These past two years, accusations, charges, summons to Quebec, all had been slammed on him with surprising violence. Gouverneur Callière having recently passed away, le Marquis de Vaudreuil had been nominated in his place, an even cooler "supporter." The truce between he and the *Jésuites* had been a sham, with the powerful Society banging on Vaudreuil's door with tales of debauchery his brandy brought to the Indians.

Oh, *oui,* voyageurs snuck in extra *pots d'eau-de-vie* to spruce up the fur commerce in spite of the infernal royal decree. But what was a man to do? The Indians demanded it, especially Cheanonvoizon, the troublesome Huron Chief who was caught sending belts to the Iroquois to incite them to rebel against the French—again. The fragile peace with the Iroquois being vital to the French commerce, he had ordered his men to build Cheanonvoizon a large French-style cabin to placate his uprising, earning the chief his sobriquet of Quarante Sols, the would-be rent for the property. So far, with the help of a few illegal swigs of firewater, it had worked.

Returning to Quebec, the voyageurs had also reported his progress; the growth and improvements to the village, the migrating of the tribes. Miffed, Quebec and Montreal's merchants had complained vehemently to the authorities. They filed protests, he counterattacked, wrote to the Court, pleaded with

Pontchartrain, ranted to Vaudreuil and damned the *Jésuites*. Both sides were far too uncompromising, wallowing in spiteful loathing, blind to the other's redeeming qualities, both clamoring their own innocence.

If only he could have pushed past his hatred and appreciated the benefits of the labor of the Jesuits. These zealous servants of Christ penetrated primeval forests with a total disrespect for their lives and comfort to spread the words of God and teach French to the tribes. They paved the way for traders to move in and reap the gain of their conversions, therefore advancing Cadillac's own cause by familiarizing the native man to the French ways.

The "Black Robes," as the Indians called them, beheld this *Nouveau Monde* as their chance to import a purified French civilization, devoid of its weaknesses. They staunchly fought the ills brought by the trading of brandy; the cheating of Indians by avaricious trappers and traders who took unfair advantage of their inebriated brains; and the debauchery and violence its uncontrolled consumption entailed. The Jesuits often experienced first hand drunk Indians' cruelty. Many a Jesuit was slowly tortured, carved bit by bit, yet kept alive to watch his own limbs fall in the stew pot. Death came only much later, when intoxicated torturers lost interest in the game.

But Cadillac could not overcome his rage at their meddling in politics, especially when it interfered with his own aspirations and his pleasure. He was still seething over the uproar he and Frontenac had unwittingly created, winter 1694, just before his departure to Michilimackinac, when the two had organized the production of two harmless plays (*Nicomède* and *Mithridate*) by Molière, the 17th century king of French Playwrights. Thrilled by their success, they were contemplating *Tartuffe*, but rumors of its forthcoming staging enraged the clergy. True, *Tartuffe*, a biting satire by Molière, threw poisonous darts at lust, greed and ambition hidden behind a religious façade. A portion of the clergy suspected the arrows to be pointed at their chests. They protested loudly. The bishop had harangued the population against the two acolytes from his pulpit, calling them, "corrupters of morals and destroyers of religion." Instigated by the Jesuits, inflamed by the clergy and the notables, waters of treason and hatred were rolling at him, closer and closer, and he strained and shoved and lunged to free himself.

Convinced of the criminal aspect of the fire raging in the church, he bunched his fists at his side, "As *Dieu* is my witness, this terrible deed will be avenged."

Through a haze of fear, he remembered his children and Marie-Thérèse, now—and at last—carrying another child in her belly, so close to the destructive flames and the ammunition. Panic, of gigantic proportion, squeezed his chest, and he made to turn back. A corner of his brain noticed Dugué rolling powder casks out of the *magazin* with a band of recruits, and he breathed a little easier.

His eyes roamed wildly over the mass of people scurrying about, emptying buckets over the hungry flames, running to the river and the well for more, bumping into each other, spilling the precious water. There she was, outside their abode, her belly protruding. She and Marie-Anne de Tonti were counting and prodding children away from the danger zone, their reluctant charges casting mesmerized glances toward the frantic scene. She shouted an order to Marie-Anne who nodded and firmly handed the children to Rose, herself also pregnant, who led them away. Then the two women stood mute in front of their homes, shaking their heads, and Cadillac wanted to rush forwards to enfold her in his arms. But then he heard Marie-Thérèse shouting to Marie-Anne and other women, "Help me! Let's empty the houses, salvage what we can. Marie-Anne, yours first, before it's too late. Then mine."

Fort Pontchartrain du Détroit

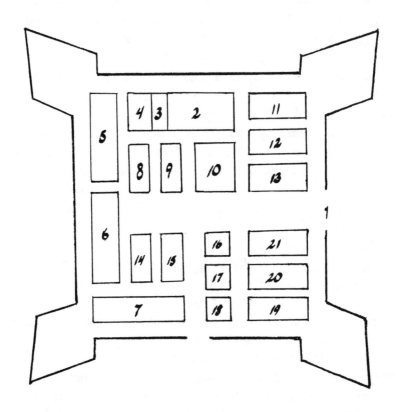

1. *Main Gate* 5. *Home of the de Tontis*
2. *Ste. Anne* 6. *Home of the Cadillacs*
3. *Sacristy*   7. *Magazin*
4. *Vicarage*   8-21. *Cabins*

He should not have panicked, Marie-Thérèse could handle whatever needed doing. Reassured, he returned his attention to the inferno. Père Delhalle's grey cassock was amongst the men dousing the burning building and he blew through his cheeks with relief. He noted that Aristide Dents Crochues and his cronies were amongst the group and his mind registered that the Indians must have seen the blaze and rushed to the fort, leaving their women behind to quickly disassemble the wigwams as need be. Someone had opened the gates, for although Indians came and went freely within the fort during the day, none except the panis were allowed inside at night.

Having devoured the church, the flames licked the vicarage as if tasting it first before engulfing it in a furnace. And then, in an enormous roar, it ignited the whole building. Stricken and helpless some dropped their buckets and sunk next to them.

Cadillac burst into action. "Don't just stand there," he yelled. "It's going to burn the whole fort, everything you own. *Sacrebleu*, it's all wood here. If it reaches the *magazin* it will blow up. *Debout*! Get up!"

He tore through the crowd. "Marsac, supervise the unloading of the *magazin*! Delorme, oversee the crews emptying my house and de Tonti's. Marsac, get teams to fill buckets and soak pelts at the river and the well! Chacornacle, form a brigade with the women and children to bring the water up! De Tonti, organize the men, dig trenches around the church and the vicarage. Let's try to contain the fire! All others douse the burning buildings with the water and the wet skins that are passed to you!"

In a chaos of French and Indian tongues, leaders shouted orders, men jumped to their assignments, dogs barked, children cried and women gripped buckets.

Someone clutched at Cadillac's arm. "The *registres* . . . in the vicarage . . . must . . . save the records!" Breathless, covered with soot and sweat, Père Delhalle tightened his hold like a vise. "The . . . parish *registres* . . . deaths, marriages . . . all there." Then letting go with the look of someone who's made a momentous decision, he darted to the men holding the buckets. "Wet me, I'm going in!"

The water punched him from all angles, soaking his grey robe, weighing him down. He stooped to dash into the building and collided with a chest—Cadillac's.

"You can't! You won't. Not when this fort needs you," Cadillac bellowed.

Père Delhalle knocked the hands holding him. "Let me through, I'm going in."

"*Non*, you're not. *We're* going in."

Both men spun to face the speaker.

"We're going in!" said Le Grand Pierre. "Wet us!" he yelled, pointing to himself and to Aristide standing by him.

"I'm going too!" Père Delhalle yanked his sodden robe up.

Cadillac's arm shot out of the night. "*Non*, you won't. That's an order, even if it means putting you under arrest!"

For a split second, Père Delhalle's eyes shone with pure outrage and rebellion. "How dare you! I . . . I . . ." He paused, breathing heavily, fighting to check his emotions. Pulling himself together, he cast a hasty sign of the cross over the two men. "*Dieu vous benisse*. God bless you," he said through clenched teeth and turned his back on the commandant.

"Get us some pelts each! Come on, more water, *encore, encore!*" Le Grand Pierre ordered. "Quickly! More!"

Wrapped in their soaked skins, they sucked in their last clear air and lurched into the inferno.

Mere seconds later an explosion of sounds erupted from the collapsing building, showering sparks over the men watching the tragic scene. Some crossed themselves, eyes glued to the burning church, hoping against all odds to see the two figures emerge unharmed.

"Keep digging!" Cadillac roared at de Tonti's men. "You! Get that water here faster!" He grabbed a shovel and started hacking the ground savagely. They worked furiously, the heat scorching their faces, tears and sweat blurring their sight and each breath more painful than the previous one.

Swooosh! The structure crumpled upon itself, a fiery tomb for the two men who had penetrated it. Horrified, they ceased all fighting, buckets and shovels by their feet, and stared at the fire. Cadillac's fingers clenched the shovel. Père Delhalle dropped to his knees, "*O mon Dieu,* welcome these two brave men into your kingd . . ."

Someone screamed, "Get the water over here! *Vite!* They're crawling out!"

Everybody left their posts and ran—even Cadillac—and they dropped by the two men sprawled on the ground, sodden and charred in places, tangled in their pelts, eyebrows and hair singed. Aristide, badly burnt on his face, arms and feet, twitched in agony.

"*Courageux!* Brave!"

"*Sans peur!* Fearless!"

"*Incroyable!* Incredible!"

For a few seconds, Le Grand Pierre soaked it all in, and then, too weak to lift a hand, his voice a ragged whisper, "My . . . beard . . . still . . . there?"

Veron Grandmesnil swatted him on the head, "One might have known your first words would be important!" He sniffed and grimaced. "It's all singed and smelly. Your wife won't like it." Le Grand Pierre winced comically; the grimy, sooty crevasses on his skin turning his face into a giant spider web. It forced a chuckle out of the tense crowd.

Père Delhalle stood on the fringe of the group, too grateful for the lives of these two men to dare ask about the records. Cadillac was not so hampered. "Did you get to the *registres?*"

Le Grand Pierre sadly shook his head.

Swallowing his disappointment Père Delhalle elbowed his way through the crowd. "You tried, you risked your life, that's what I shall remember," he cried warmly, endearing himself even more to the community.

Enough heroism! Cadillac shifted his attention back to the fire now beginning to engulf de Tonti's abode. "Let's go back to work!"

Several hours later they finally put out the fire. Ste. Anne, its vicarage, de Tonti's and Cadillac's homes were reduced to piles of charred wood and ashes. The blaze had been contained a few feet from the *magazin*, with everyone jittery about the intense heat.

The whole village and its Indian allies dropped to the ground, spirits sunk to the lowest level. But not Cadillac. He would not give in. Years of adversity had taught him to bend like a reed in the wind, never to snap or lose his footing. With his undaunted energy, the only standing figure amongst his crestfallen villagers, he cried, "We shall not be defeated. We have tamed and conquered, looked danger in the eye and crushed it. We have built and sowed and reaped some glory. We have come here to prosper and spread the glory of God and our beloved France. In their name, we shall wipe the soot and tears from our faces and salvage our pride and rebuild from the ashes." He sunk to his knees. "Let us thank *Dieu* for all the lives he spared today."

Without the fire that destroyed it, Ste. Anne would be the oldest continuous parish in the nation. As it is, it must be content with second place, the honors going to St. Augustine, Florida. Cadillac loaned one of his storage buildings as a place of worship until a humble Ste. Anne was hastily rebuilt. In 1706, during an Indian uprising, it was partly dismantled and covered with sodden doe skins to prevent its destruction by fire. Finally, in 1708, Cadillac raised the money to erect a more substantial church.

Betrayal

Having lost their homes, the Cadillacs and Père Delhalle took shelter in one of Cadillac's barns, their belongings heaped haphazardly about them. The de Tontis piled in Grandmesnil's narrow cabin.

Marie-Thérèse had tossed her children to sleep on bales of hay. Quivering with fatigue, she rummaged through her possessions, taking inventory. The men sprawled on carpets laid over the hay, tin goblets of brandy in their hands. "I have set a general meeting for two o'clock this afternoon to investigate the fire. Right now everyone is too sapped of energy. Tempers are frayed." Cadillac rubbed his stubbly chin. "It's going to be dirty. We have a case of arson."

Appalled, Père Delhalle cried, "Arson! But who? And why? How do you know?"

"I *know,* although I can't prove it yet."

"Are you certain?" Père Delhalle peered expectantly into Cadillac's somber face. The later slowly nodded. Père Delhalle slumped sadly back in his chair. "But why would one set fire to

Ste. Anne when it means so much to all of us? It does not make sense."

"Oh, it does. Let's say the criminal wants to stir trouble for the fort, more specifically for me. It's common knowledge my enemies far outnumber my friends." Père Delhalle opened his mouth to protest. Cadillac silenced him with a hand gesture. "A fire to destroy the church, the bastion of our faith so intimately linked with France, would certainly attract Roy Louis' displeasure. Very clever. The criminal wanted to create trouble, of that I am convinced." He paused to down some brandy and watch the priest's reaction.

Père Delhalle slowly digested this piece of logic. He bent toward Cadillac and whispered quietly, "But who?"

Cadillac's sharp glance settled on the priest's disturbed face. "I am certain that we'll find two criminals; the one who planned the deed and paid someone to do it, and the hands that executed it." His voice came out harshly through his clenched jaws. "But *pardieu*, I shall find them!"

"Do you suspect anyone?"

Cadillac laughed bitterly. "I can count on my fingers those I don't suspect!" It was true and it rankled so much. He poured himself another drink. "De Tonti tops my list." The priest gasped. "Hear me out, *s'il-vous-plaît*. De Tonti so badly wants this fort, it's eating at him like a poison. His hatred of me, of my authority, has taken gigantic proportions. I strongly suspect he is planning my downfall; he intends to resurrect old Du Lhut's Fort St. Joseph on the Lac des Hurons with the help of the *Jésuites*."

"*Mon fils*, I object! I will never believe our sainted Fathers to be so devious."

About to throw more accusations the Jesuits' way, Cadillac clamped his lips shut. He and Père Delhalle went back a long way and the priest had been loyal to him and the fort. "Anyhow, my ruin would bring his rise. I also suspect revenge from the two Compagnie de la Colonie's clerks I tried for cheating. I just heard from Vaudreuil that they are bringing charges against me. It's too late now to travel, the water will soon freeze over, but at the first thaw I'm going to Quebec to countercharge."

"Honestly, commandant, must you always lock horns with everyone? Bend a little, er . . ." Père Delhalle faltered, pinned to his chair by Cadillac's haughty stare.

"*Jamais!* Never! You, of all people, asking me such a cowardly course! When have I ever compromised, settled for less than a complete win?"

Père Delhalle gave a heartfelt sigh. Cadillac's energy was like a tide, sometimes retreating, but always returning with a crash, foaming and snaking, as an angry wave does to the rock blocking its path.

They settled in pensive silence, Cadillac gnawing his bottom lip. "*Non,*" he said after a while. "De Tonti is more likely to have done it." The priest wearily closed his eyes and rested his chin on his laced fingers.

Cadillac sprung out of his chair, chewing the inside of one cheek, reviewing the events that had led him to believe the fire was arson. "I caught him plotting last night. Scared him out of his wits."

He and Marie-Thérèse had gone on their customary evening stroll, chatting with the villagers, the men baring their heads and the women curtseying clumsily. Lately the stroll had turned into more of a parade. Marie-Thérèse was, at last, *enceinte* again; a little ahead of all others, early February; the Bienvenus expected for March; Pierre Roy and his Miami wife, Marguerite, close behind, in April; and Rose in June. It gave Cadillac much joy and much pride. It was only fitting that the village's first pioneer baby should be issued from its First Family. But only a fool would believe that the Sieur Cadillac would engage in a leisurely walk without an ulterior motive. *Non,* in the twilight-bathed village, his hawkish eyes scanned everything, noting what everyone was doing, making mental notes, catching tidbits of useful information. In the evening the villagers dragged chairs and benches to their doorsteps, and sitting in the last hour of daylight, fatigued by a hard day's work, whispered the latest gossip and exchanged news.

The settlement had changed since the arrival of the women; children laughed and cavorted in the streets, and the men returned quietly home in the evening to play cards and sing with their neighbors. Soldiers eagerly gathered for the mandatory parades while officers shouted crisp orders under the admiring glances of the ladies. Even the bachelors had somewhat settled down. Those who had not, and kept singing bawdy songs under decent folks' windows after a long night at the tavern, were sharply reminded of their manners by an irate wife emptying the content of her chamber pot over their heads. The women had silently but steadfastly taken charge. As Cadillac had anticipated and encouraged, the men were being quietly drilled by a formidable army. No more spitting in the one-room hut or relieving oneself on the wrong side of the cabin, *s'il-vous-pla ît*.

But last evening, as he toured the village, Cadillac had not derived his usual pleasure, *non*, an indefinite malaise, an anxiety had constricted his chest. His happy thoughts had been cut short by the sight of de Tonti, in a spot near the palisade, cloaked in semi-darkness, engrossed in a discussion with several traders, volleying hand gestures and head nods; de Tonti, who darted sneaky, worried glances at his commandant. Cadillac's mind, always on the lookout for trouble, told him to pay attention. He had keened his ears to their voices but could not catch even the odd word. In the dwindling daylight de Tonti had nervously dismissed his companions and slithered away, as the snake he was. Cadillac had gritted his teeth and sworn under his breath, "*Le bougre*! The Blackguard!"

Later, in bed, flat on his back, an arm folded under his head, he had resolved to bring about the scoundrel's recall to Quebec.

"But can you prove it?" Père Delhalle insisted.

Jerked back to their conversation Cadillac repeated, "Prove it?"

"De Tonti's guilt."

"Alas, *non.*"

"Could he be in league with a few disgruntled settlers, like the one you ordered to pay a fine to the Indian whose dog he had kicked, and whom you threw in prison when he refused?"

"Ah, irate settlers. Those who don't agree with my seigniory, my power of jurisdiction, my rights to collect rents and levies. They were happy to have me lead them to success and glory, but now they don't want to pay the price. An unpredictable, ungrateful lot sometimes, but not murderous. Power begets jealousy and spite."

Cadillac wagged a taut finger at the priest. "I promised *Dieu* and now I promise you that this vile crime will not go unpunished."

The crime remained unpunished. Cadillac could never prove it was arson, nor confirm de Tonti's guilt. Were Cadillac's suspicions correct? It is hard to say. Indeed de Tonti schemed to disgrace his superior and to surreptitiously fill his pockets; he had been accused several times of illegal trade, and the two men's hatred led them to believe the worst of each other. Cadillac could not abide a rival. He went to great lengths to hold the upper hand, eternally outwitting and dominating de Tonti who, unable to muster the skill of confrontation, resorted to devious means to seek revenge. Plotting, rebellion, ineptitude, jealousy? Yes. Arson? Maybe not.

The Baptism

In the arms of her mother, two-week old Marie-Thérèse wailed lustily, flailing angry little fists in the air. Madame Cadillac cooed gently to her.

Veron Grandmesnil chuckled. "She's going to have a temper!"

The assembly exchanged knowing looks. "What's new? Except the wife and daughter Magdeleine, the whole family has a temper."

Born on February 2, 1704, and baptized immediately, the child's energy had astonished everyone; she was always hungry, slept little, absorbed the world around her as if she were in a hurry, protested furiously at being put down, and fussed over a delay for her mother's breast. Cadillac beamed arrogantly at his daughter, Marie-Thérèse, named after her mother in thanks for the most beautiful gift she'd given the fort: the first white baby born within its palisade, albeit a girl and not a son.

It had been a tight race. He glanced furtively at the Bienvenu woman's—and Marguerite Roy's—cumbersome figures. Rose waddled beside them, an enormous belly preceding her. And only five months *enceinte*!

The child, his child, wailed louder and Cadillac grinned. Nature had a way of disposing of the weak and feeble, and weak and meek could not describe young Marie-Thérèse. *Non*, this truculent child would live.

He scanned the crowd packed in his barn for her official presentation. It should have been a bigger, more imposing one, the occasion warranted it, but the timing was not right. It was a bitterly cold winter and the trappers had long left for the season, leaving women, farmers and artisans to rule the roost. And of course, Quebec and Montreal were still sulking. In their resolve to bend him to their will, to check his power and close Detroit, they still refused to enlarge his inadequate garrison. But he could wait.

As usual, in the fall, Le Grand Pierre had fretted, torn between two worlds—on one side his bride was expecting, and Cadillac had granted him a permit to practice carpentry; and primeval forests filled with magnificent fur-bearing animals beckoned on the other. He prowled between his cabin and the river as pleasant as a grizzly on the verge of hibernating catching a would-be resident in his favorite cave. The day he kicked their pig, Rose had packed his bag, sighing, shoved him outdoors, and threw husband, gun and provisions into his canoe. "*Mon ami*, you must go." Then she returned home to sit by her newly built chimney, complacently patting her slightly rounded belly and pig, and, content, had sipped on a warm acorn brew.

Ordinarily they would have met in the chapel, but winter had rushed in too quickly after the fire to allow them to rebuild Ste. Anne. Instead Cadillac had lent this barn until a new house of God could be built. Pelts and skins were pegged against the logs to seal the drafty walls. Tools were stacked on the sides. Casks of peach brandy, cider, coarse wine and *eau-de-vie* had been set amongst dishes of nuts and sweet meats and jars of preserves on a long table covered with one of Madame Cadillac's embroidered tablecloths. Two panis filled goblets of the bone-warming liquids to a lip-smacking and guffawing group of habitants in their holiday garb; woolen tunics and doeskin leggings decorated with beads for the men, and thick woolen frocks with pretty fichus trimmed with muskrats for the women. Cheeks flushed and eyes shiny, *"Vive le Roy, vive le Seigneur du Détroit!"* they shouted from time to time in Cadillac's direction. He acknowledged their good wishes with a majestic nod. At no time did he let anxiety cloud his brow. At his bidding, any time now the most troublesome Indian chiefs would come to pay tribute to their *père*, in honor of his child. A ceremony to placate discontent, curb pride and play the Grand Seigneur.

The Cadillac clan stood in front of a roughly hewn altar that had been pushed against a wall; Cadillac resplendent in his white, blue and gold uniform, black hair powered and tied neatly with a ribbon underneath his tricorne; and Marie-Thérèse's heavy brocade dress peeking underneath a luscious otter stole wrapped around her shoulders. A heavy silver cross shone between her breasts. The children, well-rehearsed for the occasion, fidgeted somewhat yet remained silent, wiggling their toes in their rabbit fur-lined high moccasins. The godparents, Bertrand Arnault and Geneviève Le Tendre, smiled over the baby.

The guests had brought their own chairs, but while the Cadillacs were standing no one dared to sit. The officers in their dapper habits hovered around the commandant, wives by their side, their lacy *hautes coiffes* bobbing up and down.

Père Delhalle moved from group to group, a breviary in hand.

A wonderful aroma wafted in the barn, tickling growling bellies. A firepit, lined with smooth rocks, had been dug in the center of the shed. Dancing flames stretched around a gigantic, bubbling cauldron of smoked caribou stew flavored with maple syrup and dried morels, licking snowflakes that plunged down from the smoke hole in the roof. Next to it sat Rose, ladle in hand. "Who wants some stew?"

Laplante ambled over, wooden plate in hand. She dished him out a generous portion of the gut-sticking stew. "Want any fish?" she motioned to the slices of smoked sturgeon, eel and whitefish skewered on birch sticks laid on raccoon pelts.

"*Non*, but I'll have a crêpe."

"Françoise, *une* crêpe!" she yelled.

Françoise, the Cadillacs' live-in maid, tottered over with a black *poële*, a flat pan. She held a large bowl of thin batter, a little flour and a few eggs from Cadillac's precious hens all mixed with water, not milk since they still had no cattle.

"Attention, *messieurs et mesdames*, Laplante is about to toss his crêpe," she announced, clapping her hands.

Laplante flushed a bright red and swayed a little; sieur Cadillac served a *sacrée eau-de-vie*! He tossed the remains of his drink in his thirsty mouth.

L'Esperance refilled his goblet. "There, take another one for the work."

The habitants teasingly gathered around him, clapping and singing, "*Allez*, Laplante, go!" Children pushed and shoved to get the front view. Françoise melted a nut of bear grease in the *poële* over the fire. Meanwhile Laplante rubbed his hands.

A ladleful of batter in hand, Françoise cocked her head, "Are you ready?" Laplante nodded. She poured the batter in the pan and handed it over to him. He twirled the liquid around to spread it evenly and replaced the *poële* over the flames.

"*Allez*, Laplante, *allez*," his audience continued.

At last he removed the piping hot pan from the heat and shook it to loosen the batter, and then with an expert flick of the wrist he tossed the crêpe high in the air, "Ooooooh," went the crowd. The crêpe twirled and flipped over and landed back in the pan. "Aaaah!"

"Bravo!" People applauded and children shrieked.

Pan in hand, Françoise called, "*A qui le tour*? Who wants a turn?"

In a corner of the shed Marsac retrieved his fiddle, "How about a little *Dance Carrée*?"

Instantly chairs were pushed aside, men put out their pipes

and women hastily wiped greasy fingers on their petticoats. Cadillac bowed grandly to his lady, "Madame?" She handed the baby to Geneviève le Tendre and curtsied gracefully.

Skirts were hitched and women twirled, and rumps were furtively patted. Veron Grandmesnil invited all the ladies, which brought a grin to Cadillac's face, except on his own wife's turn; then a thin purple vein pulsated on his temple.

In the midst of a twirl the door was wrenched open and a gust of snow and frigid wind whistled in. "*Fermez la porte!*" yelled L'Esperance, stomping closer to the fire. Cadillac breathed deeply, all senses alert.

Flanked by elders gripping their buffalo skins tightly around their chilled bodies, the newcomers stepped in regally, four chiefs in full regalia of vermilion paint: Quarante Sols the Huron, Jean le Blanc and le Pezant, the heavy one, the two *Outaouais*, and one Miami, all bearing symbolic gifts.

As directed by a magic wand, the dancing and bantering suddenly ceased. The tribal rivalries, ancestral hatred, and deceit among the four had caused enough problems at the fort to make Chacornacle reach for his sword's hilt. Cadillac placated him promptly. As if one man, his officers nimbly jumped into action, escorting the chiefs toward their superior, smoothly spacing them, subtly placing the most difficult one at the head of the procession.

Quarante Sols solemnly walked toward the commandant, raising a *calumet* in his hand. "*Mon père*, our custom, as you know, is to use *calumets*; hence we present one to you. We invite you to receive it with the eyes of friendship and goodwill. Tell Onnontio, your Governor, we pray that the sky and the sun may ever be calm and ever bright, and that no cloud may darken or hide it."

Smooth words. A total allegiance to the French and a public renouncement to instigate more Iroquois trouble would have pleased Cadillac more, but a seasoned soldier, his somber face did not betray his skepticism of the wily chief's speech. He bowed.

Jean Le Blanc and Le Pezant followed. Cadillac's eyes narrowed; these deceptive two must be separated soon. Tribal enemies of the Miamis, they shrewdly spurred each other to inflict misery and humiliation on that tribe and blamed it on the French, to the great delight of Quarante Sols, who fed the animosity.

Le Pezant spoke for both, a belt across his palm. "We beg you to permit us to bring you this belt to remind you of the belts we exchanged, one with another, to fuel the Council fire here, that our minds may ever be enlightened for the utterance of wise thoughts, and that all may hold ever the same opinion."

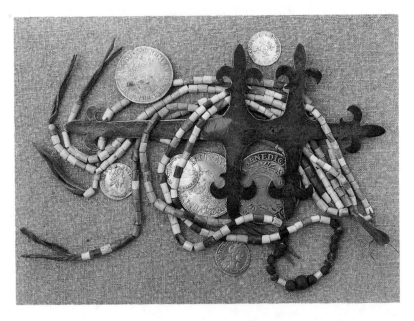

from the collection of Carl Gennette

Objects of the Era
These wampum beads were sacred to the Native Americans.
The French silver cross and coins are from the early 18th century.

The Miami chief had listened to Le Pezant, scorn carved on his face. At last he took his turn, no less cunning than the other three.

"*Mon père*, accept this robe of beaver skin in return for having taken care of the bones of the Chief of the Miamis who died in your village last winter. He could not wish to die more comfortably than amongst his brothers. We leave him, hoping that he will be safe there and at rest."

Oui, and a *sacrée* difficult task it had been to juggle the sorrow of the Miamis and placate the joy of the *Outaouais*. Regal, Cadillac raised an imperious hand and bowed grandly. He would be no less manipulative as the others.

"*Mes enfants*. I am obliged to you for having remembered the promise you gave your *père*, and for coming here with your gifts. I rejoice to see that the land is united, and that tranquility reigns among you. I shall instruct my officers to give you a belt to exhort you ever to be of the same mind, and provisions for your elders because they have obeyed my voice."

Formalities over, the chiefs looked at Cadillac expectantly. He snapped his fingers. Père Delhalle winced, others ignored it. The panis quickly spread thick fur blankets around the fire. Chacorn-acle, well-versed in the protocol, grabbed a cask of brandy from the table. Cadillac bid the chiefs and elders to sit, his officers diplomatically sneaking in between. Soon the *calumet* was lit and the talking stick passed around. Made of wood and feathers, the talking stick was passed from man to man, as each described his dreams or visions.

The others resumed their dancing until well into the night.

The Return of the Trappers

Late April, 1704

Several days of sunburst had melted the ice and the river flowed freely. A new makeshift Ste. Anne was being rebuilt above its ashes. Parties of trappers and Indians started to trickle into the fort, jerking it back to life. Furs, furs, furs; mounds of soft, shimmering, thick furs. The stench of raw pelts pervaded the village; no one took any notice. Furs were the lifeline of the fort, the means to fill pockets and placate growling bellies.

Officially the Compagnie de la Colonie could purchase only furs harvested by holders of proper *congés*, or licenses, but for the right price clerks were not adverse to memory lapses. *Coureurs de bois*, mostly half-breeds, were seen bartering pelts at the trading post and squandering their profit at the tavern, their Indian concubines and raggedly blue-eyed, copper-skinned offsprings squatting at the door. Where the "money" came from nobody asked, except Cadillac, who eyed them speculatively, taking mental notes.

In the *magazin,* piles and piles of furs had been stacked in every available space. Rose idly ran her fingers through a marten pelt and, the pink tip of her tongue wetting her lips, watched the silky hairs ripple back. Suddenly, a glob of spit landed with a "pang" and deadly accuracy in the middle of a *poële* on a nearby shelf.

She clumsily whirled around. "Le Grand Pierre!" she screeched, a hand on her enormous belly. A broad grin spread on Le Grand Pierre's hirsute face.

"Eh! No spitting here!" Veron Grandmesnil darted forward and pushed a wet rag on Le Grand Pierre's chest. "Here, you big *rustre*. Clean that up and get out!"

Winking at Rose, Le Grand Pierre wiped the pan clean with mock fastidiousness, and the task done, dangled the rag daintily under Grandmesnil's nose who snatched it and ambled away mumbling under his breath, "Trouble is back. . . ."

Indeed trouble was back, but so was fun. That night the Cadillacs' barn was packed with men puffing on their pipes, listening, spellbound, to the extravagant *contes* of Le Grand Pierre. Their oldest son, Joseph, by their side, the Cadillacs nodded regally at each arrival—Cadillac tightly. An acerbic message from Gouverneur Vaudreuil intimating a recall had arrived with the first packet of voyageurs that morning.

Little Marie-Thérèse snoozed in Françoise's arms. Madame Cadillac, unaware yet of her husband's trouble, perched gracefully on her favorite oak chair, a memento from more comfortable days in Quebec. A fine pair of scissors, specially made by the whitesmith, dangled from a ribbon tied to her *jupon*. On her lap rested the pockets she was embroidering for her husband. Garments did not include sewn-in pockets, instead they hung outside by a belt.

The officers and Grandmesnil had squeezed inside, resting their shoulders against the rough logs, their ladies sitting in front of them. Père Delhalle settled on a bench near the roaring central fire, his grey cassock tucked around his legs. A tight circle of children, including the younger Cadillacs (Antoine, Magdeleine and Jacques), had gathered cross-legged at the feet of the voyageur, drinking in his every word, faces upturned.

Rose waddled over and dropped heavily on a bench near her husband. In a corner, one-month-old Joseph Bienvenu suckled at his mother's breast. Pierre Roy gloated over Marguerite's drooping belly; the birth of their first child was imminent.

Le Grand Pierre faced his audience standing up, his rich baritone voice holding it enraptured. He paused now and then to puff on his beloved pipe and gauge his narration's impact on the listeners, wrapping the truth—as was expected of him—in a blanket of high drama.

". . . And the snow begins to fall, hiding the sun behind its puffy, dense clouds and setting darkness in the woods. We feed on caribou and deer, and the snow continues to fall, quietly, relentlessly. Laden, the trees creak and hunch against the onslaught, the branches droop and snap under their heavy burden. We sink waist-high in the thick snow in spite of our huge snowshoes, its weight sucking us deeper and deeper still, sapping our strength. We struggle to free our frozen bodies and crawl on the cruel blanket covering the earth. We have no provisions left and our clumsy efforts alert the keen eyes and ears of the animals and they escape our guns. We retrace our steps and dig and scrape to unearth the carcasses of the animals we'd eaten weeks ago. We boil them in melted snow over meager fires and gobble these pitiful morsels with clawed fingers.

"Soon famine sets upon us, twisting our bellies and dulling our eyes. We take our snowshoes apart and simmer the gut to make a broth. Soon that is gone also and we must cut squares of our skin leggings and coats and throw them in the pot to survive. Our dogs whimper and crawl weakly in the snow. We seize our blades and kill them for mercy and for food. So hungry and cold are we that we tear at their still-warm flesh and devour it raw, guts and all, sucking in their life-giving blood. Our stomachs, empty for so long, heave and we retch upon the white snow. Scooping our meal for the second time, we force it down our throats to give us strength."

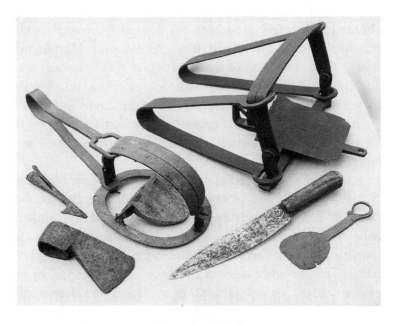

Trapping Tools
Hand forged animal traps, beaver or muskrat harpoon,
butcher knife, trade axe, and iron hide scraper.

The children's mouths slackened. The ladies fanned themselves. Half of the room winced. Cadillac remained impassible,
his mind engaged in developing arguments in his defense to the
Ministry at Versailles. The Intendant Beauharnois had joined
rank with Vaudreuil, turning the conflict over the *commerce des
fourrures* into a gigantic political squabble. But he banked on
the strength of his ally Pontchartrain, his own persuasive
powers, and the greed of the French Treasury to convince the
Crown to maintain le Détroit. The wings of "le Faucon" were
not yet clipped.

". . . When the dogs' flesh is gone, we boil the bones and
gulp the broth. Next we burn the fur off the skins with coals and
scrape them clean. We simmer them over and over to extract all
the juices. And then we have nothing, we can barely stand."

He paused for more effect. "By then we fear the woods have become our graveyard. We claw at the frozen ground for roots to chew on. We pray to *Dieu* for mercy. Those who have enough strength sing to hide the pitiful cries of the sick. Our gums bleed from chewing on wood. As more days pass, one lost his nose, and another his fingers. Death stalks over us. Most of us dig feebly in the snow and lay in makeshift graves to await it quietly."

Le Grand Pierre knew precisely when he held his audience in suspense and, being a tease and a born actor, took his time, sucking on his pipe and scratching his beard.

"What happened then, how did you survive?" Sans Rémission shouted.

One more exasperating puff.

"*Allez*, Le Grand Pierre, tell us," L'Esperance begged.

At last Le Grand Pierre opened his mouth. "A dog belonging to a tribe of Chippewas sniffed us out, leading its masters to our camp. Upon seeing us so weakened, they said they'd return with food and blankets. Two more days pass; our breath is becoming weaker and each man is making peace with his maker. And then, when all hope has deserted us, a most beautiful sight—women loaded with baskets, wood and blankets. At first we think it is a vision, that death has taken us to heaven. The women quickly assemble a lodge and drag us in one by one. Some gentle copper-skinned hands cover us with warm furs. While life returns to our frozen bodies, we watch them light a fire and boil corn and rice."

"Gentle copper-skinned hands" got Rose's attention. Six months in the wild was a long time. She pursed her lips and eyed her husband suspiciously. Had he or hadn't he? Can one trust a man with a female body tattooed on his chest? Le Grand Pierre read the expression and grinned back ambiguously. Had he or hadn't he? Winking naughtily, he resumed his narration.

"The men sit quietly by us. When we grow stronger they take us back to their winter camp and share their dwindling food supply for the rest of the season. We trade our guns and powder and they heap our canoes with furs. We jump in our canoes at the first thaw." He bowed. Pierre dropped on the bench next to Rose. Bunching her petticoats, she squirmed stiffly to make room for him. He burst into a broad smile and nudged her teasingly. The realities of life dropped on the spellbound listeners who, shaken out of their reverie, peppered him with questions. He answered each query with colorful details.

Each spring, trappers came back with harsh tales of horror and brutality, of endurance beyond limit. Yet after a summer of roistering and squandering their hard-earned gains, each fall saw them vault into their crafts without a single glance backwards.

Cadillac prepared to leave; he would interrogate Le Grand Pierre on his whereabouts privately, drawing sketches of uncharted areas, untouched tribes. He was halfway through the door when Le Grand Pierre hailed him. "Ah, M'sieur Cadillac. I have a message from the Outagamies—*les Renards*—elders. They thank you for your invitation and will consider it."

Cadillac briefly nodded to Le Grand Pierre. So at last, the *Renards* might make a move. *Bien.* The "Foxes." They called themselves the Meskwahkihaki "the Red Earth," and like many others, had fled their ancestral East Coast ancestral lands to escape the violence of the Iroquois. They had settled west of Mishigum, on the Wolf River Valley (Wisconsin). He counted on their migration to the west of the fort as a block against the Sioux and Illinois, who were beginning to encroach on the French fur routes.

Dark Clouds

Again, le sieur de Lamothe boarded his vessel for Quebec. The summons from Vaudreuil and Beauharnois had requested his immediate departure—weeks ago—which he would have heeded sooner had he not been emboldened by a reassuring letter from Pontchartrain. The Ministre had written that "Roy Louis intends to give you the command of the post and that the trade be yours, but his *Majesté* insists that the trade be limited to fifteen to twenty thousand *livres* a year." A warning had been added, "Leaving you absolute master of the area, I hope that your behavior will in no way provoke the Iroquois."

Intentions, intentions—when will Roy Louis turn them into concrete orders? Pontchartrain, Cadillac trusted and held in the palm of his hand, but Louis? And twenty thousand *livres* of beaver pelts! A fortune for many but not quite enough for all his troubles and his indomitable ambition. Still, he'd settle for now. In the meantime he must keep his enemies at bay, the Compagnie de la Colonie, livid over his profit in the *commerce des fourrures*, was pressing more charges against him.

The *sacrés* conceited fools in Quebec thought him permanently removed from le Détroit! If their wishes were granted, the rising star of the Northwest and its founder would be clamped down—forever. They had gone so far as to accuse him, Ruette d'Auteuil[6] and the Gouverneur de Montreal of plotting to "usurp the Compagnie of all fur trade au Détroit." And if that were not foolish enough, even of planning to trade with the British!

He'd written to Pontchartrain again, entreating him to hasten the king's decision, promising a share of his profits of the *commerce des fourrures* to La Compagnie de la Colonie as soon as he was reinstated at its head.

Pontchartrain sought the advice of Champigny, a former Intendant of Nouvelle France (1686-1702), and of a financier, Bouvier, before making a decision regarding le Détroit. Champigny advised of the necessity of the new colony while Bouvier confirmed the worst fears of Vaudreuil, the Jesuits and wealthy merchants of Montreal and Quebec: le Détroit lay in the heart of the Indians' nations. Nouvelle France justly believed that the master of that area will become the absolute ruler of the whole beaver trade. And of course, Bouvier was right. Cadillac had outrun and outhought them all. That, they could not forget nor forgive, and therefore clamored for the closure of the post.

He'd had internal problems to settle; Quarante Sols still plotted with the Miamis to wipe out the *Outaouais* village and blame it on the French. The *Outaouais* planned revenge and scared the settlers. News of the skirmishes had reached the authorities and the *Jésuites* who, grasping for reasons to provoke the closing of his post and his downfall, protested loudly.

He had penned letter after letter of protestation, even reported his arguments with the *Jésuites* to Raudot, the Inspecteur Général de la Marine. To no effect. So here he was, boarding his vessel under the gloating eyes of de Tonti who thought him

---

6   Procurer-General of the High Council in France. Ruette d'Auteuil and Cadillac most likely were friends or at least acquaintances. D'Auteuil signed the Cadillacs' wedding certificate.

defeated and definitely out of the way, defiantly leaving Marie-Thérèse and the children behind as a proof of his impending return. He gave de Tonti a hard warning stare. Beware! Le Faucon had folded his wings temporarily—to better soar over his nest.

Cadillac would be detained in Quebec from November of 1704 until June of 1706, much longer than he anticipated. The battle of wills would be ruthless, noisy and virulent. His superior intellect, free thinking, fierce independence and arrogance had earned him many enemies. They formed a solid wall between him and success. He would dismantle it, stone by stone. Not a man to settle for less than a complete victory, he spared no energy to defend his cause. He vociferously battled his detractors, brazenly knocked on doors that would have preferred to remain closed, trampled on many toes and crushed many proud egos.

Soon after his departure from Detroit, the Miamis and Ottawas engaged in sporadic bloody battles that de Tonti could not quell. Fearing for the Cadillac family's safety, Vaudreuil sent a sieur de Louvigny, Major de Quebec, to fetch its members. Marie-Thérèse and her brood would weather the storm in Quebec by her husband's side.

A few men, mostly bargemen, joined the fort in 1704.

September 28, 1705

A triumphal moment for Cadillac: at long last the Court had bowed to his arguments. On this glorious day, and by order of *sa Majesté* and his government's full support, Cadillac was exonerated of any wrongdoing and declared absolute master of the *colonie* and the *Commerce des Grands Lacs*, the Great Lakes trade. The contract was signed at the *château du gouverneur*. We can imagine the scene; Cadillac jubilant and arrogant, Vaudreuil and company bowing stiffly and resentfully to his majesty's wishes. Cadillac had voluntarily agreed to "hand over

40% of the furs gathered at Detroit, all of good quality." Pontchartrain had tersely reminded everyone that "this establishment (Détroit) is the only way to stop British encroachments and the Five Nations (Iroquois) to penetrate deeper in this continent."

Back at Fort Pontchartrain, de Tonti was struggling with more problems: rumors that Quarante Sols planned to join the Iroquois at Michilimackinac tormented him.

A large contingent of pioneers, again mostly bargemen, came to settle.

1706

The friction between Cadillac and the Jesuits and merchants of Montreal continued. Bitter over Cadillac's victory, the Jesuits claimed that Cadillac was a "bold and enterprising officer who believes his authority to be unlimited and let it be known that he will rule over the Jesuits."

The accusation did not trouble Cadillac very much, he was too busy rejoicing in another success: at long last, and after many personal requests, de Tonti was removed from the fort. Le sieur de Bourgmont would act as commandant interim until Cadillac's return.

In May of 1706, Marie-Thérèse became *enceinte* again.

On June 9, François Dauphin de la Forest received orders to serve with the commandant at Detroit.

June 20, 1706, Cadillac returned to Detroit with his family, de la Forest, and 144 settlers (voyageurs, farmers, soldiers and craftsmen: a tool maker and a gunsmith), the largest group of immigrants yet. This group included such settlers as La Liberté, Gatineau sieur Duplessis, Morisseau, and Parent.

Back at the fort:

In January of 1706, de Tonti was forced to leave Fort Pontchartrain. Sieur de Bourgmont, a rough man of limited leadership, took over.

By June 2, 1706, Cadillac had not yet returned. De Bourgmont was still in charge (until August of 1706). His lack of
understanding and bigoted attitude toward the surrounding tribes
set the perfect conditions for a tragedy. Spurred by the interim
commandant's inadequacies, two Ottawa chiefs (Le Pezant and
Jean Le Blanc) plotted to prey upon the Miamis. . . .

Ralph Naveaux of the Monroe County Historical Museum
in the uniform of a Compagnie Franches de la Marine soldier

Attack

Jealousy was eating at the hearts of the *Outaouais*; they felt the French favored the Miamis, their tribal enemies. On that day, an *Outaouais* brave reported to Le Pezant that a small band of Miamis had impudently strayed close to the *Outaouais'* village.

A nasty glint lit the chief's wily features. He sent words to his acolyte, Jean Le Blanc. They rallied a bloodthirsty war party and, thrust forward by hatred, applied their vermilion paints. They seized their guns, tomahawks and arrows, and on silent but deadly feet went to prey upon the unsuspecting Miamis.

The battle was swift, bloody and totally uneven. Only one Miami brave, Pacamakona, escaped the onslaught, and while the Outaouais whooped and triumphantly brandished bloody scalps in the air, he sprinted unnoticed to the fort.

But seconds before he collapsed within its compound and, in a ragged voice, spilled the details of this vicious assault, an unfortunate episode was unfolding in the commandant's quarters. . . .

There was no sound as the door was opened, just a soft treading. Unobserved, the *Outaouais* slipped quietly in the room and padded to the desk—Cadillac's desk.

Ever since *le Père* had left in 1704, the fort had lacked
direction, a strong managing hand. Dugué and Chacornacle had
been recalled by Quebec and Marsac had switched his energy to
farming. The tribes Cadillac had contrived to control by sheer
will and personal charisma had reverted to scheming and
plundering one another during de Tonti's conceited and unimagi-
native leadership. And now de Bourgmont, a brute and a
supreme idiot who lived a dissolute life with the woman
Tichenet, a half-breed, bullied his way around; a perfect setting
for an explosion.

Le Père had been gone long, too long, reflected the Outaouais
as he snooped around, searching for he did not know what, since
he could not interpret the white man's magic writing. He groped
around for signs, anything that would suggest Cadillac's
reappearance to the area and its consequential return to order.
He knew the place would be empty, for apart from sitting
behind the desk during councils, it was common knowledge that
neither de Tonti nor de Bourgmont had felt at ease in what was
essentially Cadillac's place. While they all aspired to fill his
shoes, they found them intimidating and a few sizes too large.

The *Outaouais* lifted a map. This, he recognized. Cadillac had
drawn the fort in 1702 and explained it to the tribes. He shuffled
other documents with his index finger, unsure as to what to do
next. Suddenly, the floorboards vibrated under him, heavy
booted feet pounded past the building; agitated voices cried
outside. He ducked behind Cadillac's high-backed chair and
cocked his ears. "*Outaouais*! *Traîtres*! Traitors! . . . All dead
except Pacamakona!" Then de Bourgmont roared, "Search the
fort!" On the parade ground the bell burst into a warning din.

The *Outaouais* froze, muscles taut. The words had been
succinct, yet he rapidly grasped their meaning; an *Outaouais*
raid on the worthless, insolent Miamis; his only regret: not to
have been there to tear the heart out of his enemy. It also meant
an abrupt decline in the worthiness of his life.

A deep, disturbing awareness of danger alerted his senses.

Out! Out! he must get out. Crouched behind the chair, he rapidly reviewed his options, and then, in mid-thought, he felt, more than he saw, the door being pushed open. His ears caught a soft padding and sniffing. Holding his breath, he peered behind the back of the chair just as de Bourgmont's vicious mutt savagely leaped on him, barking and snarling, and anchored his teeth deep in his forearm and tore at the flesh.

"*Qui va là?* Who's there?" he heard a sentinel shout. Swiftly the Ottawa unsheathed his knife with his free hand, slit the dog's throat and sprang across the room, leaving behind a chunk of his arm in the dog's jaws.

Feet running, voices approaching, closing in on him, "*A la garde!* Guard!" In a wild bid for escape, the *Outaouais* wielded his bloody knife at the doeskin stretched across the window and tried to vault through its opening. "*Un Outaouais*, here, catch him!" With Cadillac he might have stood a chance. But with de Bourgmont, it was act now, think later.

A hand jerked him around. The voices, the fists were on him. The butt of a musket caught him on the temple, and another and another. A tomahawk sliced off one ear and part of his nose. They clung to the blade for a second then dropped on the floorboards where they were trampled. His head spun this way and that way, blood gushed on his chest, on his opponents' vests; vicious boots kicked him in the belly, anywhere they could reach. Over the sickening crunching of bones, he dimly heard de Bourgmont spit, "Kill him!"

They kicked him till his body ceased to twitch. "Throw him out!" growled de Bourgmont as he bent to pick his lifeless dog. And they did, just outside the gates of the fort. His body rolled in the ditch under the horrified stares of Le Grand Pierre and Aristide, who were returning from a five-day expedition down the Lac Erié, totally unaware of the fomenting drama. Jaws set, Aristide hauled his tribesman over his shoulder and walked somberly back toward his village, Le Grand Pierre shaking his head helplessly.

Le Pezant and his warriors were boisterously celebrating their successful raid on the Miamis with liberal swigs of illegal *eau-de-vie*. When Aristide dumped the inert body of their tribesman at their feet, they pounced up drunkenly, wielding wobbly tomahawks above their heads, cursing and ranting. Their drunkenness had reached the dangerous point not quite beyond oblivion, when driven by alcohol-induced boldness, one grabbed the right to do anything, everything, without sparing a thought to the consequences.

With a blood-curdling yell, again Le Pezant rallied his warriors and led them on the path to reprisal, Aristide amongst them. They hacked and whooped and trampled anything in their path, streaming through the forest in a disorderly manner.

Père Delhalle and a soldier were leisurely making their way back from a small Oppenago encampment when they were stopped in their strides by the violent cacophony. The soldier yanked Père Delhalle behind a white pine. Too late. The swish of the *Récollet's* grey cassock had caught Le Pezant's attention. The party leaped on the two men and tied them to the tree, taunting them with tomahawks and spitting in their faces.

Jean Le Blanc flinched. Aristide shrunk from the group. Death to the Miamis brought him joy, but the "Grey Robe" had become a familiar figure, in and out of their village, teaching the children, listening to the elders, quietly speaking of his God. Through his friendship with Le Grand Pierre, Aristide had discovered the value of the Grey Robe to white people. They revered him. The *Outaouais* could not agree to harming him. Besides, his people had no disagreement with the Grey Robe. His death was sure to provoke Onnontio's wrath.

And yet, dared by their drunken buddies, warriors hideously toyed with the two Frenchmen, slicing their skin at random, ripping clothes, opening gashes. The soldier gritted his teeth. The priest stared in the faces of his tormentors, uttering his prayers in a clear, strong voice. He was ready—a wilderness missionary was always ready.

In a flash Aristide stood beside the *Récollet*. "My brothers," he began. Jean Le Blanc shoved him aside and silenced him with an imperious glare. He turned to Le Pezant. "My brother. Have I not always been at your side? Have you not always counted on my support?" Le Pezant nodded. "Our quarrel is with the Miamis. I say let the Grey Robe go. Let him go to the white man's fort and carry a message to its commandant: do not interfere. Keep off your fire and do not give ammunition to the Miami dogs. Let us settle our dispute."

Le Pezant shrewdly reviewed the proposition. "My brother," he finally declared. "I have listened to your wise words. I agree. The people from across the Big Salted Lake must let us sort out our difficulties. Free the Grey Robe and his brother!" The two were untied and prodded with sticks to within a short distance of the fort. Relieved, Aristide walked beside Père Delhalle's stumbling form.

After Pacamakona's dramatic arrival and the discovery of a snooping *Outaouais* within its compound, the fort had been somewhat readied for a possible assault. De Bourgmont had panicked and issued confusing and often contradictory orders. If truth be told, Cadillac's uncompromising ways were sorely missed. Many had resented him—indeed, hated him—but they recognized his soldiering competence. He would have barked orders no one dared to brook and pulled the fort in one direction. There would have been no stumbling, no panic, and no nervous fingers clutching triggers. He would have imposed peace and clear thinking.

Instead, Le Grand Pierre had organized the partial dismantling of the two-year-old Ste. Anne and other buildings, covering them with layers of sodden doeskins to protect them from an eventual fire. Trading had ceased and Indians went back to their villages. Soldiers had assigned themselves their own duties with the help of Marsac. They guarded the bastions, fidgeted with their muskets, mounted their new *baïonettes*, rolled barrels of powder out of the *magazin*, and locked the gates. Habitants scrambled for arms, hearts beat savagely, and women hid their children under beds and up lofts. No one knew exactly what to do. The village bordered on hysteria.

De Bourgmont had climbed to a corner bastion. When he saw the warlike approaching group and its staggering victims, he shouted, "*A la garde! A la garde!*" and jittery soldiers cocked their muskets. Just then a young warrior kicked Père Delhalle viciously in the back. He plunged to the ground. Aristide leaned over to draw him up. De Bourgmont yelled, "Fire!"

A bullet caught Aristide straight in the heart. Enraged, an *Outaouais* raised his tomahawk, another fired at point-blank in Père Delhalle. The blast snatched the *Récollet* off his feet and propelled his body several feet forwards. A third one blew a hole in the soldier's back. A bloody rain of entrails and shattered bones showered the *Outaouais*.

In the bastions, the Frenchmen momentarily froze. Then, jaws clenched, they peppered the murderous band with their muskets. Le Pezant yelled a hasty retreat and bolted in the woods as fast as his obese body permitted it.

Then silence, a God-forsaken silence. Gates were slowly opened and four soldiers recovered the Frenchmen's bodies. Le Grand Pierre sadly hauled Aristide over his shoulder and dared walk into the *Outaouais* village to hand him over to his people. Back at the fort, he grabbed a cask of *eau-de-vie*, and without a word to his wife, climbed into his *pirogue* and disappeared up river. With great sorrow, the village prepared its priest for burial. He was gently placed in his coffin, his customary hair shirt on. They buried him in the little cemetery adjoining Ste. Anne with no priest attending and no proper funeral service.

The *Outaouais* soon realized the folly of their action. Jean Le Blanc accused Le Pezant of having led them into trouble. The tribes feared Vaudreuil's retaliation; the chief had become an embarrassment. He was more or less requested to vanish into the wilderness for the safety of his people. A band of *Outaouais* withdrew from le Détroit to beg for the governor's mercy. On their way they sought refuge at the Michilimackinac mission. Meanwhile, three more Frenchmen died at the hands of the rebellious *Outaouais* at Detroit. Cadillac, who had just returned there, requested more troops and immediately recommended a punitive expedition against them. Miscouaky, another Ottawa chief, and brother of Jean Le Blanc, pleaded to Vaudreuil for his clemency. Vaudreuil accorded it. Cadillac relented, settling for the delivery of Le Pezant to the French in exchange for his pardon.

Le Pezant still wielded power over the tribes; they hesitated to turn him in. Finally, September 1707, he was delivered by his tribesmen to Cadillac for trial. Now it was the French's turn to find themselves in a tricky situation. On one side they had to appease the Miamis' wrath, and on the other they could not afford to further alienate the *Outaouais*. Cadillac chose diplomacy. Le Pezant was imprisoned, tried and found guilty, which pleased the Miamis, but he conveniently escaped during the night. This satisfied the *Outaouais*, and relieved the French, who most likely boosted the obese chief over the palisade or surreptitiously opened the gates.

Minutes before Cadillac's return, de Bourgmont took off into the woods, taking with him the Tichenet woman and several other deserters, including Jolicoeur and La Roze.

Père Delhalle was mourned by everyone. They cherished his memory and enshrined him in their folklore (George Paré). In 1723, Father Bonnaventure, then Fort Pontchartrain's Récollet missionary, had his remains solemnly disinterred, properly blessed, and placed to rest under the platform of the church's altar. In 1755, when Detroit had grown enough to warrant a larger church, his body was transferred to the new building. In 1805, a fire destroyed this more imposing Ste. Anne and in 1817, its grounds were excavated and several bodies conveyed to two common graves on Congress street. No records were made. And so the body of Père Delhalle lays somewhere in an unknown spot.

Le Nain Rouge

Under the moonlit sky, Sieur and Dame Cadillac ambled beside the river, lost in their own thoughts, Cadillac morose, Marie-Thérèse a little sluggish; she'd given birth to Jean-Antoine on January 18, and had announced another child for December of the same year only two weeks ago.

Cadillac stroked his mustache pensively. On June 20, 1706, Vaudreuil had at last signed his orders to return to le Détroit. "Do not trade outside the fort. Do not allow intermarriages, and do not distribute brandy. These are *sa Majesté's* conditions," he had admonished. More directives were subtly implied: Don't complain, don't fight back. Hand over your profits. Control the Indians, stop the skirmishes and massacres. Orders only one unfamiliar with frontier life could issue. Still, he'd diplomatically agreed, having very little intention of complying, glad to be reinstated.

By then the fort, having had two consecutive incompetents at its helm, like a ship without captain, had struck one disaster after another and became more or less a wreck. Now, *bien sûr*, they expected him to reconstruct and put it back on course, all without one *livre* of theirs and amidst the most bitter adverse conditions.

In August of 1706, he and his brood had set foot again on le Détroit's soil. His steps had been long, strong, and determined; his gaze piercing, arrogant and very predatory. And no one—no one—had blocked his way. Dugué and Chacornacle had not been reassigned to the post. He would miss them sorely. François Dauphin de la Forest, an ineffectual sort of man, had come in de Tonti's stead. A new addition had been made to his troop: Michel Filie, sieur de Therigo, a sergeant commissioned to bear letters between France and Cadillac. He expected to be excessively busy.

Never had the fort seen a more impressive flotilla as Cadillac's return: canoes, *bateaux* and his own sailing vessel, all laden with goods and the largest contingent of immigrants: one hundred and forty soldiers, habitants and craftsmen, and at long last a *chirurgien,* Dr. Henri Belisle and his gentle wife, Marie-Francoise. They brought cattle and poultry—no horses. Cadillac would not allow it yet; the renting of Colon brought him a round little income. Père Dominique de la Marche, another *Récollet*, had come to replace Père Delhalle.

The larger *colonie* had required much attention and Cadillac had applied for an assistant to the outstretched *Récollet*. Père Cherubin Deniau, a Sulpician, had arrived recently to fill that function.

Busy months, these past nine. First, the fort was enlarged to accommodate a larger population. It now had eight bastions, and the streets had been extended. Cadillac's new home, an embellished version of the first, more worthy of his status, graced Ste. Anne street, just at the corner of the parade ground. Then came de Bourgmont's desertion, and another *Outaouais* attack on the fort, in August of 1706, which had cost three soldiers' lives and a nasty warning from Vaudreuil. During March of 1707, he had recorded the villagers' land grants[7]. In April, Quarante Sols, the turbulent Huron chief, had simmered down and converted to Christianity a few hours before his death.

And now, under his administration, Fort Pontchartrain and he enjoyed prosperity again. This was a success he had to grab fiercely with both hands and wrestle from adversity. While the habitants benefitted from the comfort and peace he had established for them all, they surlily resented his lifestyle and manners. That knowledge was vastly vexatious. Murmurs of "too haughty . . . gauging . . . demanding" came to his ears. He was in command here and it was blatantly obvious that everyone's safety and livelihood depended on him. *Sacrebleu*, if he collected a reward, he well deserved it. He alone supported the cost of this establishment. The habitants should have been acutely aware of that fact. How quickly they had forgotten who had cleaned up the mess and established a *colonie*! Their rancor inflamed his Gascon blood, increased his ruthlessness and blinded him to reason and caution. The more they resented him, the more he barked and squeezed. Marie-Thérèse had advised him against excess—it would only find him more enemies, and he had already too many.

He was forty-nine, when most men started slowing down. Not he, he could not afford to, did not want to. This *colonie* was worth fighting for; it deserved every morsel of his energy and *Dieu* knew he had plenty of that! His family was forever increasing, anchoring their grip on the land, and his older son, Joseph, was seventeen and an *enseigne* in his own troop. Cadillac fully intended to establish him master of the area when the time came for himself to surrender the command. But not before he'd subdued this ungrateful lot, he promised himself. His jaws hardened and his hands bunched into fists.

He pressed Marie-Thérèse's elbow. "*Ma mie*, shall we return?

---

[7] See list at the back of the book

The gates will soon be closed."

Marie-Thérèse sighed deeply, glancing one last time at the quarter moon's reflection on the undulating river. Marsac and Le Grand Pierre were beaching their *pirogues*, returning from the evening check up of l'Ile aux Cochons[8], the island Cadillac had deeded to the habitants to protect their hogs and cattle from the wolves. Two Hurons, Trou-au-Bras and Grande Gueule emptied their fishing nets while Michel Campau chatted with them, puffing on his pipe.

"It is so beautiful here! As beautiful as the St. Laurent." She smiled pleasantly at him, pretending not to notice the two deep creases between his brows. "Tell me, *mon ami*, about your own river, La Garonne, the one from your boyhood. Tell me again about tickling the fish's bellies with your hands."

Tonight he felt old, gloomy and mentally fatigued, for once nostalgic for harmony. He peered at his companion. Ah, staunch Marie-Thérèse, so sweet, so understanding, so bent on distracting him from his worries. Only she knew the real Cadillac.

They began their ascent toward the fort. "I used to go with my Péchagut cousins, my mother's landowners' side."

A rustling sound, a crackling of twigs startled him. "What is this?" he ejaculated, quickly throwing a protective arm in front of his breathless wife. A raspy cackle burst from the bushes on the left. "*Qui va là*? Who goes there?" he snapped.

Marie-Thérèse's alarmed shriek made him swivel at the hip. There, next to his wife, crouched a most hideous creature, about three feet tall, swathed in dirty crimson rags, red eyes glowing in the dark. He withdrew his sabre. Poof! the creature vanished. He and Marie-Thérèse exchanged perplexed looks. Had they imagined its appearance?

Suddenly Marie-Thérèse screeched horribly again, "*Là! Là!*" and pointed behind him. He spun around. The creature hobbled

---

[8] Belle Isle

around him on spindly, gnarled legs, sneering and taunting. He raised his sabre.

"*Non!*" cried Marie-Thérèse. She grabbed his arm. "*Non,*" she muttered frantically between her teeth, "For pity sake, *mon ami.* I . . . I think . . . it is the *Nain Rouge,* the Red Dwarf, the one *la sorcière* warned you never to harm."

Her words stopped his arm in midair. *La Sorcière?* The fortune-teller who in Quebec, years ago—before le Détroit—had pushed her way into the *château des Gouverneurs* where he and other officers had been bid by Frontenac to enjoy a congenial dinner, and insisted on reading their future? They'd good-humoredly acquiesced and laughed whole-heartedly at her comments, except when his turn had come and she had shrunk back from his palm, eyes dark and wild. "*Le Nain Rouge,*" she spat. "Beware of *Le Nain Rouge,* he brings harm and disaster to all he pursues. Cross him and success will elude you, your heirs will never inherit what you built." She had stumbled back to the door, warning him one last time, "Remember gentlemen. *Attention au Nain Rouge!*"

Bah! he had laughed then, and would not believe in such nonsense now. This malevolent figure was nothing more than a misshapen Indian banished by his tribe. He pivoted on his heels. With a poof and a twirl the figure vanished again. It booed him from behind his wife, fixing him with his demoniac glare, reaching for Marie-Thérèse with claw-like fingers. Cadillac leapt forward. "Go, devil. Do not bring your mischief here!" And faster than ever he struck the creature with the back of his sword. With a mocking, diabolical screech, the dwarf—was it human, was it demon?—evaporated, leaving behind an untidy heap of rags. Cadillac pinned them to the ground with a rageful thrust of his blade.

Marie-Thérèse's legs seemed to fold under her. Cadillac caught her to his chest. She gripped his shoulders. "*Mon ami,* what have you done?" She choked down tears. "*Le Nain Rouge* will seek revenge. We are doomed. He will cast an evil spell on us. All this," she swept a glance at the fort over his shoulder, "Will be for naught."

He shook her angrily. "Madame, take hold of yourself. It was nothing but a misshapen Indian playing a trick. The *Nain Rouge* exists only in the mind of weak people." She kept shuddering. He jerked her more violently. "Madame, do you hear me? There is nothing to fear. We shall *not* talk any more about it."

He spun her around. His arm clenched like a vice on her elbow, he started marching her back to the fort, but she freed herself with surprising force. "Commandant Lamothe," she began in an icy voice. His title spelt trouble. He jutted his chin out belligerently. "Fi, Commandant Lamothe, do not think for one moment you can hoodwink me. You struck *le Nain Rouge* and you know it. Your rashness will bring disaster to this family. Now, *excusez-moi*, I am fatigued and will retire." Lifting her frock she stomped away.

Seriously miffed, he watched her go, swearing under his breath. *Sacrée femme!*

Many fearful legends kept early habitants on their toes. *Le Nain Rouge* brought disaster to anyone who crossed his path, as he did to Cadillac who scoffed at the *sorcière's* omen and struck the creature. It terrorized habitants who feared sighting him. The *Nain Rouge* outlived French and British rules, and has appeared in odd places as late as 1981, before a thunderstorm.

Maypole

Louis XIV had—if somewhat vaguely—granted him a seigniory and Cadillac took all the power, duties and privileges the title conferred. He had cleared the land and encouraged his tenants to settle it. Within weeks of their arrival he had erected a watermill for their grains and a fort for their protection.

A seigneur was a vassal, and as such Cadillac should have had to declare *foi et hommage*, Faith and Homage, once a year to his master, Roy Louis XIV. But as can be expected, he had escaped the practice. Louis reigned from a distant land, and so far no one had had the pleasure of seeing the indomitable Gascon on one knee. Cadillac had no one to bow to for his fief on a yearly basis, which suited him marvelously.

No such luck for the tenants to whom he had granted land on his fief. They had to profess *foi and hommage* to their seigneur and agreed to pay him *cens, rentes et lods*. He collected these high rents, and had the monopoly of grain grinding, fishing and hunting (he could demand one fish out of eleven caught, which he sometimes did). Cadillac cashed in on the practice of crafts that by virtue of his status belonged to him (blacksmith, silversmith, swordsmith, etc.). He had granted contracts inside the village for housing, land on both sides of the river for farming, and several gardens around the fort.

To his daughter Magdeleine he accorded a fief with "three leagues frontage on the river, to extend from the river Ecorse inclining toward Lake Erie, with Grosse Isle and other islets which there are in the front of the concession.[9]"

Magdeleine, who with her father's position, her own prettiness and sweet temperament, could attract many suitors in a couple of years, wished to become a nun. Her father had seen to her comfort, enough to establish her own *couvent*, a great asset to the new *colonie*, one he encouraged.

Early Detroit landowners presented *foi et hommage* in May during a special ceremony as stipulated by feudal rights.

Excitement filled the air. A large crowd was assembled outside the Cadillacs' home, all dressed in their best clothes. The new house had been considerably enlarged, offering all the comforts of a seigneur's home: down pillows, expensive carpets, china and furniture imported from France. A far cry from the prodigious châteaux of France's noblemen but by contrast with the habitants' modest abodes, this residence had acquired a touch of grandeur rarely seen at a frontier post. It reigned supreme on Ste. Anne and the parade grounds. Garlands of spruce and wild flowers decorated the front gallery. Under it, the door remained resolutely closed.

A hole had been dug in the parade ground to hold a stately pole, trimmed of all its leaves, except at the top. "The bouquet" lay by its side.

The crowd parted, and one could tell from their expectant faces that a special event was about to take place. Fafar Delorme stepped through, very dignified, the chief participant in an established ritual. He knocked on the door, which was opened by a pani. "Sieur Lamothe Cadillac, *s'il-vous-pla ît.*"

---

[9]   Burton, MHPC, vol 33, p 381

Cadillac, who'd been waiting in the hallway, stepped outside, his gold and blue uniform immaculate, his wig neatly set under the white-plumed tricorne, his gorget shiny and his cravat frothy. François Fafar Delorme removed his hat and fell on his knees while his wife and children watched him from the crowd. "Sieur du Détroit, Sieur du Détroit, I bring you *foi et hommage* for my fief of Delorme on your seigniory du Détroit and I offer to pay my seigniorial dues. Will you accept me in faith and homage as stated?"

Cadillac agreed with a formal nod.

"The Maypole I am to provide every year is ready. Will you approve of it?"

"I approve."

Fafar Delorme turned away and the two Campaux, L'Esperance, Langlois, Marsac, Pierre Léger, Joseph Parent and three Rivards, amongst many others who had also been granted fiefs, paid their homage in turn.

The Cadillac family sat in the shade of the gallery, surrounded by privileged officers and their wives. All were dressed in their best fineries, although they were not as splendid as when they attended a soirée at the commandant's residence. Then, for a few hours, they tried to recapture the glamour of Quebec and displayed their silks and laces and stepped lightly to the steps of the fiddle playing a minuet under Cadillac's hawkish perusal.

A musket was fired to announce the beginning of the ceremony. An elected group of settlers approached. Louis Gatineau, their spokesman, bowed low. "Sieur du Détroit, will you grant us permission to plant the Maypole?"

"*Oui.*"

Eager, sinewy hands partially raised the pole. Little blocks of wood had been pegged to its side to allow someone to climb it. Marsac attached the Colors of France. *Le tambour* played "Le Drapeau," the Flag Call. As the pole rose, the Fleur-de-Lys floated in the air, calling all eyes and hearts to follow its movements.

The pole was finally embedded in its hole. Cadillac stared at it, so reminiscent of a distant July 24, 1701, when he had thrust the Colors of France in this soil for the first time. He cleared his throat. "Père Deniau, will you give the blessing?"

All fell to their knees. Hat against his chest, Cadillac bowed his head. He should have been thanking *Dieu* for this glorious day yet a rebellious corner of his mind reminded him that little had been given. He had struggled in a reeking swamp of suspicion and treachery, and if his hands were not lily-white any more—were they ever? It was because some of its murk and stench had clung to them.

He faced the crowd squarely. "Let us 'water' the pole." A servant handed him a silver goblet filled with *eau-de-vie.* "*Vive le Roy!*"

Every year a youth was chosen to climb the pole. This year one of the Bienvenus' sons had been elected to "make up" for the loss of their two-year-old toddler a few weeks ago. "*Vive le Roy, vive le Seigneur!*" he shouted. *Le tambour* rolled.

"*Vive le Roy, vive le Seigneur Cadillac!*" echoed the assembly, tapping the casks of peach brandy.

Up and blessed, the pole was ready to be blackened.

De la Forest handed Cadillac a musket loaded with powder only. He fired it at the pole. Everyone took their turn in order of their social status in the fort until the pole was blackened its whole length.

A feast was laid on the parade ground, fiddles broke into dancing tunes, skirts were hitched and women twirled. Joseph Cadillac and young Magdeleine Fafar Delorme danced three times together and disappeared once. She returned flushed and fanning herself. Her father planked himself by her side and did not budge—young Cadillac was hot-blooded and bent on dallying. Fafar had other plans for Magdeleine.

Races were organized and bets tallied. Children shoved and screamed and babies fell asleep on their mothers' broad laps. Baby Jean-Antoine Cadillac in her arms, Geneviève Le Tendre gossiped with Marie-Françoise Belisle while keeping an eye on her own progeny. Marguerite Roy, the blue-eyed copper-skinned child born to Pierre Roy and Marguerite, his Miami wife, just a few weeks after three-year-old Marie-Thérèse Cadillac, caressed the latter's rag doll and Marie-Thérèse, her mouth stuffed with sweetmeats, shoved the girl in the dust and thumped her on the head with it.

The three-year-old Le Pennec twin boys, Pierre and Joseph, like their parents, Rose and Le Grand Pierre, towered over their playmates on sturdy legs. Inseparable and precocious, with a propensity to scuffle and explore, and a temper to equal their size, they distributed hefty punches here and there with huge, hard fists, spreading terror amongst the younger village boys. When he was not whacking their behinds out of sheer frustration, Le Grand Pierre tossed them in his canoe and paddled them up river on hunting trips, walking them until they dropped. Rose sighed and prayed. What can one expect from boys whose father displays a shameful tattoo on his chest?

The Huron, Grande Gueule, challenged Chesne and his buddies to a foot race. Trou-au-Bras recruited baggataway players.

A little apart, Veron Grandmesnil chatted languorously with *la veuve*, the Widow Marie Lepage, his gaze roaming hotly on parts of her figure his hands so obviously itched to touch. Cadillac frowned. He had suspected an illicit *affaire de coeur* for some time, a dangerous behavior in a rigorously pious community.

Whilst Veron Grandmesnil could flirt with the cream of the crop (not too openly), Marie Lepage was not quite the cream. She and her presumed husband, Beauceron, had arrived the summer of 1706. They were an odd couple, she, a rounded, handsome brunette and he, a coarse, short man of limited intelligence. Soon the man had departed for Montreal. A few months later, she claimed to have learned of his demise. *La veuve* did not languish. Marie had been very "good" to the bachelors and to several others who had no business visiting her home. One could argue she served a social function. She worked at the tavern during the day, where her pert ways drew a large crowd (good for business), and discreetly pursued "friendships" at night. The bachelor population was more settled, less blows were exchanged.

So, when Cadillac had officially registered the land grants last March, and she had applied for her lot at the corner of St. Antoine and St. Louis, he had agreed. She paid her rent on time, was kind (she had cheerfully agreed to be Godmother to several Indian offsprings), lively and enterprising, and, thank God, outwardly behaved with propriety. So far, apart from pursing their lips and chastising leering husbands, neither wives nor clergy could pin any scandal to her chest. Cadillac meant to keep it that way. He made a mental note to talk to Grandmesnil at the first opportunity.

Trou-au-Bras and Le Grand Pierre organised a game of baggataway. Marie-Thérèse strolled by. Cadillac seized her arm and, together, they strolled about, nodding, stopping to say a few words here and there, Cadillac very much the grand seigneur he knew he was born to be. Following the demoniac creature's apparition a few days ago, an unshakable cold had settled between him and Marie-Thérèse. She had become jumpy and superstitious, crossing herself furtively, fear fleeting across her face, hugging Jean-Antoine fiercely. She lived in dread of *le Nain Rouge* and feared a loss or a disaster. It hurt to think she would silently blame him for it. She had relaxed only a moment ago. He had seen it in her eyes in the peculiar way she glanced at him when all was well. When the ceremony was almost over she had realized no catastrophe was to happen; maybe, just maybe, all would be well for years to come.

And he prayed to God it would be so.

He was wrong.

Clairambault D'Aigremont

How Cadillac would remember this day of July 15, 1707 and the nineteen ones to follow! *L'enfer*! Hell!

He was in his quarters, penning his *mémoire* to Pontchartrain who, by then, should have read the latest, rather inflammatory, report written by the Gouverneur and the Intendant (Vaudreuil and Raudot) on his protegé.

It was a hot, sultry day. No air penetrated the room. The commandant had pulled his hair in a tight queue and removed his *justaucorps* for comfort, mopping his sweaty face and hands from time to time. The door was closed against the army of mosquitoes buzzing on the outside. He had felt a noose tightening around him for some time now. His enemies were joining rank and pressing their attack.

The *Jésuites* accused him of being bold and enterprising (*bien*, he would have thought that a quality required to establish a new *colonie*); of giving himself too much power (the only power they tolerated was theirs); and of acting without permission (he was a seigneur and a commandant, besides, what else could he do many leagues from Quebec?). No one mentioned the increasing Indian conversions, which had pleased him and were, after all, the *Jésuites'* primary goal.

A few of the habitants, not all of them—one could always rout jealous, discontented souls—had complained of his heavy levies and grand style. Roy Louis did not donate one *livre* to this establishment, even for the troops, whom he fed and clothed. The conflicts between the Miamis and the *Outaouais* had cost Cadillac several thousand *livres*, a big dent in his profit from the *commerce des fourrures*. He deserved a reward, the type of reward, financial and social, that other officers and officials enjoyed without fingers pointing at them.

Pontchartrain, all senses alerted, required a full report from Raudot and Vaudreuil. The two, detecting trouble at last for the ambitious Gascon, jumped at the opportunity to discredit him. They wrote, "M. de Lamothe is hated by the troops, the habitants and the Savages. . . . He gives *congés de chasse*, hunting and trapping permits, which he is forbidden to do. . . . No one knows what happens to the plentiful beaver pelts he gathers. . . . He reports only a small harvest to the Compagnie." Then the most damning of all, "He still distributes *eau-de-vie* to the Savages in spite of *Sa Majesté's* orders."

Here he was, carefully penning his defense when a knock on his door startled him.

"*Entrez!*" Guignolet ceremoniously opened the door, letting a man whose somber clothing and frigid bearing suggested a dour and critical temperament.

The Gascon's face was stone. While Guignolet quietly exited, the two rapidly inspected each other, instant dislike springing between them. The heinous cackle of the *Nain Rouge* briefly echoed in Cadillac's ears. He forced it to the back of his mind. Cadillac slowly stood up and bowed politely, his brain on the alert. "Commandant Lamothe, *à votre service*."

The man bent rigidly at the waist, "Francois Clairambault D'Aigremont, Inspector of the Northwestern posts. Here," he handed Cadillac an open letter, "are my orders from Monseigneur, le comte Pontchartrain, Ministre de la Marine, to investigate this post and report my findings."

The news socked him low in the belly. The first sign of Pontchartrain's misgivings, quite a coup for his detractors. Yet apart from a little pulsating vein on his temple and the hardening of his jaw, not one muscle twitched. He needed all of his wits, he *would* be in control. Anger, frustration and bitterness turned his innards bilious but he still took the time to review Pontchartrain's document. In spite of the irrefutable proof of the Ministre's lack of faith, it was hard to believe the order. The noose had tightened one notch. Still, he would not let it squeeze further.

D'Aigremont took the indicated chair. The *commissaire*, well prepped by Vaudreuil and Raudot, frostily faced the man whose wiles and mercenary soul he had come to expose.

Pardieu, contempt and criticism were all too plainly written on the *commissaire's* face! Behind his desk, Cadillac nonchalantly crossed his legs at the ankle and shoved his hands into the pockets of his culotte in a fairly good imitation of indifference. D'Aigremont's mouth tightened, a reaction that pleased Cadillac immensely. "What would you like to see?" he drawled in fake politeness. "What can I make available to you? Can I explain any . . .?"

D'Aigremont broke in curtly. "I shall investigate on my own, without your assistance."

The men locked stares, Cadillac all too visibly reining in his temper. A dark scowl clouded his brow. D'Aigremont received the full impact of the Gascon's powerful withering glare. The *commissaire* did not flinch, his expression hardened. "Who keeps records?" he continued.

Cadillac fiddled with his quill, peered into the ink pot, coolly provoking. Without looking up he replied, "Veron Grandmesnila capable man." He busied himself sharpening a quill that looked perfect. "Still," he pursued, his voice dangerously soft, "To understand the wheels at force behind the *commerce des fourrures* and the new *colonie*, here, au Détroit, it is vital to speak with its founder, *Moi.*" Raising his eyes, they collided with D'Aigremont's hard stare.

D'Aigremont stiffened considerably and jumped up, choking on loathing. "My orders come from the highest, *Monseigneur* himself, does Commandant Lamothe doubt his wisdom?" Cadillac swallowed a nasty retort.

"I have just set out from Fort Niagara, which I successfully investigated," snapped D'Aigremont. Cadillac sniggered. Ignoring the slight, the other man continued, "I feel confident I shall prove worthy of this one." He began to leave the room. Cadillac pointedly remained seated. Almost at the door D'Aigremont halted and pivoted to face him, wagging a finger. "Do not interfere. Stay out of my way." The *commissaire* yanked the door open and stalked out of the room.

Cadillac, his wrath boiling within him until he expected steam to puff from his ears, banged his fist on his desk. *Sacrebleu*, if he had not been an unwise participant in a bungled confrontation!

D'Aigremont remained nineteen days—nineteen days of hell. Ferreting everywhere, opening bags, doors and books, he scribbled and recorded feverishly. He had arrived filled with suspicion, and suspicion he kept throughout his stay. He saw only what he wanted to see, setting his own interpretation to every act, never asking for any explanation, accumulating as much damning evidence as possible, and ignoring the truth when it suited him.

Cadillac, after much reflection, had wisely decided to cool. The facts, when examined without context and explanation could be damning. It was to his advantage to enlighten the *commissaire*. D'Aigremont icily rebuked his advances every time. Once, walking by the *magazin*, Cadillac thought he caught a glance at the grotesque *Nain Rouge* sneering diabolically from behind a barrel. *Non*, such nonsense!

Important visitors normally resided at the commandant's. But not D'Aigremont. Cadillac had foisted him on de La Ranée, who, caught between his short-tempered superior and the frosty *commissaire*, trod carefully between the two, the pressure almost unbearable. The feud, evident to everyone, separated the village into two factions, the loyal and the disgruntled. D'Aigremont eagerly invited the discontented to depose their grievances and never recorded any positive comments. When he left, everyone sighed with relief and business resumed as usual.

Cadillac, meanwhile, continued his *mémoire* to Pontchartrain, preparing the *ministre* and himself for disastrous results. D'Aigremont had refused him the courtesy to read his report. He anticipated trouble, what else from a man who blatantly found him guilty without examination. He wrote:

> *"Monseigneur,*
> *It might be published that I have enjoyed a large profit since I am au Détroit. And if it is so, one should consider the pains and care I have applied to this establishment. . . .*
> *I regret that sieur Clairambault D'Aigremont refused any communication with me. I would have like to explain my decisions. . . ."*

Cadillac would have to wait almost two years for the results.

A Council of War

Jaws set, Cadillac swept dark, assessing glances at the four persons present in his council chambers; two officers, D'Argenteuil and de la Ranée, sitting beside him, and two soldiers, Guignolet and Francoeur, guarding the door. Arms tightly crossed, de la Ranée watched him cunningly, trying to read his mind. D'Argenteuil sat on the edge of his seat. The two soldiers remained cautiously silent, sweating heavily in spite of the pervading cold. De La Forest, his second in command, had just left on a mission to Quebec.

Wind and twirling snow drummed against the logs, a gloomy day pierced through the window. One could hear the scraping of ice creepers as villagers hurried to their business. Inside the small room, the dancing light of the fire licked Cadillac's stern face, making him look unreal, satanic, and very alarming. His wig formally set on his greying hair and *epée* resting on his desk as was the custom when he rendered justice, he indeed cut a somber figure.

A couple of weeks before, months after their desertion, and immediately after he had heard word of their whereabouts at the Grande Rivière du Lac Erié, he had sent de la Ranée at the head of a search party to bring de Bourgmont and his men back for trial. De Bourgmont had slithered between their fingers. They'd returned almost empty-handed, except for one poor soul, La Roze, whom they had dragged back in.

He despised desertion, an act of treason, of weakness; a vile crime that undermined authority and sapped other soldiers of their strength. Every soldier, however simpleminded, knew its price, but *he* would have to issue the sentence, an act very unlikely to increase his popularity. He glared into the light-speckled room, cursing the foolishness of man.

Cadillac was a seigneur, and as such he acted as a judge. He enforced law and order and dealt with day-to day civil cases and petty offenses (Lower and Middle Justice), collecting fines and sending offenders to ponder over their crimes in the garrison jail. He also enacted legislation as needed at the post. Sometimes serious cases came his way, as in the case of Le Pezant, and he dispensed High Justice and dished out appropriate sentences. Generally, in the wilderness, the word of the Seigneur ruled supreme. If displeased, one could always appeal to the royal courts of first instance at Montreal, Quebec or Three Rivers, and from then on to the Sovereign Council, as he knew only too well, having been recalled several time to answer accusations.

Having no tolerance for the meek, the weak or the intractable, he was harsh, decisive and merciless. Confronted by his commanding presence and piercing gaze, not to mention an incredible talent for debate (he was perforce well practiced after all), the accused rarely presented their cases well. Heavy sentences cracked over their heads. Resentful and unable to cope with Cadillac's unyielding temperament, they resorted to sending sneaky letters of appeal to the royal courts. The steady flow piled on the delighted authorities' desks and galled Cadillac—it all helped to build a case against the unshakable Gascon and reinforce D'Aigremont's most likely incriminating report. But military transgressions came under his full jurisdiction.

"Francoeur, bring in the prisoner!" His voice boomed, breaking the oppressive silence.

All heads turned to the door, where they could hear a scuffle. La Roze was dragged in, his uniform filthy and torn by months of rough living, eyes roaming wildly over the assembly. "*Votre nom?*"

"Bertellemy Pichon, dit La Roze." His voice came out thin and shaky. A rose was tattooed on Pichon's left cheek, hence his *nom de guerre.*

"Your age?"

"Twenty . . . Twenty-three . . . Twenty-four."

Cadillac winced inwardly. His face prematurely lined, La Roze resembled hundreds of nameless Frenchmen who enlisted to escape famine. Roy Louis, permanently engaged in waging wars and building a sumptuous Versailles, ignored the needs of his common people. Gut-twisting hunger and misery stalked France, pushing peasant men to draw a clumsy cross on a contract binding them to serve Louis for many years, in the case of La Roze for life. La Roze had joined the Compagnie Franches de la Marine, the one guarding France's interest in the colonies, Cadillac's own troops. Unlike the regular Army which required seven years, the Marine pushed enlistment for life. If soldiers commonly served until they were forty or older, the Marine offered enough advantages to make up for its long commitment. It appealed to the more adventurous type of men and promised a better life after discharge, for they were given a piece of land and encouraged to settle in the *Nouveau Monde.* The marines were garrison troops. They did not travel on campaigns like the regular army. Part soldiers, policemen and settlers, the marines made up a substantial part of the population, sharing feast and famine alike with the villagers. Upon joining their *compagnie* they were given a "Nom de Guerre," or sobriquet, by their comrades, as in this case, La Roze. *Oui*, for men like La Roze, *le Nouveau Monde* and he, Cadillac, offered an escape, a new beginning. But not from desertion. No power could shield a man from such actions.

"It's de Bourgmont's fault!" La Roze cried pitifully and fell to the ground in a begging heap. The officers sat mute. Francoeur and Guignolet dropped their eyes. Francoeur hesitated to hoist him up, as if he would be sullied by his contact.

La Roze's eyes darted frantically over the men, and resting on Guignolet, he crawled on his knees, thrusting his bound hands toward the soldier's heart. "Save me!"

Guignolet recoiled noticeably. La Roze scrambled up and spat in his face. The spit landed on Guignolet's forehead, descending spider-like toward his brow. He did not wipe it off or strike back, he stared at his comrade with a mixture of intense horror and pity, a sticky blob of crystal spit hanging from his eyelashes. He hauled La Roze up and prodded him Cadillac's way.

"*Non! Non!*" shrieked La Roze, his body rearing from Cadillac as if he were the devil.

Cadillac stiffened considerably, eyes glittering icily. A deadly hush fell over the room. The moment seemed trapped forever. Then, his voice vibrating with cold rage, Cadillac spoke, enunciating every word. "Bertellemy Pichon, you are accused of having willfully deserted your post in the Compagnie de Cortemanche at the Fort Pontchartrain du Détroit in the company of a soldier named Jolicoeur and an officer, Sieur de Bourgmont. Desertion is punishable by death. What have you to say for your own defense?"

Jumping like a jack rabbit, La Roze screeched, "De Bourgmont did it, M'sieu! 'Promised to pay my return to Quebec and a place on a fishing boat to France if I helped him and the Tichenet woman gather bundles of beaver pelts."

"*Pourquoi?* Why?" Cadillac kept a closed expression.

Shivering violently, La Roze swallowed hard.

"*Pourquoi?*" repeated Cadillac in a clipped tone.

Guignolet jerked him roughly with arms of steel.

Propelled by a gut-wrenching fear, La Roze twisted wildly and burst, his voice cracking with despair. "*J'veux mon pays*, I want my homeland! No more cold and savages to scalp me." He butted his head toward Cadillac, "You have the good life. A full belly and a dame to warm your bed. *Moi*," he beat his chest, "I'm alone, I'm alone!"

Loneliness! Everyone present in the room had experienced its devastating grip. This *Nouveau Monde* offered a new beginning but it exacted a high price. Poor souls like La Roze sometimes snapped under its weight. Still, a heinous crime was being tried, with all its repercussions. Cadillac straightened and refocused hard on La Roze. "What happened to your companions?"

La Roze hesitated, ". . . Sonderot drowned. Leveillé killed Bacus in a fight and . . . and . . ."

"And what?"

La Roze's Adam's apple bobbed up and down. "We . . . We ate him. We had no food . . ."

Appalled, the five witnesses to this horrible confession visibly hardened. Cadillac, his face unreadable, bore deep into La Roze's white face. "Do you know de Bourgmont's intentions?"

"Go to *les Anglais*," mumbled La Roze, just before he abandoned the fight and went all limp in Guignolet's steely hands.

Cadillac fiddled gravely with his *epée*, deliberating silently. Finally he murmured to his officers who nodded their heads in agreement. The three faced La Roze stonily. Cadillac cleared his throat to pass judgement. "Bertellemy Pichon, on this day, the seventh of November, the Council of war finds you guilty and convicted of the crime of desertion, and even of murder, and hereby sentences you to have your head broken till death follows, by eight soldiers, being first degraded of your arms."

"*Non! Non!*" shrieked La Roze crumbling to the ground, a wet patch darkening his pants.

Imperturbable, Cadillac stood up. "I declare this *Conseil de guerre* ended. Take him out." He gathered his *epée* and papers, nodded curtly to his officers and exited without a glance backwards.

New France had the death penalty, but for years no one had volunteered to be the executioner until a death-row convict was offered full pardon in exchange for the job. Not surprisingly, the offer was accepted. Except for the military, no death penalty was carried out in Detroit.

De Bourgmont and his companions continued their dissolute life on the shores of Lake Erie, constantly hunted by French soldiers. He then lived for fifteen years on the Missouri river among the Indians. In 1720, he was appointed commander of an expedition to make peace with the Indians of New Mexico and founded a post on the Missouri (the French Court had convenient memory lapses).

A New Ste. Anne

The previous fall Cadillac had ordered the felling of white oaks and had let them age in preparation for this day, a welcome diversion from the constant stress D'Aigremont's visit had placed on his shoulders. At the first thaw, and between jobs, men had started cutting and mortising the lumber. The new Ste. Anne would truly deserve to be called a church; no more green warped logs, mud floor, bark slabs and flat roof. The previous one had been dismantled a few days before.

It had taken three days to erect the walls, thirty-five feet long, twenty-four and a half feet wide, ten high, of logs carefully joined on one another, saddled at two ends to accommodate the ridgepole.

Cadillac bore the expense for all this, Roy Louis having firmly denied financial support, stating "You should in the future maintain the almoner, the surgeon and the medicines. The building of the fort and the church are in the same category. It is not right for *Sa Majesté* to defray expenses at a place which is not to yield him any return." No return? What about the forty percent of his profits the Compagnie, directly under Louis, pocketed?

Statue of Antoine de Lamothe Cadillac
Wayne State University
Detroit, Michigan

Cadillac, with his usual determination, had not yielded to a mere shortage of funds. Come what may, Ste. Anne would be rebuilt. He had collected rents, fees for the use of his mill, leased his horse, exacted hefty taxes from the villagers who practiced a trade—the whole bordering on extortion—and saved his profits from the *commerce des fourrures* until he had accumulated enough silver coins for the new endeavor. Le Détroit had grown in importance, the fort had been enlarged, the *commerce des fourrures* flourished, and the population increased, so much so that he had just recently accorded more land contracts. He felt the cause justified the sacrifice, both his and the habitants', and he had made the decision without requesting their opinion. The habitants, fighting for their own rights, had surprised him by the vehemence of their complaints, filling his chambers for a hearing. To no avail. He had not budged.

Profoundly religious herself, between tending Marie-Agathe, born December 28, and sickly toddler Jean-Antoine, Marie-Thérèse had backed the project.

Gathered in a bunch by the west side of the church, eighteen men in buckskin leggings and open-neck chemises listened to Le Grand Pierre giving them instructions; the voyageur had finally settled to the carpentry trade. It had rained during the night and the ground was soggy and slippery.

It seemed the whole village had dropped their chores to dawdle in a lively circle around the workers, the men in rolled-up sleeves, at the ready, and the women restraining their progeny with work-roughened hands. Scores of Indians of mixed tribes loitered around them, fascinated by the animation. Marie-Thérèse rocked baby Marie-Agathe. Magdeleine had hitched frail Jean-Antoine, all bundled up, on her hip. Joseph, Antoine and Jacques stood by their father. The two priests, Père Deniau and Père de la Marche, hovered nervously by the walls. Rose, heavily *enceinte* again, watched her twins closely; they'd wrestled a spot on the front row. She did not notice, however, the worms they stuffed in young Marie-Thérèse and Marguerite Roy's pockets. Veron Grandmesnil had shut the *magazin* and idled cautiously on the opposite side of Marie Lepage, their eyes straying to one another, exchanging brief glazes hot enough to shrivel the sodden ground into sand on impact.

A long ridgepole, ropes and leather straps wrapped around it, lay in wait by a side wall, six lean maples, skinned and cut, were stacked nearby. Once an imposing white oak, silent witness to centuries of nature's mysteries, now stripped of its foliage and bark, the ridgepole was destined to carry the burden of the roof and listen to mankind's inner secrets.

Surveying the height of the walls, Cadillac chewed on the lining of one cheek. The ridgepole had to be hoisted perfectly horizontally ten feet high, pulled up the rafters and placed into the saddle at the crest. The ridgepole could slip, drop and roll at any time, crushing existing work, snatching lives.

Back in Montreal they would have used a team of oxen or horses to haul it up. Here, besides having only one horse, there was not enough space; men would pull and strain and bleed.

Le Grand Pierre separated his men into five teams. Three two-man crews (Pierre Léger-L'Esperance, Jacob Marsac-Jacques Langlois, Michel Campau-Grande Gueule) would wedge the maple trunks under the oak and help shake it off the grasp of the earth and boldly raise it above their heads. One six-man crew (Louis Normand, Claude Rivard, Rencontre, Joseph Parent, Louis Gatineau, Deslorier), straddling the roof rafters on the west side, hands tightly coiled around the ropes and straps of the ridgepole, would lift it up and take over from the ground crew. Another six-man (Pierre Mallet, Pierre Chesne, Jean Casse, Jean Raymond, Pierre Roy, Jacques Campau) would ride idly the east side rafters, waiting to pick up the slack from the other six men once the pole rested on the topmost log before its ascent up the rafters. Le Grand Pierre stepped back in the middle, eyes flashing keenly from team to team.

The crowd had turned silent. Twelve-year-old Jacques Cadillac nervously chewed his fingernails.

"Are you ready?" Heart pounding, Le Grand Pierre turned one last time to his crews. The raising of the ridgepole, a critical and dangerous task, offered a man the chance to show his skill, to prove his mettle. He breathed in deeply. Cadillac raised his eyes to the saddle, so high above the men's heads, balled his fists and blew through his cheeks.

On the sidelines wives quickly crossed themselves.

"At '*trois*' we go," warned Le Grand Pierre, plucking his

tricorne off. "*Un, deux, TROIS!*" He whacked it against his leg. All at once, the ground crews grunted and moaned, straining and heaving, slipping on the soggy ground, sweat already trickling down their faces and the hollows of their backs. The ridgepole quivered and lifted. Up the rafters, the men tightened the slack.

"Pull on the right! . . . More! . . . Watch the slack!" Le Grand Pierre's Adam's apple bobbed up and down. He wiped the sweat off his face with the back of his hand.

Cadillac swallowed hard, his fingers bit into Jacques's shoulder. The boy yelped. Cadillac did not notice.

Up, up, went the ridgepole; over thirty-five feet of menacing, crushing weight should it slip. The men's muscles knotted and bluish veins bulged under their skin.

"Pull, up there! *Encore* . . . More! Get it up!"

It rose above the ground crew's heads, out of their reach, and for a split second, when their fingers first unclenched and before the team above tightened their grips, it dangled perilously. The crowd gasped. One more heave. The ridgepole grated and squeaked as it settled on the topmost log. On the rafters, the Louis Normand team paused briefly to catch their breath. On the other side, the Pierre Mallet team climbed to the saddle. The first team threw them the end of the ropes. Pierre Mallet grunted his team to pull while Louis Normand and his men pushed the pole up the rafters. Before construction, holes had been hollowed with drill braces and bits every foot of the north and south rafters. Now, each straddling one, Claude Rivard and Rencontre followed the pole's ascent, inserting one foot-long pegs inside the holes behind it, to stop an eventual roll down. Heave after heave, they climbed, grunting and pulling, sweat dripping and making the straps oily and slippery, pain exploding everywhere in their bodies.

The echo of their suffering bounced off the wood and anchored in the viewers' hearts. Cadillac caught himself grunting. Embarrassed he hid it in a cough. Suddenly, when it seemed that neither workers nor spectators could take any more, the ridgepole fell into its mooring with a thud.

"*Là*, we made it!" Michel Campau shouted from the top. Le Grand Pierre threw his tricorne in the air and whooped and hollered. Breathless, his teams collapsed in a tangle of chaffed ropes and wet leather straps, straddling rafters and ridgepole. The spectators screeched and clapped.

Cadillac let out the breath he'd been holding and relaxed his hold on Jacques. Nobly, he walked to Le Grand Pierre and shook hands, "Good work." Both looked up at the ridgepole, no longer threatening, but anchored securely in its saddle, and nodded appreciatively.

Two days later, the church was complete. Above, it was "boarded entirely with oak rafters in a good ridge, and below of beams with square joists. Its doors, windows and shutters, and sash frames measured twenty squares each; the whole building closing with a key."

The ground was boarded and benches were lined one behind the other. Rose, Marguerite Roy and several other women applied beeswax to the wood. Gigantic walnuts grew plentifully in the region, and during the winter Le Grand Pierre had lovingly fashioned a beautiful altar and two credence tables out of the honeyed wood, carefully smoothing it to a lustrous patina. He had also fabricated a platform to rest them on, and there they sat, in the center of a thick green carpet, the altar shining between the two tables.

During the past winter Mesdames Beaubien, de La Ranée, Lamothe-Cadillac and D'Argenteuil had embroidered a fine linen cloth. Marie-Thérèse carefully unfolded it over the altar. Père Deniau deposited a gilded tabernacle and brass crucifix in its center. A large picture of the Blessed Virgin of gilded wood, especially ordered from an artist in Quebec, was hung behind it, and a tin sanctuary lamp suspended from the ceiling. Magdeleine put in the finishing touches: a large candlestick of painted wood on each side of the tabernacle.

The congregation trooped in to worship. The Cadillacs sat at the front on comfortable chairs, officers and their families followed, the more affluent habitants behind. The others piled in at the back, families first, bachelors and converted Indians last. Chesne and Xaintonge hesitated, they were married but their wives had refused to join them.

Later that year, in July, François Clairambault D'Aigremont "dropped by" to check on the *magazin* on his way to Quebec to depart for France with his report. On that day, the village was celebrating the baptism of the Pierre Mallets' son. The parents quickly adjusted to the situation, politely begging the uninvited but influential guest to be Godfather, hurriedly renaming their baby François in Clairambault's honor, bumbling into a faux-pas: pious Magdeleine Cadillac stood as Godmother, her parents at her side. Cadillac gritted his teeth, somewhat loosened like everybody else's by too many bouts of *mal de terre*, throughout the ceremony.

The rivalry between Cadillac and the Jesuits intensified. The commandant openly favored the *Récollets* missionaries, some-times ruthlessly according his favorites a post promised to the Jesuits. Father Marest, missionary of the Society of Jesus at Michilimackinac, complained bitterly to Vaudreuil of Cadillac's offensive actions; only the Bishop of Quebec could appoint missionaries. Cadillac claimed to hold Royal permission.

Truth be told, Cadillac, with an elephant's memory and grudge to match, obsessively made a point throughout his life to "put a spoke in the Jesuits' wheel," especially at Michilimack-inac. Although in 1697 France had decided to pull back from western posts, including Michilimackinac (precipitating Cadil-lac's founding of Detroit), it had remained a powerful Jesuit mission and trading center. Both Cadillac and the Jesuits, each for their own reason (Cadillac, the fur trade, and the Jesuits, conversion) had vied fiercely for the settling of the tribes around their own post, a dirty battle over "body count."

Cadillac's aversion would follow him to his grave.

The Report

François Clairambault D'Aigremont dropped his report on Pontchartrain's desk. Pontchartrain, who, ten years ago, had fallen under the spell of the energetic and dazzling Gascon, hesitated to open it. *Oui*, he had ordered the investigation, he could hardly have done otherwise—the *colonie's* authorities had pushed him against the wall—but he apprehended its content, the confirmation of his worst fears. To all appearances, he had backed an adventurer—an imprudent political move on his part.

Pontchartrain had been tormented with dread during the fall of 1707, after receiving his protegé's *mémoire*. Lamothe had protested vigorously of D'Aigremont's antagonistic demeanor and unilateral enquiry, preparing him for a disastrous report by smoothly admitting some excesses.

Pontchartrain shrugged his shoulders, nothing new. Born to privileges, all his life he had rubbed shoulders with the high-born and powerful, most of whom indulged in excesses as a way of life, his own family included. Louis XIV's court was strife with luxury and dissipation and courtesans' plots.

None drew as much furor as Cadillac, the black sheep whose cunning, brilliance and palpable ambition had affronted so many, the one no one wanted to succeed. The Gascon had warned of the danger of closing the western posts, of France's neglect of her colonies; he insisted on tightening the French's control loop over les Grands Lacs. Worse, he had done it and proven them wrong. An unforgivable act. Now, bloodthirsty, the pack of wolves, having cornered its victim, bared its teeth to tear at its flesh. Only, he, Pontchartrain barred their way.

Resolute, Pontchartrain tore at the seal, reading quietly. At the end his shoulders slumped. Steepling his hands on the document, he rested his chin pensively. *Delicat!* One faux-pas and his own career could plunge downwards with that of the Gascon's.

The accusations confirmed his misgivings. ". . . The sieur de Lamothe is nothing but an adventurer whose politics threaten France's control of the western trade. . . . He is a despot over a colony which is much smaller than what he describes and in a state of disrepair . . . There are only sixty-two colonists. . . . Only three hundred fifty-three arpents have been cultivated. He is an extortionist. . . . Hated by everyone. . . ."[10]

What to do? He could hardly continue to endorse Cadillac even if he still could not help admiring the man's wits and audacity. Yet a clear withdrawal of his favors followed by severe sanctions would pinpoint his error of judgement, certain to bring him disgrace. Pontchartrain pursed his lips.

Two days later, his decision, a compromise between saving his neck and dropping a man in whose ideas he still believed, was firmly anchored in his head.

---

[10] For whatever motive, there is no doubt that D'Aigremont manipulated numbers and facts. An official inventory of 1711 mentions a fort of eight bastions, thirty cattle and one horse, 400 arpents of cultivated land, and 143 holders of concessions at a low ebb of the colony.

Fort Pontchartrain, April 9, 1709

Boum! . . . Boum! . . . His tricorne limp and sodden, his drum wrapped in black, the *tambour* solemnly beat "l'enterrement," The Burial. A heavy, icy rain had pelted over the village for three days and now the wind had added its fury.

The bell started tolling. One by one the habitants somberly left the comfort of their homes to gather outside the Cadillacs' residence. Skirts and pants hitched up, moccasins and clogs in hand, they trudged through the ankle-deep mud. Small clusters of Indians trickled into the fort, bent against the bluster.

The door, covered from above by a black cloth, slowly opened. Cadillac and Marie-Thérèse stepped out, he tired-looking and grave, she white and clutching his arm, Magdeleine and Jacques behind, noisy and boisterous Marie-Thérèse Jr., already five-years-old, for once subdued, wringing a corner of her sister's cloak. They turned to face their entrance.

Joseph and Antoine came out, carrying the pitifully small coffin of fifteen-month old Jean-Antoine. Marie-Thérèse gave a dry little sob and pressed a balled handkerchief to her lips. Cadillac's jaws hardened. She had given birth, thirteen days ago, March 27, to François, their twelfth child. To pacify the incompetent de La Forest with whom he argued constantly, he had named him Godfather. Exhausted, frail and sorrowful, she had insisted on accompanying Jean-Antoine to his resting place. Their maid, Françoise, had returned to Quebec, a new one took care of Marie-Agathe and the baby.

Slowly the *cortège* took shape, coffin and bearers ahead, *tambour* behind, Boum! . . . Boum! The village followed painfully, fighting the sucking mud, rain pounding on their frigid bodies, wind toying with their hats and unfurling their capes. Cadillac had not bothered to order the cart to be hitched to Colon, it would never have budged.

After the ceremony, they stumbled to the cemetery adjoining the church, and watched with horror and heart-shattering sorrow as the little wooden box was lowered in a pool of mud and water. The hole had been dug the day before, but the rain and wind kept eroding it, partially filling it with murky liquid. It made a strange sucking sound, obscene and shocking, as it bubbled around the box, seeping in. *"Non!"* screamed Marie-Thérèse and made as if to plunge in to retrieve her son. Cadillac seized her, and eyes closed, pressed her sobbing body close to his chest.

The next day—the rain had not relented—Michel Filie, Sieur de Thérigo, returned from France with a message from Pontchartrain, ordering the withdrawal of most of the garrison, announcing a decision regarding the post within a year.

Cadillac banged one fist on his desk and swore savagely. Another blow. *Pardieu* if he could not see right through Pontchartrain's move; the Ministre was severing his fate from the man who had placed one of the richest fur-bearing regions within the grasp of France. *Sacrebleu*, that blackguard D'Aigremont, whose words had prevailed over his! Unaware of the disparaging description of his establishment, Cadillac attributed his disgrace to the collusion of his detractors, jealous of his power and stamina. The rest, his rights, his privileges, what his enemies would define as "excesses" had been no more than other seigneurs'. They were just rewards for his vision and hard work, and were certainly much smaller and fewer than the ones perpetrated at the Court.

Cadillac stalked about his quarters, working out his resentment, analyzing and plotting, age having shrunk neither the length nor the vigor of his steps. Not once did he consider, that maybe, just maybe, he had seized unparalleled control, that in his search for fame and fortune he had trampled ruthlessly over other people's interests, and that had he been less arrogant, less mercenary and impossible to deal with, his success would have been admired instead of coveted. Just the day before, in a heated argument with de La Forest, when his frustration over the man's imbecility had overpowered him, the commandant had booted his second in command back to Quebec.

Bah, Pontchartrain could not close this establishment, he concluded—not after having endorsed it. A man of action, of tomorrow, having analyzed the problem, instead of dwelling on it, Cadillac planned his next move. *Un jeu de patience.* A game of patience, let the tempest blow over, he would weather it.

Several days later, another kind of turbulence came to plague him. He had just received confirmation from his envoy to the *Renards* that, at last, they had accepted his offer to migrate to the fort. Pondering over the reaction of the surrounding tribes, he was drafting a plan of action. The *Renards* had a reputation of arrogance and quarrelsome disposition. The rain had at last ceased to beat against the logs, and it was that time of day when a man reaches for one final pipe before setting home. A loud pounding made his door rattle and tore him from his thoughts. *"Entrez!"*

The door was wrenched open. Veron Grandmesnil, bareheaded and grey-faced, charged in, hastily shutting the door, resting his back limply against it. Startled, Cadillac dropped his pipe and reached for his *epée*, ears cocked, listening for trouble. Painful, ragged breaths racked Grandmensil's chest. He weakly waved his hand down to appease his concern.

Cadillac poured a generous helping of Armagnac in a pewter goblet and, raking a shrewd glance over him, passed it to Grandmesnil who gulped it at once. Resigned, Cadillac drew a chair. Grandmesnil slumped on it. "Well?" prodded the commandant sharply as he rested a hip on his desk, his train of thoughts interrupted, his return home delayed, and his mood swinging for the worse.

Grandmesnil mopped his brow. "It's Marie," Cadillac's lips tightened to a thin line, "She's *enceinte* . . . Five, six months. It hardly shows . . . Except," Grandmesnil reached for another drink. "Except, this afternoon, the wind, er, the women noticed her protruding belly."

"Pardieu," Cadillac exploded, retrieving his Armagnac, "Did not I warn you, *non*, requested that you stop this folly? *Sacre-*

bleu, this is trouble." He strode about way, as if the room would never be able to contain his annoyance.

A scandal, all he needed. Grandmesnil, a calculating lawyer and efficient *commis de magazin*, had been closely associated with his own endeavor, in fact advising him on most legal matters. And then, "What did the women say or do?" he blurted.

The lawyer's dallying was of little importance to him, except that in a rigidly pious community, rules could not be broken with impunity. The women, whose coming had helped stabilize the male population as planned in 1703, had suspiciously kept a close tab on Marie and their men, sensing possible trouble. Although it was alien to the Gascon's temperament to abandon an ally in trouble, their reaction would somewhat influence his own.

Grandmesnil shuddered. "Short of having me drawn and quartered," he replied gravely and yet with a touch of wryness, "They dragged her to Père Deniau for confession and will bring charges against me and Marie at the church." He paused to rub his eyes.

"Of course, you will pay the price," the commandant stated flatly.

The lawyer shifted uncomfortably. "They, er, want me to marry her."

"You have no other choice." Again, it was woodenly declared.

"I . . . I have better plans for myself," Cadillac raised an eyebrow. "My father is a lawyer. I plan a brilliant career for myself," after a short hesitation, Grandmesnil concluded, "It does not include a woman of Marie's past, however pleasant she might be."

Cadillac did not bat an eyelid; the confession held no element of surprise, it reflected the belief of their time. There were two categories of women: the one you had fun with and the other you married. Whilst grooms brought to the marriage bed a not-inconsiderable experience, they expected their brides to be virtuous. *Pardieu,* to marry a woman of sullen reputation was sure to curtail a promising career. Grandmesnil had been warned.

Still, Cadillac did not relent. "You must marry her and save some honor, the village will see to it. I cannot interfere, but shall grant you my continued support. Better options are now closed to you, rumors of an illegitimate child travel fast. Parents of more suitable demoiselles will not let you approach their daughters."

Grandmesnil opened his mouth to protest, then shut it darkly. Cadillac returned to his desk and started shuffling his documents. Clearly dismissed, the lawyer slowly got up and exited quietly, a pugnacious tilt to his chin.

Veron Grandmesnil did not do "the honorable thing." He stealthily scaled the stockade during the night and made his way back to Montreal where he joined his father's office and was later appointed Cadillac's trusted agent and lawyer, holding the post for several years.

Marie was left to face the music alone. Two kind persons braved the village's wrath to become her daughter's Godparents on July 24, 1709: Dr. Henri Belisle and Marie-Thérèse David, wife of Sieur Desrochers. Marie later married a Jacques Baudry.

A "Promotion"

Having shown his displeasure by ordering the removal of most of the garrison from le Détroit, Pontchartrain mulled over part two of his decision. The wolves, set to devour the Gascon, would trample anyone in their way, and he, Pontchartrain, the last hand leashing in their fury, had better relinquish his hold to remain unscathed. And yet . . . it is men of Lamothe Cadillac's mettle, bold, energetic and shrewd, who accomplish missions others would not dream of, men whose intellect and ambition threaten weaker opponents, make them impossible to deal with.

Le Détroit had turned into too much of a nuisance. Pontchartrain pursed his lips and perused an unofficial report on de La Forest's performance at the fort, pretty mediocre. *Bien.* He smiled slyly. The right man to succeed the troublesome Lamothe Cadillac. A few months under his leadership and the fort would dwindle and close, freeing him of a most embarrassing situation. And the Gascon? Well . . .

Le Détroit, October 1710

Abandoned by his sponsor, stripped of most of his garrison and his best officers, the indomitable Gascon continued his fight for Le Détroit, his creation, his seigniory and provider for approaching old age—he was already fifty-two.

Cadillac stroked the stubble on his chin. Marsac's rooster had crowed a couple of hours earlier. He had pored all night over maps and documents, the stinky, smoky light of the bear grease burning his eyes. No sign yet of the *Renards*. The Sioux and Illinois were growing bolder, the *Renards* would block their way, just here. His finger circled an area to the west of the fort, perfect. Unique Algonquin, he would use them to entice their tongue brothers, the Sauk, Mascoutin and Kickapoo to resettle under his "protection."

"*A la Garde*! *A la Garde*! *Bateau* approaching, flying our colors!" His face darkened with discomfiture, he was in no fit state to greet a visitor. *Non*, much better to tidy these documents, make a few last notes, and amble back home to his man for a shave and sustenance. Then he would come back here to relax or better still, enjoy a bout of fencing with his oldest sons. At twenty and eighteen, Joseph and Antoine's fast reactions kept him on his toes. He had taught them well. Last March, Marie-Thérèse had presented him with another son, René-Louis, and their house was always filled with babies' wails and young children's noisy romping, hardly a place for repose.

Done. Stretching his legs under the desk, he yawned lazily. Suddenly, his muscles tensed, on the alert. It started with a scratching noise in the chimney behind him, similar to the scraping of a cat's claws on wood, and grew rapidly into a frenzied thumping. Cautiously swiveling around, his horrified gaze focused on a red misshapen figure, the size of a three-year-old, frolicking grotesquely amongst the dying flames. The fire spat and hissed. The hideous form cackled and sneered, his diabolical stare pinning Cadillac to his chair. Damnation! Heart throbbing, Cadillac pounced up, seized a log and cudgeled the monster savagely on the head. Bang! Bang! With a horrible screech, the creature disappeared without a trace as swiftly as a puff of wind. Cadillac's arm could not be stopped. It whacked and sliced through the air, embers flying, until its exhausted owner let it drop, his long moccasins covered in ashes, the flames extinguished. Cadillac stared at the empty fire, raking a weary hand through his hair. Nothing in there! He was just too tired, his vision had blurred.

Shaken nevertheless, he ambled to the window and rested his forehead against the cool pane, gazing outside. Escabia, Joseph Parent's pani, a cask on his shoulder and a small dog in tow, was exiting the *magazin*. Back leaning against Michel Campau's smithy, Claude and Nicolas Rivard guffawed with Trou-au-Bras and Pierre Chesne, most likely loitering to catch a glimpse of the visitor. Père Cherubin Déniau, leading a troop of white and Indian children to their religion class in Ste. Anne, stopped to call a warning to Marguerite Roy and Marie-Thérèse—Cadillac's daughter—who were trailing behind, forever arguing. His son Joseph and a heavily cloaked man were walking up Ste. Anne. Hell and damnation, they made for his quarters! For one brief moment he hoped to warn his guard and sanction any intrusion. Too late.

"*Entrez!*" he growled after the guard's knock.

The man, his hair heavily powdered, bowed obsequiously, bringing an ironic glee to Cadillac's weary features. Father and son exchanged a brief speculative glance. Joseph imperceptibly shook his head and dawdled, reluctant to miss an interesting scene. Cadillac dismissed him.

"Commandant Lamothe," the man bowed again. "Permit me to introduce myself. Jacques Charles Renaud Dubuisson, at your service." Cadillac raised a questioning eyebrow. Dubuisson's mouth took on a fatuous grin, "I have come on orders of Monseigneur Vaudreuil and Intendant Raudot to serve as commandant interim of this post." Cadillac's thunderous scowl made him step back a fraction. Dipping again at the waist,

Dubuisson smoothly babbled on, "No doubt Monseigneur feels your talents," a quick glance at the Gascon's wooden features, seeking softening there, "Would be better employed elsewhere. I, er, came in the stead of Sieur de La Forest, who is indisposed, till he can take his post." Retrieving a document from one of his many layers, he handed to Cadillac.

Brain racing, trying to assimilate Dubuisson's words and their impact, Cadillac tore at the seal. Instantly recognizing Pontchartrain's elegant writing, he tried to ignore the growing alarm within him. Somehow he managed to keep a closed expression as his eyes scanned the letter's content. "Removed . . . de La Forest in your stead . . ." Bitterness. Incredulity. Anger. Swallowing the violent emotions threatening to overpower him, Cadillac willed his heart to slow its pace. Leave? Renounce ten years of hardship? Of wrestling a *colonie* out of the wilderness to hand it over to less competent hands? To have his rights so grievously trampled upon? Still, the news should not be such a surprise, the bastard was saving his skin. And de La Forest, an inept officer to take his place! His chest constricted, each breath burning more than the precedent. Think! There was more to Pontchartrain's decision than a mere run for cover. Think!

Under Dubuisson's fascinated stare, Cadillac strode about his quarters, document in hand, stopping now and then to reread a passage. And then, something undefinable lit his features, a barely suppressed excitement, a glimmer of victory. *Bien sûr*, it made sense. De La Forest, the perfect choice. It had been all planned, orchestrated by a masterly mind. The fort caused the *ministre* much embarrassment. What better than send a fool to command it? It would dwindle, become a liability. Pontchartrain would order its closure and forget about the whole episode. The comfort of one man would prevail over the economics of France.

And Cadillac's work, the closing of the control loop over Les Grands Lacs, would loosen, opening the area to many coveting hands—*les Anglais*, Iroquois, Sioux and Illinois—all to relieve

Pontchartrain's mighty headache.

The discovery made him feel as if he had been kicked in the belly. Fingers clenched, mastering his feelings somewhat, Cadillac cast a perfunctory glance over the rest of the missive. Dubuisson, meanwhile, let his assessing eyes roam over the room, mentally calculating the value of its content, visualizing himself sitting behind the desk, salivating at the power.

One written word arrested Cadillac's attention.

Later that day, the repast had been strained. Marie-Thérèse and he had always encouraged their offspring to lively conversations. At times, he regretted this decision. His dark mood threw his daughters into nervous twittering. On edge, his sons remained cautiously quiet. From her end of the table Marie-Thérèse frowned slightly. Finally, scowling at his daughters, he bellowed, "Silence." They finished their meal in a stifling hush. Grace over, he stalked out of the room, Marie-Thérèse's speculative glance following him to the door.

He was downing his second Armagnac when she entered his study, having at last settled her brood with the maid. Thirteen pregnancies and frontier life had thickened Marie-Thérèse's body and lined her features, but had not curbed her forthrightness; she could tackle problems with great courage. She faced him squarely.

"Well?"

He poured a third drink and lifted his eyes from the amber liquid. "I heard from Pontchartrain today," he searched for better, softer words to tell the outcome and found none. "I have been recalled. De la Forest has been named in my stead."

After a devastating, silent interchange with her husband's glance, when the depth of his words sank in, she slumped on a seat. Mustering enough courage to face the whole truth, she whispered softly, "Forever?"

A violent pang of longing pierced him through. "For now." Banging his fist on his knee, "*Ma mie*, I promise I shall fight it.

But not now. Later. This is not the time. I shall do it, if not for me for our . . ." The sentence remained unfinished, his gaze wandering about him as if seeing the village beyond the walls, not imagining a life without it.

Reading the sadness in her husband, Marie-Thérèse's hand crept to her heart. For years he had sunk his energy, his hopes in this endeavor, this lifetime achievement. She grieved for the man who had made this venture possible, the part of him that had made an exceptional leader.

A tear coursing down her cheek, she reached for him on her knees. Her head fell on his lap and, closing his eyes, he stroked it gently. The gloating faces of Vaudreuil and Raudot danced in front of him. Jaws set he forced the picture away.

Suddenly Marie-Thérèse shrieked, "*Le Nain Rouge!*" and pulled away from him. He savagely hauled her against his chest.

"*Non!* *Le Nain Rouge* does not exist. This," he exploded, "This recall is the work of a collusion of envious souls and a man who is saving his *sacré* neck, not of an imaginary creature." He paused, and changing strategy, quietly stated: "Marie-Thérèse, do not fail me now."

Her chest rising rapidly, Marie-Thérèse visibly fought her emotions, her husband's dark eyes boring deep in her face, her soul. Taking a gulp of air, she said, "Tell me everything." She sensed his relief, his hands loosened their grip. Stonily, he related the morning's event.

"But where is Dubuisson? You have not introduced him to us."

Cadillac shook his head. "I have foisted him on Sieur du Figuier, as Major interim himself, he will take care of him. I felt that I, er, we, needed privacy tonight."

"What happens to us now?" she whispered softly.

"We'll have an inventory made of all the buildings I have built, tools I have amassed, anything pertaining to the fort and we shall sell it to my successor. We shall pack only our personal belongings."

Slowing digesting the news, her eyes still large and moist, she insisted, "But where do we go from here?"

"Ah, that is another thing we must discuss. Pontchartrain had a suggestion." Remorse, most likely, he thought privately. "Louisiana." He paused to let the word sink in.

"Louisiana!" she gasped. "But, er, but it is the poorest of France's colonies, hot and untamed, with only three or four hundred habitants at most . . ."

"Which is more than here." He interrupted.

"It's so far, so hostile, so new."

"D'Iberville established it more or less at the same time as I formed this *colonie*."

She looked at him, quizzically. He held her stare without blinking, she could read him so easily.

"It's a citadel of lewdness, of sickness."

"Together we can change all that. I shall request a missionary and women. You will look after the sick, Magdeleine will help with the teaching of the Indian women. Our sons will be in my troop. *Ma mie*, please see this as a new venture."

Marie-Thérèse cast desperate glances about her. "I am too old, too fatigued . . ."

"I am twelve years older."

Propelled by a formidable vitality, equal only to his ambition, her husband had always lived hard, often in defiance of authority and normal social strictures. Courting danger was second nature and at times it had paid off. Cadillac, she could tell from the coiled energy animating his expressions, the resolute jutting of his chin, was on the brink of being seduced by another adventure. She tilted her head closer to his, searching for a sign of relent, of she did not know what, "But why Louisiana?"

Cadillac pounced up, outwardly excited. Had he any other choice? Easy, do not overdo it, warned his unbending pride, no one must perceive the depth of your disappointment, least of all Marie-Thérèse, "France is on the brink of bankruptcy. Roy Louis is too engrossed in his wars, he is neglecting the colonies, especially Louisiana. It has become an unmanageable burden he wants to unload. Rumors have it in Quebec, that he would like to pass it on to Antoine Crozat, one of France's wealthiest financiers."

Marie-Thérèse sighed. At an age where most people sat by a chimney corner to review their lives, they would traipse into unknown territories. Her husband's energy knew no bounds, no age, no defeat. And she envied him.

"Maybe I shall contrive a contract with Crozat, explore mining possibilities, make our fortune."

In complete surrender, she asked only one question, "When do we leave?" Her voice sounded surprisingly calm.

"Oh, *Dieu*, Marie-Thérèse!" It was almost like a prayer. She had accepted his reasoning. His arms coiled around her, "You frightened me. I need your support."

"You shall have it," she said softly, brushing aside all her doubts, her fears. "When do we leave?"

"Timing is important, it requires thinking."

Level-headed and smart, Marie-Thérèse understood the volatile world of politics and business. "*Bien*. I shall inform the children." A tremulous smile hung on her lips. She left the room very dignified. Just in time. The door closed, she stifled a sob with the back of her hand, teeth pressing into the flesh. After her exit, Cadillac blew through his cheeks and slumped in his chair, reaching for another generous Armagnac. It was one thing to hoodwink Marie-Thérèse, but another to fool himself.

On November 10, 1710, Cadillac was "promoted" to Gouverneur de Louisiane, an advancement of dubious honor. Pontchartrain ordered him to go directly to his new post.

Adieu

They came to watch him leave, mostly curious, some gloating, others grieving, all awed and anxious, sensing the end of an era. "Le Faucon," after deploying his wings in full glory, was forced to veil his predatory gaze and release from his talons a most precious quarry: his coup de maître. Brilliant, despotic, ruthless and ambition-driven, his excessive emotions had engendered in others reactions as violent as his own. One did not "like" Cadillac, one hated and feared him, or admired and followed him.

On November 1710, in his typical one-mindedness, he had blatantly ignored Pontchartrain's orders to join his new post immediately. Instead, he had flatly refused to surrender his own residence and quarters—established in the wilderness by his own sweat. He had dogged Dubuisson's every move, contradicted him on every possible occasion and showed him for the fool he was. In brief, he made an impossible nuisance of himself. Then, conveniently detained at the fort by the non-navigable season, sniffing a possible scheme, Cadillac had planned his next move at great leisure.

"*Ma mie*," he had told Marie-Thérèse in November, once he had made his decision and tossed Pontchartrain's missive to the side. "We are not leaving."

She had gulped. "What about Pontchartrain's orders?"

An impatient waving of his hand had dismissed her question. "I shall go to Versailles and meet Crozat . . ."

"*Mon ami*," she interrupted, jumping up, agitated. Once Cadillac had set his mind, nothing, no one, could veer him off, the man feared no authority. "Think. At the Court, you will walk straight into your detractors' net, meet the Ministre again. Ignoring his wishes is bound to bring you grief. Let us leave."

"Madame, my mind is made up." No mistaking the authority in his voice. "I have lost my vast domain in Acadia to *les Anglais*, Michilimackinac and its *Jésuites* have been a constant thorn in my life, and I am being divested of my seigniory. Would you have me relinquish all hopes of a better fortune?" She opened her mouth, he raised a quelling brow, she gritted her teeth and reined in her temper. "Being Gouverneur de la Louisiane is not enough. It still places us at the mercy of the Court's capricious whim. I have studied maps and reports, talked to the tribes. There are good mining prospects there. Crozat is very wealthy, I want to interest him in a mining venture. I cannot accomplish this from afar. We shall leave for France in the spring."

The Gascon had style, no shabby exit for him. As if by special request, the sun shone brightly and the stinking, clinging mud from the spring thaw had dried. Buds had started sprouting and anxious farmers checked daily on their crops of fruit trees, especially the pears that were so delicious. Jules, the pani, opened the door.

"*En garde!*" yelled sieur de Budemont, the new lieutenant. De la Ranée had passed away in November of 1710. The skeleton garrison stood to attention.

The crowd—an arresting mix of colorful Indians and less

flamboyant habitants—quieted, craning their necks, shifting uncertainly. One did not witness a commandant and soon-to-be-Gouverneur's final *adieu* without qualms.

Cadillac stepped out in full regalia, blue and white uniform immaculate, gorget sparkling in the sunrays, and gaiters stiff and neatly pulled over his souliers; his only concession to informality, his queue tucked in an eelskin bag instead of a hot, scratchy wig. Flanked by his three older sons he paused. In full white and blue uniform, although less resplendent as befitted their much lower rank, Joseph (twenty-one) was an *enseigne* and Antoine (nineteen) and Jacques (sixteen) simple cadets. The three, well-schooled, contained their feelings. If the sons' pewter buttons did not dazzle the assembly as much as their father's gilded ones, the resplendent group created an impression striking enough to widen eyes and shorten breath.

Marie-Thérèse followed in their shadow, one-year-old René-Louis in her arms, Marie-Agathe (four) and François (two) clutching her lustrous damask frock. Magdeleine (eleven), of a sweet disposition, rubbed her right hand. Marie-Thérèse (seven) had just pinched her.

Le tambour ahead, they fell into a *cortège*. Renaud Dubuisson, sweating like a pig under his heavily powdered wig, tagged along gleefully—at last the power would be his!

On the parade grounds "l'assemblée" rallied the soldiers for inspection. The flag bearer stood at attention, the blue and gold Fleur-de-Lys hoisted high. The crowd gathered around them, all eyes on Cadillac.

He would not betray his feelings. Years of struggles, of honing body and mind, had prepared him well for moments as this, containing the bitter edge of disappointment, of wounded pride, in a blanket of merciless self-control. *Adieu le Détroit!* Farewell le Détroit! pumped his heart, twisting his innards until they threatened to burst. His soldiers! He stared at their weather-beaten uniforms, a strange mixture of French and Indian apparel, their rugged faces grave under their tricornes. He forced himself to march by, Dubuisson in tow, taking time over each man, stopping to exchange a few words with his old guard, like Jacob Marsac, the sergeant of the 1701 expedition, who had settled at the fort.

Oui, he was departing, but his pride had outwardly been salvaged. Simple souls saw in him the Gouverneur-to-be, the one they wanted to view, to touch in spite of their grudges, the closest they would ever be to one so high. Already the Indians called him "Onnontio," and if the new rank held little glory to the more enlightened, he would not disillusion common folk.

It was a bizarre procession that accompanied him to the small harbor, *drapeau* and *tambour* first, Cadillac behind, two Hurons by his side, troops and the main throng following, children skipping ahead. A few red-eyed and stinking *coureurs de bois* attached themselves to the group, just for the fun of it. They were passing through, trading in their pelt harvest, squandering their earnings. Their Indian concubines—wrapped in ragged blankets, thick raven hair lustrous with bear grease—shuffled behind, and a lively brood of blue-eyed, cinnamon skinned youngsters pranced about. The men had drunk at the tavern most of the night and huddled on decent habitants' doorsteps to snooze in the early morning. Rose, opening her newly-painted green Dutch door, discovered one peeing on it and had whacked him away with a broomstick.

The river's edge had changed much since that first day, July 24, 1701. Birch bark canoes and *pirogues* still lined the beach, but his own small sailing vessel and several *bateaux* were tied to a wooden pier.

At its foot Cadillac turned, and setting his family around him, prepared to bid his *adieux*. One by one they filed by him, at least those who had been part of the struggle or knew all about hardship and new beginnings. To each person Père Deniau, on Cadillac's last order, handed religious medals and Jesuit rings from a wooden chest, gifts normally reserved for trading or converting the tribes. Le Grand Pierre, Rose and their four sons were amongst the first, somber-faced, fearing tomorrow, yet short of other options. Grande Gueule and Trou-au-Bras brought him a beaver blanket and a pipe ornamented with beads and feathers. When eyes strayed now and then to the new fatuous commandant, Dubuisson, not one breast rested easy.

Cadillac's three older sons stepped into the craft, and turning to his younger ones, he patted each on the head. Then Marie-Thérèse, bravely containing tears. Marie-Thérèse. Setting on the eve of a new battle, he left her to fight an old one. Weeks ago, they had agreed to his early departure. She would stay behind with the younger children to dispose of their properties. Marie-Thérèse had always handled their affairs successfully during his many absences, a solid business head and strong appreciation of money guiding her. Their private *adieux* had been made moments ago in the privacy of their home. "Their home"—not for long. A fleeting glance of anxiety passed between them, he bent ceremoniously over her wrist. Two of her fingers surreptitiously caressed his cheek, a light, love-giving touch. Its warmth anchored in his heart. Wrenching himself away, he boarded the vessel without a word.

Ten years of his life were going. The men hoisted the sails, the Fleur-de-Lys fluttering in the light wind, the same kind of little breeze that had toyed with their hearts and the plume of his tricorne in 1701. Hurons—he noticed Grande Gueule and Trou-au-Bras—Oppenagoes, Miamis, Ottawas and a few Iroquois jumped in their birch bark canoes and paddled alongside. Part of his mind briefly remembered the *Renards* who still had not arrived, and of whose coming he had apprised Dubuisson. Le Grand Pierre vaulted in his own craft, Cusson, Bonaventure, St. Yves, Nicolas Rivard and many other familiar faces followed.

And so an eclectic flotilla of *pirogues* and canoes, whose paddlers sported a bright assortment of feathers, beads and tuques, vermilion paint and tattoos, bright sashes, buckskin leggings, tunics and loincloths accompanied him all the way to the mouth of Lac Erié. One would have trouble sorting the

French from the Indians if not by the color of their skin and the Frenchmen's beards, which still fascinated and repelled the Natives.

Cadillac glanced one last time over the village, its eight bastions and picketed gardens flanking the high palisade, the farm lands he had granted, and the budding orchards. *Adieu le Détroit!* No more. Never again would he hear its wake up call, push it over its hurdles or feel its *joie de vivre*.

On the beach, "his" troops stood to attention, Dubuisson rubbed his hands, clusters of habitants and Indians waved, others watched, a few women wiped their eyes. Hurons, Miamis, Oppenagoes and *Outaouais*, each group apart from the others, started a slow beat of their drums. Young Marie-Thérèse screamed and his wife pulled her close, their other four children gathered around her. Some families had bunched together, the Bienvenus, Roys, Delormes, Langlois, Des Rochers, La Jeunesses and Mallets. Others faced the new era alone, Chesne, Livernois, Bisaillon, Casse and many others. The women of the large Campau and Rivard clans, all brothers and cousins, held hands, taking strength from each other.

A sturdy lot, the survivors of nature's harsh selection, they had joined him for a new beginning, to snatch themselves a small piece of freedom and comfort. Stormy power struggles blew over their heads, but shoulders hunched, the habitants outlasted the gale. "*C'est la vie,*" they often said when life dealt them another blow. Just last evening, as he had stood by his window in the dwindling twilight, absorbing for the last time the sounds of the village preparing for the night, a violin broke into a tune, raucous laughter burst from the tavern, and an aroma of crêpes wafted into the street. He had realized then, that the village had developed its own energy, life would go on. Without him. The habitants would endure. Unless . . . unless France closed the fort and abandoned them. Another reason to fight for Le Détroit. *Non*, neither Louis XIV nor Pontchartrain had heard his last.

Cadillac After Detroit

After a tortuous summer at le Détroit, Marie-Thérèse and her children joined Cadillac in Quebec. It was with great trepidation that the whole family—except the oldest daughter, Judith, who again, elected to be pensioned off at the Couvent des Ursulines in Quebec—embarked for France, a country Marie-Thérèse had not yet seen.

Cadillac's business required him to stay at the Court, a familiar surrounding. He jumped back into its capricious demands as if born to it. Not so for Marie-Thérèse. Daughter of a *Nouveau Monde* whose harsh surroundings bred an "earthier" type of women, aged by thirteen pregnancies and an arduous life, she felt gauche and provincial and was constantly reminded of it by the condescending sneers of the pack of wolves disguised as courtly beauties.

Eloquent and persuasive, the indomitable Gascon pursued his goal: to attract Crozat, the wealthy financier from Toulouse, his birth region, to a Louisiana commercial partnership. Soon, like

Pontchartrain before him, Crozat was seduced by Cadillac's panache and convincing mining prospects. He agreed to a joint venture. Crozat would bring most of the capital, Cadillac his expertise.

The whole family arrived in Louisiana, near Mobile, in early June 1713, after a horrifying voyage of endurance: five months of battling a raging sea and furious winds. Their miserable arrival in Louisiana was punctuated by high temperatures and excessive humidity alternating with violent thunderstorms. Sand and debris blocked the entrance of the port and the Cadillacs were forced to fight their way in. When finally they disembarked, their hearts sank, at least those of Marie-Thérèse and her progeny—Cadillac could always find something to be excited about.

Fort Louis (later renamed Fort Condé), although three years old, was in a state of disrepair. Its destitute colonists, seeing a ship for the first time in two years, jostled and fought to view its cargo and grabbed whatever they could. Appalled, Cadillac ordered a distribution of goods. Marie-Thérèse, a woman of the North, learned to a cope with the torrid heat and hostile fauna, crocodiles and snakes. She applied her energy to creating a new home for her family.

Meanwhile, Cadillac struggled to tame Louisiana's many problems: diseases spread by mosquitoes and heat; famine brought in by swampy soil that refused to grow wheat and healthy cattle; intrigue, loneliness, and depression in the fort. Sometimes survival hinged on a good crop of watermelons whose seeds had originally been imported by the Spanish, and a lump of cornmeal—all alien to the French stomach, especially one of a Gascon. Bienville, the former governor, angry with Cadillac's nomination, fought with the new governor at every opportunity, almost to the point of exchanging punches. Bienville behaved as Cadillac had with Dubuisson in Detroit. Starved of white female companionship, the men fornicated openly with the Natchez women, and Father Le Maire filed angry reports on the subject. In a memoir Cadillac, with his usual bluntness and deadly accuracy, described Louisiana as "a monster without a head or tail, lacking direction . . ." The Court was not amused. On the business side, Crozat and Cadillac battled bitterly over conflicting business ideas. The financier advocated creating posts along the Mississippi to trade with northern tribes, the new Gouvernor championed developing the area surrounding the river to trade with the nearby Spanish colonies. As usual Cadillac expressed his opinion rather forcefully. Crozat held the purse strings, a formidable advantage. While not one to stop the Gascon in his track, he trampled on the feet of anyone adverse to his views. An irate Crozat planned his removal from their venture. Unsuspicious, far too engaged in the heat of discovery, determined that success lay in the exploitation of mines to trade with Mexico, in 1715 Cadillac and his son spent several months prospecting in the Illinois country. They struck lucky and discovered copper mines. When they returned, Cadillac faced his discharge from the Crozat-Cadillac venture.

Embittered, once again fighting for his ideas and survival, Cadillac quarreled incessantly with his associate and everyone else. Exasperated, Crozat requested his immediate and permanent removal from the colony. Cadillac retorted that only he knew the location of the Illinois mines.

On July 23, 1716, Cadillac was recalled but would not leave before May of 1717. That left him with a few months to learn Crozat's next move: to sell his monopoly on the Louisiana colonial trade to John Law, a Scottish financier involved in the creating and selling of shares. Smelling a rat and a failure, Cadillac ranted against the scheme, to the great annoyance of the Regent, who approved the project on behalf of the young king. The shares of the new company were eventually sold to greedy and enthusiastic Europeans at such inflated prices that the new venture crashed in 1720. This fiasco was later called the "Mississippi Bubble," and again proved the Gascon right.

Shortly before their departure, Cadillac's oldest son, Joseph, having inherited the father's impetuous temperament, fought an illegal duel over a woman. After thirty-four years in the colonies fighting for the glory of France and searching for personal fame and fortune, Cadillac embarked on a frigate without as much as one official word of appreciation, only disgrace. He would never return to this continent.

Meanwhile in Paris, King Louis XIV had died in 1715 and his political cronies were replaced by the new Regent. The King, Louis XV, great-grandson of the previous one, was only a child, and Philippe d'Orleans assumed the regency.

A foot hardly set in Paris, Cadillac was accused of speaking against the government (the John Law enterprise) and the state of the colonies. His son and he were thrown into the Bastille. Marie-Thérèse fended for herself in an unfriendly and unfamiliar world. Soon, unable to build a case against him, and feeling guilty over the shabby treatment of the sixty-year-old soldier, the Regent ordered his release and slapped the "Military Croix de St. Louis" on his chest.

The interior of Cadillac's courtyard at Castelsarrasin

Free at last, Cadillac hurried to his home village, St. Nicolas-de-la-Grave, to settle his inheritance (his parents had died in 1699), and dashed back to Paris to defend his rights to his Detroit property. Marie-Thérèse and their other children stayed with his relatives. One wonders at the ability of this woman to adapt to so many different situations.

In 1722, Cadillac sold his seigniory of Detroit to Jacques Baudry de Lamarche, a Canadian living in Paris. With this money he purchased the post of Gouverneur of Castelsarrasin, a large town close to St. Nicolas, and established his family in their new residence. A circle had been completed. Son of Gascogne, he returned home to spend his last years. However, after thirty-four years in a vast world, life in a mid-size town proved to be somewhat restrictive and dull. Not slowed by age, the sixty-four-year-old spent most of his time in Paris, fighting over rights and recognition for his work. Surrounded by a provincial aristocracy, Marie-Thérèse, an outsider, felt more isolated than ever.

On October 16, 1730, close to midnight, at age seventy-two, tired and bitter, Le Faucon veiled his predatory eyes for the last time. In anticipation of his death, he had purchased a plot in the church of the Carmelite Fathers. And there, a great fighter and visionary, **Antoine de Lamothe Cadillac, seigneur of Doua-quec and Mount Desert, former Commandant of Forts Michilimackinac and Pontchartrain, founder of one of the nation's largest cities, former Governor of Louisiana, knight of the military cross of St. Louis, former Governor of the town of Castelsarrasin**, was quietly laid to rest.

Marie-Thérèse, his most devoted companion and supporter, faced old age in a foreign world. In 1731, she moved in with her son Francois and his wife. When she died, in 1746, at the age of seventy-five, for unknown reasons, her family did not bury her next to the man she had faithfully followed and shouldered. She was placed in a little cemetery across the road from him. History has been unkind to Marie-Thérèse. The first pioneer woman to come to the northwest, she was thrown into obscurity. We do not know for sure how many children survived the Cadillacs. Only three are mentioned in the records of Castelsarrasin: Joseph, Marie-Thérèse and François, all married. Magdeleine had joined a convent. The trace of all direct descendants disappear with a Granddaughter, Marie-Thérèse, daughter of the older son, Joseph, when she came with her husband, more or less destitute, to New York and Boston to claim her rights to her Grandfather's lands in Maine (Massachusetts at the time, 1787). The family died on Mount Desert, one of Cadillac's early possessions, around 1810.

Shortly after Cadillac's death, in 1731, his only married daughter's husband somewhat cantankerously requested an inventory of the deceased's possessions—probably to check he had not been cheated on Marie-Thérèse's dowry. Two portraits of the Cadillacs are mentioned. No one has been able to trace them.

The old carmelite chapel was turned into a prison in 1813. Then in the 1950's the town decided to improve its paving and started digging around its entrance. Human remains were exposed and the Archaeological Society of Tarn-et-Garonne was alerted. Careful excavations proceeded under its supervision. It soon became clear that under five strata an area had been hollowed out to contain burials. A skull that appeared to belong to an old man was discovered. Unfortunately, during the night, an unauthorized digging disturbed and damaged the other parts of the body beyond reconstruction. Was it Cadillac's skeleton? Although we can assume it was, the truth still eludes us.

Enveloped in a cloak of assumed identity and past, as mysterious in death as he was in life, Cadillac continues to tease us from the grave. Scoundrel or visionary? A man of gigantic emotions, he engenders in others reactions proportionate to his actions. In life, one did not "like" Cadillac, one despised or admired him—all feared him. Dead? Yes. But Le Faucon does not go meekly. Centuries after his death, the Gascon's panache lingers on, spinning a seductive web around us. While historians argue over his true character, we can feel the heat of his hawkish stare and challenging grin bore through our souls, because, in spite of everything, Cadillac emerges victorious. He has accomplished what many of his detractors have not: a lasting masterpiece—the city of Detroit. He has achieved immortality.

Detroit After Cadillac

After Cadillac's departure, le Détroit suffered two decades of mismanagement, but none as savagely destructive as the year immediately following his exit.[11] No sooner had Cadillac disappeared downriver that Dubuisson, free at last of Cadillac's restraining leash, began to flex his muscles to prove his power. He threw half the village out of the fort. The unfortunate lot included Madame Cadillac and her progeny, Père Deniau, the doctor, the King's interpreter, and a few prominent citizens—Cadillac's old guard. This was a poor move; these people wielded some influence and were rather well-liked. The village overruled Dubuisson and forced them back in. Rapport between Dubuisson and the colony heated considerably, and we are left to ponder over Dubuisson's intentions.

But he had not done his worst yet.

In 1712, led by their chief Pemoussa, and in answer to Cadillac's invitation, a thousand *Renards* and a few Mascoutin, Kickapoo and Sauk arrived at the fort and clamored loudly for the commandant. Unfortunately the Foxes' arrogant and belligerent reputation had preceded them. The Hurons, Ottawas

[11]   Much of this section is adapted from Woodford and Woodford's *All Our Yesterdays*.

and Miamis balked at their coming. They stormed the fort and promised an all-out war if the Foxes were allowed to remain. One look at the tribes' determined features and the Foxes' equally fierce behavior, and Dubuisson, whose reasoning and diplomatic skills were as limited as his garrison (thirty men), panicked. He weakly apprised the Foxes of Cadillac's departure and dismissed them, banging the doors shut behind them. The Foxes dug their heels in, camped outside the fort and threatened a war if not allowed to stay.

Stuck between the two, Dubuisson, instead of using diplomacy, resorted to flexing his muscle once again, and barked an order to leave. The Foxes swore to burn the fort and besiege the village. Habitants hurriedly dismantled the church and other vital buildings and covered them with wet doeskins to stop them from catching on fire. Meanwhile, the Foxes began their siege and shot flaming arrows at the fort. The war continued for several days with the colony trapped, quaking, inside its palisade. Finally large bands of Hurons and Ottawas returning from war raids in the west besieged the Foxes' camp.

The battle continued for nineteen more days, after which the Foxes decided to withdraw and flee up river. Not content to be rid of unwanted guests and driven by blood lust, the French garrison, under Dubuisson's command, and the Hurons, Ottawas, Miamis and several others, chased after them. The frenzied band pursued, wildly shooting, knifing and tomahawking until the river ran red and only a few escaped to safety. A thousand Indians may have been slaughtered that day.

When de la Forest finally assumed his post, the village sighed with relief.

However, as Cadillac had shrewdly predicted, Pontchartrain continued sending ineffectual commanders in the hope of ridding himself of an embarrassment (passable Sabrevois succeeded de la Forest in 1714). When the new Regent took power after Louis XIV's death, Pontchartrain fell into disfavor. France, debt-riddled, stalked by famine, and on the brink of bankruptcy, did not spare much thought and support for her North-American colonies, even less for the little village of the Straits.

But again, Cadillac's prediction came true. Le Détroit, moved by its energy, continued to grow and survive. Indian skirmishes and rivalries plagued it now and then and when French people were killed, it was mostly from getting in the way, trying to settle peace.

Finally, toward 1730, after a string of run-of-the-mill leaders, tragic events in Acadia (Nova Scotia) brightened Detroit's future. Centuries of conflicts had raged between France and England. Every time the two mother countries went to war, the colonies followed. Acadia, too close to British colonies, was often captured. When many Acadians moved to escape the onslaught, several trekked to Detroit. 1755 was to be of paramount significance in the history of both the Acadians and Nova Scotia. That year the British conquered Acadia and decreed the expulsion of all Acadians from Nova Scotia. The stunned Acadians were rounded up, allowed to retrieve only what they could carry, and expelled from their lands. The Acadians never recovered their properties.

The British continued their progress westward toward more French possessions, hungrily eyeing Detroit. France began to recognize the importance of her colonies, and to the delight of the Quebec authorities and the Detroit habitants, she decided to strengthen her little outpost as a barrier to British encroachments. Encouraged by this surge of official interest, many displaced Acadian families migrated to Detroit. Several of them belonged to the educated and prominent class and injected a new vigor in the village. Robert de Navarre, of royal blood, established himself as the colony's notary and retained his position through British and American rules.

For fifty-nine years after Cadillac's founding, Detroit continued her destiny under French rule. Her habitants tended to their occupations with their usual *joie-de-vivre*, quite integrated to their environment and neighboring tribes, warming their insides with occasional swigs of homemade peach and pear brandy.

By the mid 1750's, the French and Indian war had flared up drastically. This bloody struggle waged between England, who coveted the Ohio Valley and the Great Lakes area, and France and her Native Allies, who defended them. The French built a series of forts from Lake Erie to the Ohio fork to protect her possessions. On October 1758, British General Braddock, assisted by the colonial forces of a young George Washington, took over Fort Duquesne (Pittsburgh), then Fort Niagara, forcing France to withdraw from all her posts east of Detroit.

The fort had never been under direct attack, and news from Quebec and Montreal traveled slowly, so the habitants continued business as usual, ignorant of their disintegrating world.

On November 29, 1760, Robert Rogers, accompanied by his horde of rangers—a couple of hundred mean-spirited, toma-hawk-wielding roughnecks—and Captain Donald Campbell of the Royal American Regiment from Pittsburgh, banged on the fort's doors and demanded complete surrender to the British forces.

Caught unaware, de Belestre and the habitants refused, requesting an explanation for this hoax. Rogers extracted the orders from his pouch. He explained that British General Wolfe had defeated French General Montcalm on the Plains of Abraham, just outside Quebec, that both men had died in the battle, and that the fall of Montreal had followed. France had then been forced to surrender her possessions. England engineered a massive gathering of the previously disorganized Iroquois forces and rallied them to their side, a formidable foe for the underpopulated French colonies and her Indian allies.

Skeptical and accustomed to centuries of conflicts between France and England, the French bowed, merrily thinking that a few months hence, all would return to normal and Detroit would regain her French nationality. So, on November 29, 1760, the *tambour* beat "l'assemblée" one last time, and the blue and gold

Fleur-de-Lys was slowly taken down and the Union Jack raised in its place. French troops marched out, Detroit had surrendered, her habitants had suddenly become British subjects. At the time of surrender, only 80,000 French subjects lived in the colonies, compared to 1.5 million British.

Overcome by their distaste for their hereditary foe, several Detroit families left the area to return to predominantly French Canada (by culture if not by nationality any longer). Most, like the Campaux, Rivards, Beaubiens and Chesnes, had invested too much time and effort in their Detroit endeavors to abandon them. Besides, they did not really believe in the continuity of the new ownership. They grumbled somewhat and carried on with their lives, hoping for an impending turn of the situation. Indians, whose livelihood depended on the fur trade, cheered the region's new masters, their next business partners.

Rogers and his roughnecks left and Captain Campbell remained to rule the roost. Campbell, a Scot, possessed great gaelic charm, good manners and astute diplomatic skills. The French remained cool to their British conquerors, but the captain scrupulously kept his troops in check, wisely kept Robert de Navarre at his post, extended many invitations to prominent families and gradually defrosted the atmosphere.

Soon, however, the British's conquest soured; the coveted prize had turned into a pain. Trouble erupted from many corners. Some of the French started taking on the cause of a new breed of men: the American rebel; if France could not have the Detroit, neither would England. The tribes' hopes soon vanished, smiles disappeared. The British had no intention of integrating. They refused to distribute gifts and ammunition, and felt no obligation to provide medical care. Their traders surpassed the French in unscrupulousness and, unlike the *coureurs de bois*, did not deign to share a roaring evening of drinking and yarning with their native partners. Captain Campbell excepted, most officers were rather snooty and looked down their well-bred noses at the native man.

Another dramatic conflict was in the make.

Disenchanted with the British, Indians started to listen to a shrewd Ottawa chief, Pontiac, who advocated ousting the intruder from the area by forming a confederacy of the tribes. Once united, he planned for the confederacy to attack and destroy all forts and settlements, reserving for himself the richest plum of all: Detroit.

After much planning and conniving, on May 7, 1763, Pontiac was ready to make a move. He called for a parley with Major Henry Gladwin, who had assumed command of the fort in 1761 and had kept Campbell on as a second in command. This would allow many warriors to penetrate the fort. Once inside, they would draw their sawed off muskets and dispose of the whites.

Unfortunately for Pontiac, his conspiracy was not the best kept secret, and Major Gladwin had heard of it. Pontiac and his men were let in, to be surrounded by a well-prepared garrison. They were promptly escorted out and warned not to present themselves at the fort again (one could not kill such a powerful chief as that).

A few days later Pontiac demanded admission. When he and his warriors were denied it, they declared war on the British. And so began a string of atrocities perpetrated on white settlers. Women and children were slaughtered and scalped, and a few victims eaten. Captain Campbell fell into their hands. His death was not an easy one. Knifed by the jealous Saginaw suitor of his Indian sweetheart, he suffered many horrible mutilations.

In July the colony's spirits sank low. Captain Dalzell and his reinforcement troops had almost reached the fort when hidden Indian confederates pounced on them. Only ninety men survived. Buttoned up, the fort braced itself for the continued onslaught and siege.

Finally, October 1763, news of a peace treaty between France and England reached the fort. France was transferring all of her North-American possessions to the British, with no further allegiance to the Indian tribes. Pontiac lifted camp and went back to his ancestral home on the Maumee River, never to return to Detroit.

Peaceful days at last.

Not for long. The American Revolution was spreading. The British would use Detroit as a base to send troops and Indian raiding parties to the most troublesome areas: Kentucky, Pennsylvania and New York. Captain Richard Lernoult vainly tried to keep the garrison under control, but the arrival of cruel Henry Hamilton, the "Hair-Buyer," triggered a bloody frenzy. Raiders butchered thousands of families, sometimes bringing back prisoners whom the habitants tried to ransom. Daniel Boone had the dubious honor of being one of the British-Indian's alliance "guests." He eventually escaped during transit.

In 1778, the Americans organized an offensive, under General George Clark, to control the British-Indian attacks. Clark and Hamilton met in southern Illinois and Indiana. Clark trounced Hamilton's forces and sent the "Hair-Buyer" to rot in a Virginia prison. Hamilton was eventually exchanged and promoted by Britain to Governor of Bermuda.

By then the American Revolution was in full bloom and Captain Lernoult feared an imminent attack on Detroit. He recommended a bigger, stronger fort. In 1778, its position was staked out, overlooking the town, at the crossroads of present-time Fort and Shelby streets. Named Fort Lernoult after its founder, it was renamed Fort Detroit by the Americans, then Fort Shelby in 1812 in honor of the Kentucky governor and his men who freed it from a brief British re-conquest. No longer required, it was taken down in 1827.

The Revolutionary War ended in 1781 but not for Detroit. Michigan had been assigned to the United States, but admission to the Union progressed slowly. The British were loath to hand over a lucrative fur trade. They delayed the process by claiming the United States had not fulfilled its treaty obligations. British commanders continued to sponsor Indian war parties in Ohio and Indiana, a situation the United States could no longer ignore. President Washington sent an army under "Mad Anthony" Wayne to defeat the confederacy once and for all. They met at the Battle of Fallen Timber in 1794 (near Toledo). Wayne crushed the Indian forces and proceeded to Detroit to establish American ownership. British troops evacuated Detroit in the spring of 1796. On July 11, 1796, American troops reached Detroit and the Stars and Stripes were raised over the small town.

Descendants of the original settlers now acquired American citizenship. Although they had gone through two foreign nationalities, their French culture and language had survived. Their lifestyle still centered around their church (the first Protestant priest came only in 1783). By then Detroit had a distinct cosmopolitan flavor. The first "foreign" family, the Michael Yacks, from Germany, had been taken prisoners by Indians and ransomed by the Detroit habitants in the 1730's. They were given land to settle on. The first Jew, Abraham Chapman, had arrived around 1761. Add to that a few Dutch, English, Irish, Scotch, Africans[12] and the native tribes and the picture becomes very international.

Although made up of many nationalities, Detroit remained predominantly of French culture for many years, well into the nineteenth century. Unfortunately, as mentioned before, it is not in the French temperament to emigrate. The French community suffered from lack of new blood. Its number increasing in small quantity compared to other nationalities, it gradually became engulfed. Ironically, the French language remained the tongue of the elite until the turn of the twentieth century, especially to the British. They spoke French during their soirees and went to great length to send their young ladies to French parochial schools, the most-sought school being the St. Clare Institute,

---

[12] At that time Detroit had about 150 slaves, half of whom were Indians, the other half Africans, all spoils of the Revolutionary raids.

founded by two French nuns in 1833.

In 1792, an invitation from the Bishop of Baltimore allowed a young Sulpician Father to escape the French Revolution: Father Gabriel Richards, one of Detroit's most prolific intellectual and humanitarian contributors. He arrived at Detroit in 1798 and with unwaning energy brought changes to the growing city: the first printing press and newspaper, and a new and grand Ste. Anne church. Richards fought for the establishment of the first university (University of Michigan), was elected to Congress, thrown into jail, elected bishop, and gave his life caring for the victims of the 1832 cholera epidemic that ravaged Detroit.

Nineteenth century Detroit's booming economy attracted many immigrants, mostly Europeans, Italians and Poles among them. The next century would bring in races from around the world, Arabs and Asians and large contingents of African-Americans, all drawn to a thriving auto industry.

Where have the tribes gone? According to a 1990 census, 55,658 Indians live in Michigan, half of whom have elected to live on tribal lands, the others assimilate with the rest of the population. Sault-de-Sainte-Marie's Chippewa reservation counts the highest numbers of native people. Seven tribes have been federally recognized, most of them Chippewa (nineteen bands), one Saginaw and one Ottawa. Except for a few dotted numbers, Hurons, Miamis, and Pottawatamies migrated to other states during the resettlement drive of the mid 1800's.

Nowadays if one hears French being spoken in Detroit, it is most likely by a tourist. The last regular mass in French at Ste. Anne was celebrated in 1942. The French population has been absorbed amongst millions of Michiganians. They have left us with the biggest gift of all: the founding of a city on a prime geographical location, a city with one of the busiest waterways in the world that allowed it to grow into one the nation's largest industrial centers. Many streets are named after the first land owners, and many Michigan names were given by the French, either from their own language (Grand Rapids, Au Sable River,

Grosse Pointe) or from an Indian tongue (Michilimackinac, Michigan). French expressions "a propos, RSVP, deja vu" have slipped in our conversations, and when we "do-si-do" to the sound of a fiddle we are stepping into the "souliers" of the first habitants and their *Danse Carrée*.

Where once a little fort graced the river bank, an imposing financial district now stands, with high office buildings, luxurious hotels, gigantic exhibition halls, shops, universities and theaters. In the cultural center, one can soak in International culture in the magnificent Detroit Institute of Arts, visit the innovative, hands-on Science Museum, and hop over to the extensive Detroit Public library and its priceless Burton collection of historical documents. One must walk through the streets of the "Old Detroit" recreated in the basement of the Detroit Historical Museum and inhale the old-worldly scents of its boutiques, and discover the evolution of Detroit at the marvelous "Furs to Factories, Detroit from 1701 to 1901" permanent exhibit. A few minutes away, discover Historic Fort Wayne and its restored barracks.

In 1701 men and women of different venues, nations and races came to share one area, stretching tempers beyond limit, each staunchly defending his or her own rights, sometimes infringing aggressively on the others. Time has passed, humanity is learning to cohabit more peacefully, but has not yet eradicated the occasional dispute.

Like every major city Detroit has complex problems, but unlike many others it has the will and the talent to overcome them. She is a city of creation, of innovation; she has always attracted the smart, bright and bold to herself and by extension to Michigan—who can forget Ford, the Dodge brothers, Joe Louis, Elijah McCoy and many others, including the creators of "Motown Rock"? Many talents have been, many are, and many more will come to keep her amongst the best. Placed on the map by a man with a vision, Antoine de Lamothe Cadillac, Detroit will always strive to stay ahead.

Glossary of French and Indian Terms

Adieu: Farewell

A la garde!: Guard!

A votre service: At your service

Allez: Go

Allons, allons-y!: Let's go

Anglais: English

Armagnac: Brandy from Cadillac's home region

Arpent: Old land measure (.85 of an acre)

Assemblée: Drum call to assemble the troops

Assez est assez: Enough is enough

Attention: Careful

Aujourd'hui: Today

Baggataway: Lacrosse

Baïonette: Bayonet

Belle vie: Good life

Bien sûr: Of course

Bienvenue, bienvenue à tous: Welcome, welcome to all of you

Bon travail: Good work

Bonne femme (une): Good woman

Bonhomme (un): Good Fellow

Bonne nuit: Goodnight

Bougre, bougrement: Blackguard, devilishly

Breton: From Brittany, a rocky coastal province in Northwest France.

Canadian: Frenchman born in Canada

Castor, peaux de: Beaver, beaver pelts

Censitaires: Tenants

Cens, rentes et lods: Rent

C'est ma femme: It's my wife

C'est tellement beau ici!: It is so beautiful here!

Certificats de confessions: Certificates of confessions

Ce soir: This evening

Chapeau (un, le): Hat

Charmé: Charmed

Château: Castle

Chemise: Shirt

Chirurgien: Surgeon

Comme c'est facile!: How easy!

Cochon: Pig

Coiffe, haute coiffe: Head-dress, tall head-dress

Colon: Colonist

Comment: How

Commerce des fourrures: Fur trade

Commis de magazin: Warehouse clerk

Commissaire: Commissioner

Compagnie de la Colonie: Company of the Colony, formed by leading Canadian merchants

Compagnies Franches de la Marine: Independant Companies of the Marine

Confortable: Comfortable

Congé: License

Conseil (de guerre): Council (war council)

Conte: tale, yarn

Contretemps: Mishap, delay

Corbeau (un, le): Raven

Coup de maître: Master stroke, masterpiece

Courageux, Sans peur, Incroyable: Brave, fearless, incredible

Coureurs de bois: Unlicensed French trappers

Cravatte: Cravat

Crêpe: a crepe, a thin, flat pancake

Culotte: Breeches

Dame du Manoir: Lady of the Manor

Dame, Madame: Madam, lady

Damoiselle, demoiselle: Young lady

Danse Carrée: Square dance, the ancestor of

Debout: Up

Delicat: Tricky

Détroit (le): Detroit, the Straits

Diable: Devil

Diane (la): Drum wake up call

Dieu, mon Dieu!: God, my God!

Dieu vous bénisse: God bless you

Docteur: Doctor

Doucement: Gently

Drapeau (le): Flag, drum call to honor the flag

Dupe: Fool

Eau bénie: Blessed water

Eau-de-vie: Brandy

Ecoutez!: Listen

Enceinte: Expecting, pregnant

Encore: More

Enfer: Hell

Enfer et damnation: Hell and damnation

Ennui: trouble

Ennuyeux: Tedious, troublesome

Erreur de Jugement: Error of judgement

Enseigne: Ensign

Ensuite: Then

Enterrement: Burial, drum call for burials

Entrez: Come in!

Epée (une, la): Sword

Et bien: Well

Excusez-moi: Excuse me

Facheux: Troublesome, contrary

Faucon (le): Hawk

Femmes (les): Women

Feu: Fire

Feu follet: Dancing light

Fille, fils: Daughter, son

Foi et hommage: Faith and hommage

Français: French

Garonne (la): River running through Cadillac's homeland

Gascon: From the Gascony province of Southwest France

Gentil garçon: Good boy

Gentilhomme: Nobleman

Gouverneur Général: Governor General

Grande Rivière du Lac Erié: Grand River of Lake Erie

Grand: Tall, Mighty

Grands lacs: Great Lakes

Grosse: Big, large

Guêtre: Gaiter

Ici: Here

Intendant: Highest civil officer in New France

Ile: Isle

Ile aux Cochons: Hogs Island (Belle Isle)

Jabot: Flowing ruffle attached to the front of a shirt

Jamais, à jamais: Never, forever

Je veux mon pays: I want my homeland

Jeu de main: Hand game

Jeu de patience: Game of patience

Je sais: I know

Jésuites: Jesuits

Joli (e, es): Pretty

Jupons: Petticoats

Jurons: Swearwords

Justaucorps: Outer coat

Là: There

Lac: Lake

League: Measure of length (2.5 miles)

Louisiane: Louisiana

Loups: Wolves, Oppenago

Livre: Old French currency (pound)

Magazin: Warehouse, powder house

Maintenant: Now

Maître, coup de maître: Master, teacher, Master stroke

Majesté (sa): His majesty

Mal-de-terre: Old French name for scurvy

Ma mère: Mother

Ma mie: My dear, darling

Mes fils: My sons

Mes enfants: My children

Mon Père: My father

Mon ami: My friend, dear

Mariage: Wedding, drum call for weddings

Mémoires: Memoirs

Merci: Thank you

Mère Supérieure: Mother Superior

Ministre de la Marine: Minister of Marine

Mishegum: Michigan

Moi: Me

Moulin: Watermill

Nain Rouge (le): Red Dwarf

Nom de Guerre: War or Army name

Non: No

Nouveau Monde: New World

Nouvelle France: New France

Onnontio: Title given by the Indians to high ranking officials (governor)

Ou (où): Where

Oui: Yes

Ours (un, l'): Bear

Outaouais: Ottawa

Paisible: Peaceful

Pani: Pawnee

Par ici: This way

Partir: Leave

Pauvre bougre: Poor soul

Père: Father

Perruque (une, la): Wig

Plume: Feather

Poêle: A flat pan

Pot: Cask

Pourquoi?: Why?

Prenez soin: Take care

Prêt: Ready

Prière (la), messe (la): Drum call for mass

Puant: Smelly

Quartiers: Quarters

Quel plaisir!: What a pleasure!

Qu'est-ce-que-c'est?: What is this?

Qui?: Who?

Qui va là?: Who goes there? Who's here?

Qui veut un tour?: Who wants a turn?

Qu'il est beau!: How handsome he is!

Rapport: Report

Récollets: Recollect order of priests

Regardez!: Look!

Registres (les): Records

Renards: Foxes

Restez: Stay

Rien: Nothing

Roy: King

Rue (une, la): Street

Rustre: Lout

Sabre (un, le): Saber

Sacré (e): Damned

Sacrée femme: Damned woman

Sacrebleu: Swearword

Saute, Sautez: Jump

Sieur: Sir, sire

Soeurs hospitalières: Nursing sisters

Soulier: Shoe

Sortez!: Get out!

Sorcière: Fortune teller

Sûrement: Surely

Tambour: Drummer

Tirez: Pull, fire!

Tourtière (une): Ancestor of the meat pie

Tous: All of them

Tout de suite: Immediately

Traître: Traitor

Tricorne: Three-cornered hat

Tuez-le: Kill him

Un, deux, trois!: One, two, three!

Venez: Come

Veste (une, la): Waistcoat

Veuve (la): Widow

Vexant: Vexatious

Vite, plus vite: Quickly, faster

Vive le Roy! Vive le Seigneur du Détroit!: Long live the King! Long live the Lord of Detroit!

Votre; la, le vôtre: Your, yours

Votre nom?: Your name?

Vous: You

Voyageurs: Travelers; men who guided people through the wilderness and paddled the canoes, carrying them over portages.

Genealogy

Jean Laumet - Jeanne Péchagut
Jean is a judge
Jeanne, daughter of landowners
St. Nicolas-de-la-Grave, France
Eleven children, including:

> **Antoine Laumet, dit de Lamothe Cadillac**
> b. March 5, 1658, St. Nicolas-de-la-Grave
> d. October 16, 1730, Castelsarrasin
> Soldier & explorer, Commandant at Michilimackinac
> Founder of Detroit, Governor of Louisiana
> Married June 5, 1687

Thirteen

Judith, born 1689. Articled to the Ursuline Convent on November 12, 1711 by her father. No trace.

Joseph, born circa 1690. Entered the military, may have been in Detroit and Louisiana, went back to France with the family. Married Marguerite Grégoire, two children. One of which, Marie-Thérèse, married Barthelemy Grégoire. May have had three children. Immigrated to Boston to claim her grandfather's lands in Mount Desert. Died there in the early 1800's. No trace.

Antoine, born April 26, 1692. Came to Detroit with his father. Entered the military. No trace in France.

Magdeleine, born at Port Royal or Mt. Desert. Came to Detroit—very popular. Became a nun in France.

Jacques, born March 16, 1699, Quebec. Came to Detroit with his mother in 1701. No trace.

Pierre-Denis, born June 13, 1699, Quebec. Died July 4, 1700.

Antoine de Lamothe Cadillac

Denis Guyon - Elizabeth Boucher
Denis is a shipping merchant, Elizabeth, not known
Family originated from Perche region of France
First generation Canadians, Beauport, near Quebec
Several children, including:

Marie-Thérèse Guyon
b. April 9, 1671, Beauport (Quebec)
d. June 10, 1746, Castelsarrasin
First white woman in the NW Territory
Gave Detroit its first pioneer baby
Beauport, near Quebec

Children

Marie-Anne, born June 7, 1701, Quebec. Died two days later.

A "child," born and died in Detroit in late 1702.

Marie-Thérèse, baptized February 2, 1704. First white baby born in Detroit. Married François Hercule de Pouzargues. Died February 1, 1753. No children.

Jean-Antoine, baptized January 19, 1707, Detroit. Buried April 9, 1709.

Marie-Agathe, born December 28, 1707, Detroit. No trace.

François, born March 27, 1709, Detroit. Married Angelique Furgole, a widow. No children.

René-Louis, born March 17, 1710, Detroit. Buried in Quebec October 1714.

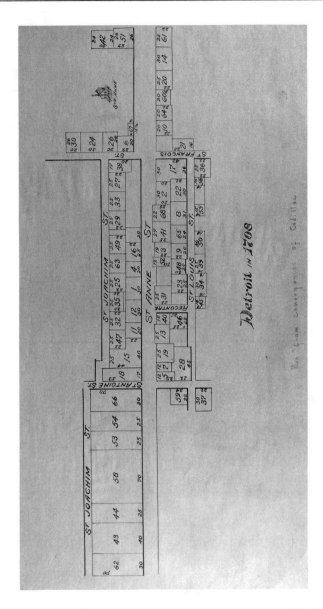

Courtesy of the Burton Historical Collection
Detroit Public Library

List of owners to match preceding map. Although the map says it was drawn in 1708, the land grants indicate that numbers 67 and 68 were granted only in 1710, so the map was likely drawn at a later date. When a lot has been granted twice or more, censitaires are listed by chronological order.

1 Pierre Chesne
2 André Chouet
3 Pierre Favreau, Robert Germain
4 Joseph Despré
5 Salomon du Vestin
  Michel Richard
  Bizaillon
6 Pierre Léger, Jacques Cardinal
7 Bonnaventure Compien
  François Livernois
8 Jacob De Marsac
9 Mr. d'Argenteuil
  Nicolas Rose
10 Jean Richard
   Jacques Hubert
11 Jean Labatier, Cadillac
12 Etienne Boutron
   Antoine Magnant
13 Pierre Hemard
   Jacques Hubert
14 Antoine Dupuis, Jean-Baptiste Duplessis
15 Jacques Langlois
16 Guillaume Bouet
   Pierre Robert
17 Michel Massé
18 Michel Campau

19 Louis Normand
   Alexis Lemoine
20 François Tesée
   Antoine Carriere
21 Pierre Chantelon
   Jean Lesueur
22 Francois Bienvenu
23 Pierre Estevé
24 Blaise Surgère
25 Pierre Poirier
26 Antoine Ferron
27 Pierre Tacet
   Jean Coutant
28 François Fafar Delorme
29 Michel Disier
   Louis de Charnie
30 Jacob de Marsac
   Charles Charon
31 Rencontre
   André Marsille
32 Desloriers
   Pierre Cornie
33 Xaintonge, Bouché
34 Jacques Dumoulin
35 Guillaume Aguet
   Pierre Chesne
36 Louis Gatineau
37 Joseph Parent
38 Martin Sirier
   Nicolas Rivard

39 Qilenchivé
  Jacques Dervisseau
40 Mr. Derancé
41 Mr. du Figuier
  Paul Guillet
42 Pierre Mouet
  Baptiste Trudeau
43 Pierre Mallet
44 Antoine Dufresne
  (Tuffé)
45 Jean-Baptiste Chornic
  Jean Chevalier
46 Jean Casse
  Zacharie Laplante
47 Paul Langlois
48 Jêrome Marlier
49 André Bombardié
  Pierre Lecuyer
50 Pierre du Roy
51 Pierre Roy
52 François Marqué
53 Antoine Magnant
54 François Bonne
55 Toussaint Dardennes
56 Pierre Bassinet
57 Francois Brunet
58 Antoine Beauregard
  Dupuis (may be one
  and the same)
59 Marie Lepage
  Joseph Seneval
60 Jacques Campau
61 Jean Serond
  Joseph Trudeau
62 Pierre Robert
63 L'Arramée
64 René Lemoine

65 Jacques Lemoine
66 Paul Guillet
67 Joseph Rivard
68 Antoine Tuffé
  (Dufresne)

Land Grants

King Louis XIV had granted a seigniory to Cadillac as part of the deal to settle a new colony on the "Détroit." In turn, the commandant granted land within, and outside, the fort to the habitants—but not without the King's permission. Although he had applied several times, this was long coming. Finally on March 10, 1707, Cadillac entered the first of the official records. As "Lord of the Manor," his name does not appear as a *censitaire* (tenant) on what was essentially his property.

The following is a list of the land grants recipients inside the fort, compiled from:

Cadillac's Village, C. Burton
Ste. Anne Parish Records
Detroit 1710 Census
Montreal Notarial Records
Michigan Historical & Pioneer Collection, Burton, Vol 33, 373-382
Cadillac's Papers

Interestingly enough, a high number of real estate transactions occurred—life was harsh and lonely on the frontier; some upped and went, a few passed through, others like the Campaux, Beaubiens, and Livernois, withstood it and procreated many generations of sturdy Detroiters. Some moved for similar reasons to present time: a bigger lot, better location and orientation, arguments with their neighbors, or just to be where the action was and keep up with the Joneses on Ste. Anne (the "in" street where most of the moves happened) and the parade grounds. Where possible occupations and dates of arrival have been included. Note the men's most common first names: Pierre, Jacques, François and Antoine.

Inside the fort in 1707

Argenteuil (d'), officer, St. Louis. Sold to **Nicolas Rose**
Bienvenu, François (dit **Delisle**), soldier & farmer, St.
Louis.
Bombardié, André, soldier & farmer, St. Joachim, sold
to **Pierre L'Ecuyer**
Boutron, Etienne (dit **Major**), Ste. Anne. Reverted to
Cadillac. Granted to **Antoine Magnant** (voyageur).
Bouet, Guillaume (dit **Deliard**), Ste. Anne. Sold to
Pierre Robert.
Campau, (Campo) Michel, farmer, 1707. Two lots side
by side on St. Antoine going to the corners of Ste. Anne
and St. Joachim.
Chantelon, Pierre, farmer, 1707, Ste. Anne. Sold to **Jean**
Lesueur
Chesne, Pierre (dit St. Onge), 1707, Ste. Anne
Chouet, André (dit **Cameraud**), Ste. Anne
Compien, Bonaventure (dit **L'Esperance**), soldier &
farmer, Ste. Anne, sold to **François Livernois.**
Despré (Guyon-Després), Joseph, Ste. Anne, may have
been related to Madame Cadillac
Disier (Dizier), Michel, St. Joachim, sold to **Louis de**
Charnie
Dupuis, Antoine (dit **Beauregard**), farmer, Ste. Anne.
Sold to **Jean-Baptiste Duplessis**
Du Roy, Pierre, St. Louis
Estevé, Pierre (dit **La Jeunesse**), also called Stebre,
soldier & farmer, St. Louis.
Fafar Delorme, François, farmer & King's interpreter,
1701. Corner of St Louis and St. Antoine.
Favreau, Pierre (dit **La Grandeur**), Ste. Anne, sold to
Robert Germain.
Ferron, Antoine, farmer, St. François.
Figuier (du), Louis Fournier, Sieur, officer, Ste. Anne.
Reverted to Cadillac. Granted to **Paul Guillet**
Hémard, Pierre, soldier & farmer, Ste. Anne. Sold to

Jacques Hubert.
Jardis, François (dit **Rencontre**), Ste. Anne. Sold to **André Marsille.**
Labatier, Jean (dit **Champagne**), soldier, Ste. Anne, reverted to Cadillac.
Langlois, Jacques, farmer & blacksmith. Two lots on Ste. Anne, one backing on St. Joachim.
Langlois, Paul, farmer, 1707, St. Joachim, next to Jacques Langlois.
L'Arramée, St. Joachim
Léger, Pierre (dit **Le Parisien**), farmer, corner of Ste. Anne and St. François, sold to **Jacques Cardinal** (voyageur).
Lepage, Marie, widow, may have worked at the tavern (1706-07) Corner of St. Antoine and St. Louis. **Only woman.** Sold to **Joseph Seneval.**
Marlier, (Marliard) Jêrome, St. Louis
Marsac (de), Jacob, (dit **Desrochers**), ex soldier, farmer, 1701. One on St. Louis, another on St. François, later sold to **Charles Charon.**
Mallet, Pierre, farmer & voyageur, Ste. Anne, backing on St. Joachim
Marqué, François, Ste. Anne. Sold to **Jean Paquet**
Massé, Michel, farmer. A long tract on Ste. Anne, corners of St. Louis and St. François.
Mouet, Pierre (dit **La Montagne**), on the Square (Church and parade ground, west side of Ste. Anne)
Normand, Louis, toolmaker, Ste. Anne, sold to **Alexis Lemoine.**
Parent, Joseph, farmer, toolmaker & brewer. Corner of St. Louis and St. Antoine.
Poirier, Pierre, soldier & farmer, St. Joachim
Quilenchivé, St. Joachim. Sold to **Julien Dervisseau (officer)**
Rancé (de), Sieur, Ste. Anne and Rencontre
Richard, Jean, defaulted, grant reverted to Cadillac who granted it to **Jacques Hubert.**

Roy, Pierre, Ste. Anne.
Sérond (Serron), Jean, (dit **L'Eveillé**), Ste. Anne. Sold
to **Joseph Trudeau**
Sirier, Martin, (also spelled Cirier), soldier, corner of St.
François and St. Joachim. Sold to **Nicolas Rivard**
Surgère, Blaise, farmer, St. François
Tacet (Tachet), Pierre, St. Joachim, sold to **Jean
Coutant**
Tesée, François, Ste. Anne, sold to **Antoine Carrière.**
Vestin (du), Salomon, Ste Anne, backing on St. Louis,
sold to **Michel Richard Bizaillon.**

Habitants mentioned as neighbors in the records (Cadillac's
papers) but whose grants are not found:

Abatis, Jean, Ste. Anne, next to Etienne Boutron
Boucherville, Ste. Anne, next to Pierre Leger
Dervisseau, Julien, St. Joachim, next to Quilenchivé
Dumoulin, Jacques, other side of Quilenchivé, moved to
St. Louis (see 1708).
Ferland, Jean, St. Joachim, next to Paul Langlois
Grandmesnil, Veron, lawyer & village and warehouse
keeper, 1701 Ste. Anne, next to Jean Serond (Serron)
Pichet, Pierre, St. Joachim, next to Pierre Tacet

Lands granted outside the fort (1707)

Bombardié, André
Boutron, Estienne
Bosseron, François (also spelled Beauceron, husband of
Marie Lepage)
Campau, Michel
Chantelon, Pierre
Compien, Bonnaventure
Disier, Michel
Dupuis, Antoine, 2 tracts

Durand, Jean
Estevé, Pierre (Stebre)
Fafar Delorme, François
Ferron, Antoine
Gorion, Jean-Baptiste
Hémard, Pierre
Jardis, François
Laloire
Langlois, Jacques
Langlois, Paul
Lamothe Cadillac, Magdalaine. **Only woman**
Langlois, Paul
Lafleur
Léger, Pierre
Marlier, Jerome
Mallet, Pierre
Marqué, François
Marsac (de), Jacob, 2 tracts
Massé, François
Parent, Joseph
Poirier, Robert
Richard, Jean
Robert, Pierre
Surgère, Blaise
Texier, Antoine

Grants inside the fort in 1708

Aguet (Aguenet), Guillaume (dit **Laporte**), sold to **Pierre Chene (Chesne)**
Bassinet, Pierre, St. Louis
Beauregard, Antoine, Ste. Anne (possibly the same as Antoine Dupuis)
Bonne, François, Ste. Anne
Brunet, François, 1705, Ste. Anne.
Casse, Jean (dit **St. Aubin**), Rencontre. Sold to **Zacharie Plante**

Chauvin, Jean-Baptiste, St. Louis (not on map).
Chornic, Jean-Baptiste, St. Louis. Sold to **Jean Chevalier**
Dardennes, Toussaint, St. Louis
Desloriers, Jean-Baptiste, St. Joachim. Sold to **Pierre Cornie**
Dumoulin, Jacques, St. Louis, moved from St. Joachim
Dupuis, Antoine, farmer, Ste. Anne (may be the same as Beauregard).
Magnant, Antoine, Ste. Anne
Gastineau, Louis, sieur du Plessis, St. Louis.
Tuffé, Antoine (dit du **Dufresne**), Ste. Anne, bordering St. Joachim
Xaintonge, St. Joachim. Sold to **Bouché**

Habitant not recorded:

La Chapelle, Robert, St. Louis, next to Pierre Bassinet

Grants inside the fort in 1709:

Campau, Jacques, blacksmith, Ste. Anne
Guillet, Paul, merchant, Ste. Anne
Lemoine, René, merchant, Ste. Anne
Lemoine, Jacques, merchant, St. Louis
Robert, Pierre (dit **La Fontaine**), 1708, Ste. Anne

Grants inside the fort in 1710:

Tuffé, Antoine (dit **Dufresne**), Ste. Anne
Rivard, Joseph, 1708, Ste. Anne

List of Museums and special events related to

French Colonial Days

Presentations:

"Fort Pontchartrain's beginning years brought to life by its First Pioneer Lady"
A variety of 50 minute presentations of the French Colonial era, in period costume, (with audience participation for schools) by Annick Hivert-Carthew, the author of this book. Write to "Marie-Thérèse Cadillac," Omega, 1717 West Hamlin Rd., Rochester Hills, MI 48309, or call: (810) 375-5464.

"Madame Cadillac Dance Theater"
A variety of programs in period costumes of dance, drama and music of the French colonial period. Dance workshops available. Harriet Berg, Artistic Director. Call company representative, Cally Kypros, (313) 881-8024.

Museums:

Detroit Historical Museum:
5401 Woodward Avenue, Detroit, MI 48202
Tel: (313) 833-1805
Permanent exhibit: From furs to factories, Detroit at work, 1701 to 1901 (trading post, bust of Cadillac, model of fort).

Historic Fort Wayne including **Great Lakes Indian Interpretive Museum**
6325 W. Jefferson, Detroit, MI 48209, temporarily closed due to budget cuts. Call (313) 833-9721 for update

Michigan Historical Museum, Lansing. Section on French missionaries and explorers. (517) 373-3559

Detroit Institute of Art, Detroit. XVII and XVIII century French paintings, sculptures and decorative of France. Native American artifacts. (313) 833-7900

Fort de Buade Museum, 334 N. State St., St. Ignace. North side of Mackinaw Bridge. Open June thru Sept. Early French and Indian period of the area. Authentic artifacts of this region.

In France:

Cadillac's museum "**Musée Lamothe Cadillac,**" St. Nicolas-de-la-Grave (Cadillac's birth place), Rue de la Porte d'Ouan. Open during summer, per request during off season. Write to: Mairie de St. Nicolas-de-la-Grave, 82210.

Places to visit and events to attend:

Windmill Pointe in Grosse Point Park was part of the Grand Marais (Great Swamp). To learn more about the history of the area call the Grosse Pointe Historical Society.
Tel: (313) 833-7900

Ste. Anne Church, Detroit, at the foot of the Ambassador Bridge. The second oldest parish in the nation, established by Cadillac in 1701, rebuilt several times.

Annual French Heritage Day, Father Marquette Memorial Park, St. Ignace, MI, (906) 475-7857

Colonial Michilimackinac, Mackinaw City, MI 49701. Reconstructed 1715 French fort and village. Many reenactments including military pageantry, voyageurs and French wedding. (616) 436-5563

Old French Town Days Festival, Monroe, MI. Annual summer event. XVIII century crafts and reenactments, music, dance and games. Call Monroe Historical Society, (313) 243-7137

Rendez-vous on the Rouge, Dearborn, MI. Annual event, usually the second week of June. Crafts, military pageantry, trappers, and storytellers. Call the Dearborn Historical Society, (313) 565-3000

"Feast of the Hunters Moon," Lafayette, Indiana. Largest colonial reenactment event in the US including voyageurs, military pageantry, crafts and Native American pow-wows. Usually in October. (317) 742-8411

"Cadillac Festival," Castelsarrasin, France. Bi-annual summer festival celebrating the founder of Detroit (3 days), parades, Mme Cadillac in her horse-drawn carriage, gourmet food, visits of chateaux, and more. Combined with an international meet of Cadillac car owners. Write to Mairie de Castelsarrasin, France, 82100.

"Cadillac Festival," St. Nicolas-de-la-Grave, France, birthplace of the founder of Detroit. Summer-long activities related to the founder of Detroit. Is co-guest at bi-annual Cadillac festival (see above). Art and flower show in the village's quaint streets. Do stop at the Cadillac restaurant for a traditional Gascon meal. Write to Mairie de St. Nicolas-de-la-Grave, France, 82210

"Feast of the Ste. Clair," Port Huron, MI. Annual event, usually in May. Many reenactments, candlelight tours, French catholic mass and authentic outdoor ball. Call the Port Huron Historical Society.

La Maison François Baby, Windsor, Ontario. House of prominent French-Canadian citizen. Houses Windsor's

community Museum. Tours in English or French.
(519) 253-1812

Associations who organize programs related to the French Colonial period, or provide research material:

Detroit Historical Society
(313) 833-7934
The DHS offers guided tours of Detroit's landmarks, and many special events and programs related to the French Colonial period. Its Speakers Bureau will help you select a speaker for a special event.

Michigan Library and Historical Center, Lansing
(517) 373-3559
Perfect for research

Burton Historical Society, Detroit.
(313) 833-1480
Housed inside the Detroit Public Library. Records and original documents pertaining to the history of Detroit and Michigan. Perfect for tracing one's ancestors.

Historical Society of Michigan, Ann Arbor
Center for teachers of Michigan History
(313) 769-1828
Offers programs and helps select keynote speakers.

Bureau of Michigan History, Lansing
Land and early farms records
717 W. Allegan, Lansing, MI 48918

Bibliography

In French

Boutonnet, Jean. *Cadillac, Regards sur la Vie de Lamothe Cadillac*. Musée de St. Nicolas-de-la-Grave, 1988.

Boutonnet, Jean. *L'Oeil des Contemporains*. Musée de St. Nicolas-de-la-Grave, 1989.

Boutonnet, Jean. *L'Oeil de l'Histoire*. Musée de St. Nicolas-de-la-Grave, 1990.

Boutonnet, Jean. *L'Oeil sur la Famille*. Musée de St. Nicolas-de-la-Grave, 1991.

Boutonnet, Jean. *Biographies contradictoires*. Musée de St. Nicolas-de-la-Grave.

Cadillac, Antoine de Lamothe. Papers—in French. Originals at Archives de Paris. Those pertaining to Detroit have been translated and published in Burton's *Mich. Historical Colls*, vol 33 & 34

Dumas, Silvio. *Les Filles du Roi en Nouvelle France*. Quebec, 1972.

Lachance, André. *Crimes et Criminels en Nouvelle France*. Montreal, 1984.

Lanctot, Gustave. *Les Troupes de la Nouvelle France*. Canadian Historical Association Report, 1926.

Mandou, Robert. *La France aux XVII et XVIII siècles*. Nouvelle Clio, Paris, 1967.

Margry, Pierre. *Mémoires et Documents*, Vol. 5. Paris, 1887.

Marion, Marcel. *Dictionnaire des Institutions de la France, XVII-XVIII.* Editions Picard, 1989

de Rochemonteix, Camille. *Les Jésuites de la Nouvelle France au XVII siècle*, 3 vols. Paris, 1896.

Toujas, René. *Le Destin Extraordinaire du Gascon Lamothe Cadillac.* Atelier du Moutiers, Montauban (France), 1974.

Trudel, Marcel. *Histoire de la Nouvelle France*, Vol. II. Quebec.

Archives Nationales, Colonies, several volumes. Paris.

Dictionaire Biographique du Canada, Vol II. De 1701 à 1740.

Journal des Jésuites, 73 vols.

Lettres, instructions et mémoires de Colbert, 7 vols. Paris, 1861-73.

Rapports de l'Archiviste de la Province de Quebec, several volumes.

In English

Arnold, Pauline and Percival White. *How We Named Our States.* Criterion Books, 1965.

Bald, Clever. *Michigan in Four Centuries.* Harper & Brothers, 1954.

Boutonnet, Jean. *A look at the life of Lamothe-Cadillac* (unpublished).

Burley, Louis. *Michigan's Pioneer of Pioneers (Etienne Brulé)*. Louis Burley Press.

Burton, Clarence. *Cadillac's Village*. Detroit, 1896.

Burton, Clarence. *Early Detroit*, Detroit.

Burton, Clarence. *Building of Detroit*. Detroit, 1912.

Burton, Clarence. *A visit to the home of Cadillac*. Michigan Pioneer and Historical Society, 38, 1912.

Burton, Clarence. *Michigan Historical & Pioneer Collection (MHPC)*: vols 33, 34. Detroit, 1903.

Catton, Bruce. *Michigan, a History*. W.W. Norton & Company, 1984.

Crawley, Mary. *Daughter of New France*. Little, Brown & Company, 1901.

Delanglez, Jean. *Cadillac's Early Years in America*. Mid-America (15), 1948.

Delanglez, Jean. *Genesis and Building of Detroit*. Mid-America (19), 1948.

Delanglez, Jean. *Cadillac at Detroit*. Mid-America (19), 1948.

Delanglez, Jean. *Cadillac's Last Years*. Mid-America (19), 1951.

Dewhurst, K. and Y. Lockwood. *Michigan Folklife*. Michigan State University, 1987.

Douville, R. and J. Casanova. *Daily Life in Canada from*

Champlain to Montcalm. McMillan, 1968, Hachette (France), 1964.

Eccles, W. *France in America.* Michigan State University, 1990.

Eccles, W. *Frontenac the Courier Governor.* Toronto, 1959.

Eccles, W. *Canada Under Louis XIV.* Toronto, 1964.

Eccles, W. *The Canadian Frontier.* Toronto.

Farmer, Silas. *The History of Detroit and Michigan.* Detroit, 1889.

Ferry, W. Hawkins. *The Building of Detroit, a History.* Wayne State University, 1968.

Fuller, George. *Michigan through the Centuries.*

Fuller, George. *Historic Michigan.*

Gallup, Andrew and Donald Shaffer. *La Marine, the French Colonial Soldier in Canada.* 1992.

Gilbert, Helen Francis. *Tonquish Tales*, vol 2. Plymouth Heritage Press, 1984.

Goodrich. *First Michigan Frontier.* University of Michigan, 1940.

Guérard, Albert. *France.* University of Michigan, 1959.

Hamlin, Marie. *Legend of Le Detroit.* Gale Research Company, Detroit, 1877.

Holbrook, Sarah. *The French Founders of North America*

and their Heritage. McClelland & Stewart (Canada), 1976.

Houlding, J. *French Arms Drill of the 18th Century.* Museum Restoration Service, Canada, 1988.

Johnson, Ida. *The Michigan Fur Trade.* Black Letter Press, Grand Rapids, 1971.

Paré, George. *The Catholic Church in Detroit 1701-1888.* Wayne State University, 1951.

Parkman, Francis. *Count Frontenac and New France under Louis XIV.* Toronto, 1898.

Parkman, Francis. *The Jesuits in North America.* Toronto, 1898.

Parkman, Francis. *Pioneers of France in the New World.* Toronto, 1898.

Parkman, Francis. *The Old Regime in Canada.* Toronto, 1898.

Parkman, Francis. *A Half Century of Conflict.* Toronto, 1898.

Pepper, Mary Sifton. *Maids & Matrons of New France.* Little, Brown & Company, 1901.

Pound, Authur. *Detroit Pound.* D. Appleton Century Company, 1940.

Seno, William J. *UP Country, Voices from the Great Lakes Wilderness.* Heartland Press, 1985.

Woodford, Arthur & Frank Woodford. *All Our Yesterdays.* Wayne State University, 1969.

Wynne, John, S.J. *The Jesuit Martyrs of North America.* Universal Knowledge Foundation, 1925.

―――. *Cadillac and the Founding of Detroit.* Wayne State University, 1976.

The French American. Chelsea House Publishers, 1988.

Index